THE 11 LIVES OF AN ABYSSINIAN CAT

Flummox

HJ HARRISON-VULLIS

First Published 2025 by Dirty Dieter LLC
Copyright © 2025 HJ Harrison-Vullis

ISBN 979-8-9986045-0-8 (Print)
ISBN 979-8-9986045-1-5 (eBook)

Cover Design and Interior Formatting by Gregg Davies Media (Pty) Ltd
www.greggdavies.com

CONTENTS

“In the beginning God created…”
— First verse.

INTRODUCTION BY LADY CONFUSION: FOR WHOM I AM

Here's a story I need to tell, a story from the heart…

People tend to view me as a wise person of wisdom: for some reason, they believe I know everything. Some turn to me with the hope that I can be their Dr. Phil, desiring that my advice can rescue their disastrous relationship – or perhaps give them the financial guidance that you won't find on any episode of Shark Tank.

I can even guide you on realizing a lousy investment and cutting your losses, even if just for a dinner date at McDonald's, or perhaps a Michelin restaurant … I call them the "M n´ M" losses.

Heck, I even shared the well-kept secret with an avid adventurer regarding how to ride a porcupine, bare ass, without possibly jeopardizing his dream of starting a family in the distant future.

See me as an oracle or a clairvoyant if you desire. No, I never consult Wikipedia or any episode from The Jerry Springer Show. Whatever you decide to call me, my knowledge and wisdom have nothing to do with magic whatsoever.

I often get people asking me where I think Witchcraft comes from. Strangely, I don't see myself as a person who would know the history of the occult, but did you know that witchery, or witchcraft, started with children playing an innocent game?

With a flicking movement, they imagined using their hands to change their friend into a different character, accompanied by sim sala bim, known as the Swedish equivalent of *abracadabra*. The children practiced this movement of the wrist and hands to perfection; the better you were at it, the faster you could win the game. After all, changing all your friends into frogs while playing hide and seek will make you the fastest spell-slinger in a town where innocence is cherished. Hands were no longer enough, and a replacement was sought due to the increased cases of CTS.

Carpal Tunnel Syndrome is a state that causes a lack of sensation, soreness, and tingling in the hand and forearm. Whatever they sought had to be something light, durable, and unique, which resulted in them harnessing the power of a "special" stick. Instead of using your hands, you can now use a fictitious magic stick. The children initially shared one among themselves until every child built enough courage to cut their twig from a wealthy farmer's vineyard.

Parents back then didn't withhold sharp objects from their children; survival of the fittest, I guess. One of the original twelve youngsters who started the game, the limping one, even took it upon himself to set standards for an acceptable stick, such as maximum length and girth. Not only did he take the initiative: he also thought it wise to proclaim himself as the official game-monitoring "police" who would eventually share a kiss on the cheek.

And so the magic wand was born. The excitement of each having their own led to some children claiming their wands had a hidden power, giving them superiority over those around them. Some no longer wanted to abide by the original role-playing structure; thus, a broom was introduced into this complex arrangement.

The broom was nothing but a broom, used to punish those who misbehaved during the role-play experience, such as claiming their magic stick having the power to dismiss a spell that a fellow player cast. In such an event, the guilty player was given two choices: give up their rights as a player and be banned for life or sweep the church's floor a Saturday before Sunday's worship of the creator.

However, all it took was for one child to notice the resemblance of an arrow to the broom. Instead of committing to sweeping the church's floor, she saw the opportunity to create a superior character that could fly away to avoid prosecution for not keeping to the agreement of sweeping the floor. This resulted in the original innocent game boiling hatred against one another and parents alike.

The whole town was up in arms with claims of bullying and mobbing, which robbed the children of their joy. One day the wealthy farmer stepped forward and demanded a reckoning on those who damaged his young vines, resulting in significant financial losses. Not only was he the richest around, but he also was a good friend to the church's leaders and economic hope. Love turned to hatred, and hatred turned to Nero as unknown darkness filled the air and bestowed itself upon a town where simplicity no longer existed.

Mist crept in from the lake, forcing all animals, big and small, all the birds in the sky to seek refuge among those that scurried along the ground. "ROUND EM UP!" he shouted, "and let the town be illuminated to mark the beginning of a new era where witches are no longer tolerated!" Innocence went up in flames: a limping child became the first tax collector to climb up a tree instead of choosing a quick drop and a sudden stop as a result of sealing their fate with a kiss. This is why you should enjoy a good glass of red in memory of the first they burnt at the stake.

Most of us want to be the best, perhaps have the best, and will even invent our special powers with the hope of having our magic stick carved by a 200-year-old blind-wise man. But are you willing to die for it? That's an entirely different game: willing to die so you can have more than you can handle.

We even look at inspirational characters from movies to guide us through life with the hope that we will be the one to receive the Oscar for Gladiator, the one reciting Ezekiel 25:17 just before we get to pop a high-velocity projectile into the skull of the boss who didn't see our potential, or even the one that kicks a messenger into a deep dark hole or from a stage while shouting "THIS IS SPARTA!"

Some even go as far as to adapt the Joker's crazy persona just so they can interrogate their version of a Batman, with the hope that they can be the next one holding the dying dog Sam in an imaginary world overrun by cognitive thinking zombies, as portrayed in the legendary movie "I was Legend", starring nonother than the Haymaker himself, Will Smith, who revealed to be more of an Orthodox than a Southpaw.

What you are about to read is inspired by actual events and isn't 25% real versus 75% fiction, but 87.2% real and 12.8% somewhat accurate. Most statistics are made up on the spot anyway, except for this. If you believe "The Exorcism of Emily Rose" and "The Conjuring" to be factual, you should stick with the opinions of those who gave both screenplays a thumbs up. We are quick to press play when we see the opening title, "Based on true events," yet we never give it another thought.

Let me say this: a story like this should never be converted into a screenplay since there's no group of actors talented enough to portray the scars, laughter, anguish, fear, desperation, joy, and tears that define the 87.2%. Damn, this sounds morbid. Take comfort in knowing that the rest of this story won't push you to reveal your deepest, darkest secrets, nor is it the aim to have you start chewing off a limb.

We all have our secrets, some moderate, and some those only a deaf and mute priest can whisper to a cardinal after a confession.

This book, or shall I say journey, is based on the life of a person with a very dark secret, as seen through my eyes, a dear friend since high school to a truly broken man. I would say his life is a dark adventure – an exceptionally dark adventure with infinite repeatability – which can be described using complex calculus equations.

You are about to embark on an adventure to solve his murder, luring, right? It's almost like a good episode of "Murder She Wrote", "Mindhunter", or a few from "Unsolved Mysteries", excluding those that discuss aliens or anything that can change shape. Your sole purpose is to establish who will kill him, if that is the correct term for making him evaporate into thin air with only a whisper left to speak in his memory.

At the end of this story, you'll come to one of two possible conclusions: this story was absolute rubbish, or you will have a longing to "re-read the book". No breadcrumbs will be left to follow: you will be left to interpret hidden messages at your own pace while pondering.

Nothing we do in life can truly be comprehended regardless of our level of education. You may bicker that you managed to master your life and understand your purpose, but rest assured, you haven't, even if you read all the purpose-driven books known by all the people from all cultures walking the earth.

You may find yourself sitting next to a very well-acquainted person and still struggle to identify the deep scars within them left by life; it makes you realize that an author undeniably governs your opinion regarding your purpose and not you. If you can't recognize the scars of a broken person, what use is your purpose anyway?

My dear friend hides his secret incredibly well. He uses his brokenness to follow in the footsteps of pioneers embarking on uncharted territories. Subconsciously, he pays attention to everything he sees, touches, feels, tastes, or smells with one purpose: to change everything to a superior version.

Some may see it as a talent, a blessing, but he experiences it as a living hell. Not because it's too much to handle but simply because he has had little success improving on the things subconsciously observed. He has the ability to access his subconscious while being fully aware of his surroundings, altering his memories and whatever he has been taught, and then returning to his conscious thoughts.

I still remember as clearly as the Saharah night sky the day he, spur of the moment, suggested an invasive solution to enable paraplegic patients to walk and super athletes to run 2 seconds faster once they've launched from the blocks. He did so by arguing medical, scientific, and mathematical facts but with one major flaw: he couldn't support the arguments weeks later since his brain had already conquered the medical problem with a solution and moved it to "file 13".

As a student, he even tutored the Fourier series but failed every test on the subject itself since his brain would typically shut down to something already conquered. Perhaps it is some protective measure his brain has to prevent him from altering things too much; perhaps the cockroach floating on a cork within his mind fell off and drowned.

Then there was the time he came up with a process to allow future Mars missions by means of human torpor using a very small device fitted in both ears, but the project had to be placed on "ice" since he altered a Laplace transformation so mush resulting in him misplacing one of the steps within a file buried deep inside his brain.

Not only does he have the ability to amend sophisticated formulas or rewire his brain, but he also has the gift of manipulating his memories during lucid dreaming, for which one such event resulted in him almost spending Valentine's Day with a few knocked-out teeth and perhaps a lacerated lip.

As the story goes, he declared his love to a girl he fancied with the belief that she and her jock boyfriend had split several months earlier. Apparently, he went deep into his grey matter during a dream and altered all possible outcomes when declaring his love but completely messed it up when he misplaced the memory of knowing she was actually already engaged. Duh, you may think that happens a lot, but let me add the following.

If you want to know if someone is lying or not, ask them to tell their version of events backwards. They won't be able to since their brain can't store something that didn't happen, but he can, not that he is lying but because he can create and alter the past, present, and future, therefore creating events. To ask me exactly how his brain works will be the same as asking someone to measure the speed of light in one direction. Good luck finding such a person!

Yes, most people certainly grasp everything consciously, but still, only a few manage in some way or another to enter their subconscious, which may drive them insane because they aren't always able to tell the difference between what truly happened and if it genuinely happened. At times, they lose the ability to tip the scales in favor of awareness, leading them to an alley of the *distorted subliminal*. What you've read leading up to this sentence may come across as confusing and unorganized, but everything will be crystal clear at the end, I promise.

I dedicate this book to people who walked the same path as him and those who dare to follow in his footsteps. All said up to now is to give you a foundation on which you can build a beautiful house, not a home, as homes have love, and a house is a structure containing furniture and nothing more.

We see it all the time when hotels market themselves as a home away from home. Do we truly feel at home when we stay at a top-rate hotel? Or do we believe we should, since if we don't, something must surely be wrong with us? Feel free to visit my friend's Manhattan Penthouse or any of his mansions if you want to know the true meaning of "as cold as a witch's tit," not because his places are cold in temperature but because it lacks love, life, and the scents associated with homes. I believe the proper definition for this would be a mausoleum.

Again, all you need to do for now is put aside your views on life and focus on solving the matter concerning his death. I would go as far as to say that you can choose if he dies or not... Nah, I'm just trying to confuse you a bit more.

Enjoy this adventure. Don't try to assign an ICD-10 code to what my dear friend is since he is a human and not a what. After all, I dare to tell his story with the utmost respect, as should you.

Every chapter starts in a unique way where my dear friend's experience and knowledge are shared, followed by actual events and dialogue, for what he does is based on information gained throughout his life, regardless of accuracy and confusion. After all, Shakespeare said: "A jack of all trades is a master of none, but often better than a master of one."

As a precaution, don't let your children read this book. Yes, your children, the ones you are trying to shield against the evils of the world since they are innocent with no possibility of them doing something wrong against others, just like Jeffrey Dahmer's parents believed as he grew up.

Who cares about your children anyway except you, who perhaps secretly watches porn while beating the bishop or auditioning the finger puppets and possibly treating your better half like crap—I guess you swiped right on the wrong one... What, beyond a reasonable doubt, makes you think they will refrain from reading this after observing your protest?

What is more rewarding than exploring what your parents warned you about? Trust me, they will investigate whatever you deem inappropriate. Wake up and smell your coffee, sunshine. After all, aren't you also the one serving the hard-boiled eggs without sharing the fact that they are eating something which popped out from the same hole, the Cloaca, which chickens poop from?

Then, there is another thing you need to be aware of: You might get offended during this joined expedition. If so, feel free to take it up with whoever said what. The characters in this journey will surely step on toes, test belief systems, and challenge thoughts. Certain things may be seen as made up with the intent to offend, which isn't the case, nor can I apologize on their behalf since I'm only the story-teller. Then again, you may conclude that the person who offended you may be perceived as unstable.

What I've learned from life is not to screw with someone who is more unstable than a Soviet-era claymore. Also, as a heads-up: consult your translation app to keep up with some foreign languages that present themselves throughout. Enjoy this story of a man with an overloaded brain generating 40 Watts of electricity 24/7, 365!

"If a man has not discovered something that he will die for, he isn't fit to live"

MARTIN LUTHER KING, JR

1

———————————

A SUCCESSFUL BUSINESSMAN

August 2023

There's nothing like a well-tailored suit, not only because it shows elegance but also because you only need to wash and iron the shirts and occasionally send the rest to the cleaners. The word cleaner or plural form can describe two things: one is a hitman for the Cosa Nostra, and the other is a business that dry-cleans suits. Only the rich understand the third meaning, which I selectively neglected to add because the difference between enslaving a person and a cheap domestic laborer is one dollar...

———

Rays of sunlight promise a beautiful day through high-rise buildings onto lower Manhattan's busy jagged sidewalks. People dressed in suits and the occasional tourist rush to the end of a maze, which leads to a return journey in the late afternoon. Taxis, Suburbans, and limos are bumper to bumper with horns honking as if communicating in Morse Code; a few short honks for getting your ass

1

moving and several extended ones for emphasizing how to get the fuck out of the city.

Food vendors are selling the best heartburn has to offer while some patrons sip on disposable coffee cups, not realizing the lack of hygiene from the pot. Shoulder to shoulder and with little emotion, they rush through a straightened Serpentine Ramp, getting one day closer to retirement or perhaps affording that one-bedroom apartment Manhattan boasts about.

A well-dressed businessman in a tailored blue suit exits the slaughter row, like a Judas goat, into a brightly lit bespoke tailor shop, De Luca Sartoria. He is Jacob Van Der Linde, a 38-year-old self-made billionaire, the proud owner of several patents, and a polyglot whose mastery of German is better than the chancellor himself. His crafted leather shoes reflect the ceiling lights as he places heels and toes one after the other on a straight path toward greater success. His posture is upright, his shoulders slightly pulled back and down but not in a forced way. His core is tight, the result of hours of Pilates, while his arms are relaxed and not showing any visible signs of his well-defined biceps. He maintains a consistent pace, with hips showing minimal movement. His face expresses confidence, the kind that a president has before he or she addresses the nation.

This is a man who got where he is today, not because of rich parents or a bank, but due to his endless commitment to learning new things with the aim of mastering them all. Suits with hand-picked stitching don't define him; rather, it is his ability to portray mystery or what some will call an enigma. MENSA members will describe him as a subject who doesn't fit within the bell curve governed by the Stanford-Binet test or the Cattell equivalent. He never saw a reason why he should take part in any form of testing to determine his intellect. Perhaps he is under the acceptable range to become a MENSA member or above.

No one will truly know since his ability to learn a new skill doesn't indicate intellect. The only number that genuinely means something to his admirers is the number of zeros added to the annual bonuses he pays to his staff.

Not only does he conform to the definition of being an autodidact, but whatever he sets out to learn happens fast, evidenced by learning English within the first year of university.

It's not as if he was never exposed to English but that he never truly cared for the one-hour weekly lesson during high school. English back then, or any other language besides his native, was solely used during rough sex or a fight; don't fuck with a kid who knows a few English words since he may just have seen the latest Bruce Lee movie and will kick your ass.

It may just be before your time when kung-fu movies were dubbed in English. If not, you'll clearly remember the movement of kung-fu stars' mouths with failed synchronization of sounds. Now imagine doing that at a schoolyard fight. That alone should make you fear your opponent, especially if you expect a right hand but get floored with a left since it sounded like he is about to use his right.

Jacob is the kind of man you want to introduce your sister to, especially knowing he has his shit together, has a six-pack, and a jaw chiseled from a 150 GPA diamond. When he smiles, he reveals his faintly visible symmetrical dimples shadowed by his five o'clock. His teeth have been complimented by some of the more renowned dentists around the Southern end of Central Park. They compel those who have always wanted to explore his lips during sunrise as he serves you breakfast wearing nothing but an apron accompanied with a subtle, raspy morning voice.

Some, not all ladies, may compare that to "I'll most likely be late for work," while others may compare the raspy voice to the film version of Bram Stoker's *Dracula* when Gary Oldman says: "Aren't you forgetting something?" Jacob always wears the same cufflinks complimenting his Ralph Lauren shirts and, at the same time, shows his love for English bulldogs.

Strangely, he doesn't wear ties from his collection of red, pink, black, or grey, which he only reserves for weddings and funerals since the dead may perhaps rise to the occasion to overcome the general shock of someone not dressing to impress just before deviled eggs are about to be served.

Regardless of the occasion, he will turn any respectable mourning woman or bride into a percolator once they get to know him. In his pocket, a handkerchief square with an embroidered crest representing the principles he stands for, his family name, and around his left wrist, a Hora Mundi 5717 by Breguet.

At 6'2, he carries the scent of a cultured man well acquainted with the different notes and chords a private Nose crafted as recommended by those who can only wish to have the private perfumer on their payroll. His stature demands respect, while his education taught him when to speak. Some may see him as a confused individual, but the cultured will recognize him as the ideal example of a metro man, a billionaire metro man.

Canvassed jackets are neatly displayed on Jersey Forms, with full suits lining the walls inside multiple dark-stained Italian oak cabinets. None of the suits on display are to be browsed since they are reserved for final fittings. Oxford leather lures any metro man for a fit in class while a seasoned cobbler patiently finishes the last stitches of what has become a creation of his trade. A junior cutter with meticulous precision drafts a chalk pattern on a piece of cloth using dot paper, while an apprentice tailor stitches buttons for a final fitting.

Whoever or whatever they are, they all wear a custom-made apron with the insignia associated with De Luca. The owner approaches Jacob and extends his soft, warm hand; he is senior cutter Giovanni De Luca, also known as the Methuselah of cutting, a well-respected grumpy old Sicilian. He is short, around 5'2, clean-shaven except for his mustache and a forehead with so many frown layers you could screw his hat on. His mustache is between a Dali and a Hungarian butcher with slightly waxed tails. This is not just any cutter; oh no, this is the man who knows more influential people than the pope knows words from the Dead Sea Scrolls.

Some argue he's part of the underworld, *if not the underworld itself*, whereas others may mistake him for a janitor version of a shorter Alfred Pennyworth as portrayed in "Batman". His mysterious persona can be compared to the beginning or end, birth or death, and possibly Spring or Fall.

Even so, his attire is simple yet perfectly tailored. His smell reminds you of someone you may have met as a child but with no memory of that friendly person. No, I'm not referring to the mothball and medication combo smell of your gran's closet but to something that you only smelled once or perhaps twice in your life.

It possibly was the faint smell of cinnamon, tangerine, or a combination of essential oils. Once you smell it, you'll close your eyes, and just for a moment, your memories drift off to the pleasant feeling of being free with the weight of the world lifted from your shoulders. We all know that smell, yet we can't place it even though it brings up good memories.

Giovanni may come across as a grumpy Sicilian who lost all his belongings to the Cosa Nostra. Still, for some reason, he always has a livelier spirit when he sees a regular, especially Jacob. Regular doesn't point toward the company of a known face every month, not only because both are genuinely devoted businessmen with little time for chit-chat but also because their business transactions are of a strange complexity, which should never be seen as a standing agreement.

***

"Good morning, my good Sir," says Giovanni in a thick Sicilian accent.

"Buongiorno maestro taglierina per abiti," replied Jacob with an accent between a Brit-Australian and a New Zealander with a hint of South African. "Did I say that correctly?" asks Jacob. Inquisitively,

De Luca responds, "Perfetto! What brings you here this lovely morning, Sir?" De Luca knows perfectly well why Jacob decided to visit but always pretends to be surprised.

Both know this dance quite well and keep to the status quo of professionalism set forth by elegant and respected businessmen, including pirate captains. With a faint smirk, he replies, "Time for a new suit, maestro." De Luca Sartoria isn't precisely the kind of place to show up in your JC Penning suit, nor is it where a high school kid high on hormones can have his suit made for prom night. No, it's so much more, a place where only the crème de la crème of New York has their suits made and not altered. Giovanni isn't the kind of man that would ever judge, but he will direct you to the store where people rent for the occasion.

Every second-fitting suit will go through his hands and receive the seal of approval, a personally stitched tag by the maestro himself. He pays more attention to detail than a teenage princess scouting for a pimple on her forehead. Legend has it that De Luca Sartoria has been there since the first cornerstone of the Fraunces Tavern was laid back in 1719 by the De Lancey family.

Thinking of it may come across as being ridiculous, but no one truly knows how old Giovanni De Luca is. Some street kids swear they've seen him turn into a bat at night, while those with needles and powder in the alleyways describe him as the original Chupacabra. Needless to say, don't mess with your barber, your barman, or Giovanni De Luca. They tend to have more information than the internet itself.

"Follow me, Sir," says Giovanni. Jacob slowly follows him as if Giovanni is on his way to competing in the annual tortoise race. Step by step, they make their way to a sizeable anti-fatigue mat with the De Luca crest pressed into it. This is where Giovanni takes his measurements, just like a trained veterinarian will inspect a grumpy English bulldog, with Giovanni being the dog. He doesn't believe in filing dimensions merely because he believes every client should always be treated as a new customer, regardless of how often they've visited.

A price tag of $20000 should always be justified by perfection, not by a quarter inch to the left or right, but with no tolerance. On the other hand, Jacob's suits are unique and in a completely different class regardless of Gucci's opinion; that's to say, he was to discover the uniqueness. Jacob removes his jacket and hands it to the apprentice. Giovanni starts the measurements carefully and with precision. "Please raise your arms, Sir," he instructs. Jacob raises his arms slightly above his shoulders while Giovanni measures around the broadest part of Jacob's chest, the measurement essential to get the right fit for his jacket.

Giovanni's apprentice records the measurement in a small pocketbook, the same kind of book your great-grandfather used to record the shopping list for his tool shop and the to-dos from his soul mate. "Lower your arms, please," he instructs. He places the end of his tape measure at the shoulder seam of Jacob's shirt and gently slides it down his arm toward his wrist. He is fully aware of his surroundings, but in the back of his head, he still ponders about the letter he has to post.

Will I be able to do it perfectly, and will it reach its intended recipient, Jacob questionably thought. The apprentice records the measurement to get a proper sleeve length. The maestro places the end of his tape measure in Jacob's armpit and pulls it down to his wrist. Jacob is as silent as the grave, a man with few words but a mind that works overtime. Next, he measures around the neck just below the Adam's apple and slightly above the collarbone. "18.5 pollici," utters Giovanni. "An ideal measurement," replies the apprentice. De Luca measures his waist, his out and inseam, and concludes by measuring his rise from the bottom of his crotch to his waist.

"I'll have it ready by next week Thursday. Does that suit you, Sir?"

"Light grey, right?"

"I never forget, Sir."

"But I never told you."

"It's the only color you still haven't chosen, Sir."

"You are a remarkable man, maestro De Luca."

"And you are a pleasure to work with, Sir."

The apprentice hands Jacob his blue jacket, and he fits it back fast and accurately, just like Superman hangs his cape in a telephone booth. "I'm off. Please send my regards to your beautiful wife, maestro."

"And you to your beautiful dogs, Sir."

"Thanks. They're the best money and love can buy, Signor De Luca."

De Luca knows it takes a strange man to name one of his dogs after a city, but at the same time, he admires the possibility that the name has a deeper meaning.

Jacob extends his hand, and Giovanni reciprocates with a firm shake. He moves toward the door facing the street just like Gaspard Ulliel would at the end of a Bleu de Chanel commercial, exits De Luca Sartoria, and back into the straightened Serpentine Ramp. He picks up his pace, ensuring that he keeps up with the "Geise" folk as he aims for a USPS box across the street from Anna-Maria's Diner. He approaches it, stops, and removes an envelope from his inner pocket. He carefully inserts the envelope and explores the opening, longer than most would, ensuring the letter has made its way into the belly of the beast.

Is that his dark secret, unable to confidently drop a letter into a postal box? Not even remotely! Whenever he posts a letter, he always spends a long minute ensuring the letter does indeed fall into the box's bag. Why, you ask? It's straightforward; he needs to ensure he did it right. As to his secret, he is allergic to love and extremely good at it. Compare him to Hannibal Lecter if you want, but know that

Jacob will outsmart the masked cannibal in every aspect of twisted psychology.

It is truly a strange spectacle seeing Jacob, the highly skilled autodidact, inserting letters regardless of whether it was in Osaka, Milton Keynes, Frankfurt, Milano, or Cape Town, where he inserted 3, 2, 3, 2, and 1 letter respectively. He has performed the same ritual to perfection, like a college kid dicing hotdogs for his cooked Ramen; it must be done with perfection.

This man can untie a bra using one hand, yet he struggles to do this basic simple thing: posting a letter. He reminds me of a crow dancing around an object even if, in his case, he is stationary. Contrary to popular belief, crows don't just stand mindlessly admiring an object. Instead, it always tries to solve some form of puzzle. He carefully crosses the street, jaywalking between the slow-moving traffic towards Anna Maria's Diner.

2

DR. JIMMY COOPER'S HOUSE

I live in a town where driving a rectangular box with wheels seems to be the "in" thing, but I genuinely don't get it, to be frank. What fascinates me more is the number of miniature plastic ducks they tend to display on their dashboards, and there is not a single scratch, even though it is supposed to be for offroad. On weekends, you'll see them driving without doors and a missing roof, even if it's lion cold.

Lion cold refers to my ex's penis after getting out of a pool when only the head and mane are visible. These drivers occasionally take their prized possessions to someone's farm to test the ducks' capabilities for gripping onto the dashboard. I will never comprehend why you would want to record a one-minute clip showing off the quasi-adventure you took on your way to the Himalayas, with the route starting on someone's farm down South and ending at the entry gate where they have a few beers and end up discussing the magnificent power below the hood of a vehicle which offers little comfort according to ex drivers.

I may be seen as a hater, which I'm not, but I'd instead buy myself a proper car that provides everything thought of just after the

Second World War, like a BMW. Did you know that BMW's insignia resembles a plane's propeller because they used to specialize in building plane engines? If you believe this, you should stick to your small pecker pickup, your ducklings, Nipon hybrid, or that thing created by a man who thinks it's a good idea to send people to Mars except himself.

So, what does the BMW insignia mean, and where did it originate from? BMW's logo originates from the State of Bavaria, where the car manufacturer wanted to resemble the State's official colors. However, using coats of arms and symbols of autonomy in commercial insignias wasn't allowed back then. Hence, BMW displays the colors in an inverted manner. By the way, Bavarians don't see themselves as part of Germany, the ones shouting "Nein-Nein-Nein" at the end of the "Inglorious Bastards" movie…

Vintage City is undoubtedly one of the most sought-after places by highly skilled medical specialists such as plastic surgeons, cardiologists, psychiatrists, etc. Most people in this well-established suburb of New York City own their homes, with price tags ranging into the millions.

Houses here aren't built from a neighborhood development plan, having a model house with financiers about to add a ridiculous interest rate for first-time home buyers. Instead, this is a neighborhood where architects can display contemporary designs and palace-like structures where pseudo-kings and queens refrain from having washing-drying lines in their garages or backyards.

You won't see any couple driving a golf cart down the quiet streets to visit their next-door neighbor with LED lights illuminating the cart's frames like the overweight Uncle Fred and his one-night stand he is about to show off, hoping to get approval from his neighbors. Ample parking spots at each house aren't reserved for sports cars but rather to give a large extended family the peace of mind of not having their cars scratched by kids in the streets riding their bikes with playing cards fixed to the rear wheels to simulate engine sounds during Thanksgiving and Christmas. Front porch chairs give you a sense of romance or sophistication while displaying imports from Bali or rocking chair craftsmanship from an Amish community in Pennsylvania.

Christmas lights during the festive season are hung by companies conforming to HOA standards, while inflatables dismiss the occult displayed during Halloween when children are well-behaved when choosing a favorite candy bar from silver designer salad bowls. Big fluffy dogs, the kind you will see in "The Never-Ending Story" or "Marley and Me", welcome guests to the French and Mahogany Palma doors with a wagging tail and a nose print. Let's agree to disagree on the dog reference for "The Never-Ending Story". Agreed, he was a dragon, yet he looked pretty much like a big fluffy dog.

Yes, Nassau County is one of the best places to live in New York and so for several reasons, excluding the ones already mentioned. This is also not a place where you'll see some secret societies or fraternity coat of arms at the front doors, nor will you see a bumper sticker boasting about a child's final year in school or one bragging about being a dad or mom of a child in a well-respected military division.

These fine folk conform to the definition of class and elegance. Other medical professionals, less qualified, will never experience the perfectly trimmed lush greenness the streets display, the front-page gardens designed by top landscapers and maintained by owners with a green thumb, or the large swimming pools, the backyard basketball courts, and even the fine country club where you can either practice your swing, swing with or without medical consequences, or pretend you have a swing.

All you can do is dream about living in such a utopia when you will eventually realize that "faking it till you make it" doesn't apply here, nor will your overtime as an hourly worker get you closer to affording the HOA fees. After all, this isn't exactly the kind of book a sophisticated person would read. Don't get me wrong, I'm not trying to say they are better human beings, but rather that we sometimes have to accept the fact that we can't live above our means.

That's how the world works, and there's nothing you can do about it. But remember this: they aren't as intelligent as you think because they never truly grasped the story of the three little pigs. I'll let you figure that out yourself. Now that I think about it, this can pretty much include every person in our beautiful country living in something that has a roof covered by shingles.

Vintage City's front yards are annually competing for the Mr. and Mrs. Wilson Garden Award, which is truly something to boast about, taking into consideration that you'll be the talk of the town among those who don't trim their bushes and those who believe missionary style is the only position since before Noah introduced the Afghan Hound after the flood.

If you compete, you must be damn sure no one else knows your secret. Last year Anny Du Preez managed to pull it off. Her secret, wait for it, was nothing more than a dedicated landscaper who is vertically challenged and uses the word "amigo" twice a day when sweating his ass off in the sun. All she had to do was to pay him handsomely and occasionally pretend she was pruning her roses. Sure, there was a massive dispute from other contestants, but she knew pretty well that her "bush" had to be trimmed just before the judge's "inspection."

As might be expected, 48-year-old Anny thoroughly understands the power of luring a male judge to the Afghan hound experience, or was that the reverse cowgirl? Honestly, I can't remember, but I do know that the judge's wife is smiling from ear to ear with the new "positions sexuelles" he introduced her to. After all, he had a good teacher. Rumor has it that Miss 48 also "had a go" with

Jimmy Cooper, the well-respected psychiatrist living a few blocks away.

How and why does this young woman push her desires onto upstanding gentlemen? Her husband is eighty fucking eight and can't keep up with her libido – nor keep it up at all. Do you blame her, and if so, why? Think about it, but not for too long. It is indeed true that age doesn't limit your hunger for intimacy, but can you do it seven times a day at the age of eighty or early nineties?

Jimmy Cooper, the highly successful psychiatrist, decided to go home early and is doing so slightly on the wrong side of the road in his X5 Beemer, which is fully capable of doing zero to sixty in 3.8 seconds while you enjoy the smell of a well-crafted leather interior. Hans and Joachim, from the BMW R&D department, also added the latest drive technology, not to mention the intelligence BMW enthusiasts long for, carefully installed by a Turkish or Greek technician. What else does a man need? Perhaps a 5-bedroom house filled with the aroma of freshly baked cookies, a loyal wife, and three kids taking turns riding on the back of a big fluffy dog. Shame on Jimmy for texting and driving at 35mph on a 20mph street!

Will he be allowed to self-prescribe mood stabilizers if he were to run a child over? Nobody ever asks that question, do they? We would want to see his license to practice revoked, or better, have him beg for his life just before the "hangman" pushes the button to release the fatal toxic nerve gas on a man strapped to a chair as urine stains the front of his pants.

What is it with us and selective vengeance anyway? Nevertheless, Cooper has had a pretty shitty day and is about to put an end to his road of destruction. This man has everything in life, or with what the good Lord can bless you with, but he has completely disregarded the fact that he started as a struggling student with a shit load of debt, late-night studies, and overcoming his past failures.

We quickly assume we are entitled to the best fruits life offers, but assumption is the mother of all fuckups. Like my mother used to say, never forget your roots. Hell, if I had Jimmy's money and influence, I'll likely also screw up as I go through life. But in his defense, how can you possibly maintain a healthy life as a psychiatrist when all you do is to work with brokenness, or perhaps you can use this as an excuse, knowing that people will sympathize with you when shedding a tear.

Suppose you can pull this off, shedding a tear while in a consensual sexual relationship with Miss 48. In that case, you'll be on your way to becoming the best con with access to the world of mastering psychological manipulation, which your wife will eventually catch up to. After all, all psychologists need a psychologist, and every psychiatrist needs a psychiatrist.

Jimmy approaches his two-story, five-bedroom house down Filibuster Street, just before the cul-de-sac. His front yard lawn is perfectly mowed with beautiful blooming plants guiding the occasional visitor to the front door. He slowly pulls up to his double garage and opens the electric door using his rearview mirror remote button. He pulls in and closes the door, which happens to stop atop the big fluffy dog's tennis ball.

So why did Jimmy leave the psychiatric clinic that early in the afternoon? Is it because he and Miss 48 are about to do the horizontal monkey dance?

I forgot to mention Jimmy just lost his job. He's on the verge of bankruptcy, and his wife decided to pack her stuff, grab the kids, and make her way to a better future. Hell, she even took the big fluffy dog. And you thought you were having a lousy day… The last thing he wants to do right now is to engage in any sexual activity, regardless of the promising adventure a perfectly shaped buttock has to offer.

What's currently going through his head is a feeling no suicide survivor can honestly describe except remembering there was total darkness, no hope, and a point of no return. Rationality leaves your soul while the devil takes complete control of the situation, or so exorcists will say. You feel hopelessly abandoned, with emotional pain running up and down your spine and deep into the darkest part of the brain, abandoned at that point by reason, the grace of God, and the purpose-driven book you read somewhere in your life.

In some cases, it may likely feel as if your heart broke as it tries to burst through your chest from pain and angst. No tablet known to man can prevent the action that follows the decision to end it all. Perhaps total peace will calm your emotions, or perhaps that is just a way for your body to give up. The shitty part is that failure brings an intense feeling associated with survivor guilt; what the fuck did I just do? Regardless, your brain will shield you as you go against the meaning of life as it scrambles to find a solution to preserve the most important thing in your life: you.

You may conclude that what I just mentioned is gibberish. Yet as I said, reason abandons you, and your brain is firing signals not meant to be fired, and nothing will make sense besides ending it all. His brain is in complete overdrive, and it doesn't seem there's a way out. At least he texted the landscaping company on his way not to show up the next day.

Jimmy exits his car, leaves the garage through the back door, and returns with duct tape, a swimming pool pipe, a few rags, and a costly bottle of bourbon. Tears are streaming from his eyes while he struggles to open the bottle. Eventually, he takes a few gulps, lights a pre-rolled blunt he confiscated from a patient's bedroom drawer, and connects the swimming pool pipe from the exhaust to a partially open back window. He tapes the pipe tightly and seals the gaps at the rear using a few rags.

At this stage, he is set to end his life. Ironic, isn't it? Everyone on this round ball we live in has a breaking point. I don't care if you're the "Queen of England" or as tough as the "Man of Steel" with an impenetrable mind; you have a breaking point, and self-destruction will find it. His arrived today with compliments from his arrogance. He gets into his car and takes several more gulps.

I'm not sure how much you know about ass, gas, or grass, but you don't die immediately when trying to gas yourself to death. There are a few stages before you reach the end, which may or may not be good. If you're lucky, you'll abandon this gamble before you fall asleep, and if you are unlucky, you'll be a vegetable wearing diapers for the rest of your life with a car no one will ever buy from you.

Several moments later a neighbor's white Lab approaches the unresponsive body of Jimmy Cooper, face up, on the perfectly mowed lawn. The dog licks Jimmy's face just as he shows signs of life. He slowly sits up, disorientated, and stares at his open garage. I shit you not; someone forcefully crawled under the partially open garage door and stole Jimmy's BMW and even the tennis ball! Imagine that, not having any luck at all. The gods have spoken, Jimmy, the gods have spoken. I wish I knew his lawn's secret—definitely not pig manure.

3

A CONUNDRUM AT A FUNERAL, TWO WHALES, AND 5000 LOAVES OF BREAD

If you ever decide to dig up an old grave, and I mean old, like pre-Spanish Flu old, you shouldn't be surprised to find scratch marks on the inner lid of the coffin. Several of these strange phenomena were even observed much later than the Spanish flu extermination.

Just what are those scratch marks from? Well, prior to modern medical science and device development, it was pretty common to diagnose a person as dead, that is, if diagnoses of being dead were ever made, which resulted in people being buried alive with a heart rate so low that it couldn't be detected.

Even though the stethoscope was invented by a French physician, Rene Theophile Hyacinthe Laënnec, back in 1816, physicians were rare, and medical knowledge was limited to those willing to steal a fresh body recently buried to practice dissection with the hope of understanding anatomy and physiology better. Hell, some even went so far as to kill drunken tavern patrons on their way home when fresh corpses weren't available at the local graveyard.

This phenomenon of being buried alive was soon realized; thus, a rope was installed in the coffin, leading to a bell. Not only was the bell used to indicate that you're still alive, but someone had to monitor these bells with the hope the person appointed to do the monitoring isn't as drunk as a lord or high as a kite on whatever shroom he picked in a forest—therefore, the famous proverbs, saved by the bell, and doing the graveyard shift.

If it does happen that you ring the bell, taking into consideration you are six feet below the surface, you should also hope that the shovel will be quick enough to lift the amount of force exerted by the soil. After all, graves dug in the 1800s were typically six feet deep but could be up to twelve feet for the sake of preventing body snatchers from enjoying dissecting you. Will he hear the bell since you won't? That's a question that will drive you insane six feet under. It seems to me that body snatchers had a way of screwing it up for everyone.

You may think that stethoscopes were readily available. However, even then, a person with a super low heart rate buried during the peak of winter can still be buried alive because gas exchange slows down significantly. Your chances of avoiding brain damage when submerged for a lengthy period in cold water are much better than being exposed to water with summer temperatures.

Ask your cardiologist or cardiac surgeon if Aortic Arch Surgery is the thing for you: your head will be packed with ice to minimize cerebral metabolism, allowing complete aortic arch replacement with considerably lower neurological complications and with a minor chance of post-surgery death. Call now, and you may qualify to have a trained technician service the ice maker before your turn under the scalpel. Message and data rates may apply…

———

It's a cold winter morning somewhere in a small eastern European town. Surprisingly, it has a large graveyard with fading lunettes on headstones dating back to the early 1600s and a few fresh flowers marking random graves. Family and friends, slightly covered by gently falling snow, are gathered next to an open grave, ready to say their last goodbyes.

The pallbearers remove a cheap casket from an old Hearse and position it over the lowering device. Tears of grief are on the faces of the family as the funeral director, with a hanging lit cigarette and green visor hat, starts the lowering. Halfway into the process, a sound can be heard coming from within the casket, and it gets louder and more frequent.

The family, in disbelief, orders the director to raise the coffin, while men forcefully try to open the lid using any nearby and available tools. The lid releases, and a man filled with anxiety and fear jumps out and starts running in a random direction with nothing but a hairy ass, a shirt, and a suit jacket. He is disoriented and crosses a busy road; a truck hits him, and he's dead.

The big question is, do we put him back in the casket or send him back to the mortuary? We are fascinated with death and the endless afterlife possibilities, especially when we read about some bizarre event, such as this, or watch an episode dealing with solving mysterious crimes. We can't wait for the next episode, which may fit in before we head off to bed, regardless of whether we have a busy day the next morning. Why do you think that is? Is it because we can no longer satisfy our partners with intellectual and stimulating conversations, or perhaps we have found our sole purpose: to solve crimes from within our living rooms?

Who is the more fascinating and morbid creature? The episode or the one sitting on a couch with no underwear, saggy breasts, or balls, and who sees intercourse as a chore? By the way, it turned out his heart rate was so low it couldn't be detected. I've seen it a few times back in the day. His wife got arrested several weeks later for foul play—bet she didn't see that coming—poison. She was so close to getting away with murder, which she ultimately achieved, but at a price.

You may ask yourself why this chapter is so short. As I said, everything will be crystal clear at the end. Secondly, I'm not remotely close to being called an author but only someone telling the story of a dear friend. Shall we continue?

4

JACOB'S COCOON AND A WORD FROM OUR SPONSOR, PART I

December 2023

Some of the dirtiest places and objects I can think of are the rails of an excavator at a mall, the handles at a restroom, the little peanut bowl at the bar, the air hand drier, and the famous blocked public toilet. My judgment is that people, specifically men, don't wash their hands after flipping it out, accompanied by silent flatulence and legs spread like giraffes'.

People don't truly think about it, but the fact is that most men only wash their hands when someone else is around. God forbid other men see you neglecting to wash your hands after relieving yourself. On the other hand, I am more concerned about the air hand dryer, not because it sucks the air from the restroom in and then directs it onto your hands, but because I know that taste buds and smell go hand in hand.

If you can smell something, you taste it too, just like wine connoisseurs will partially keep their mouths open when smelling a bottle of red or perhaps something fermented in a cask for several years. The molecules are so small, yet we can smell and taste them simultaneously. Whatever is sucked into the air hand dryer does have a smell and taste which you unknowingly direct onto your hands, with which you later touch your beautiful husband or wife's face. Then there is that special place we all know too well and avoid as far possible as the good lord allows us to: the hospital.

You may be familiar with the strong "hospital" smell that haunts your dreams and is the trademark of a clean healthcare facility. That smell is an attribute of relatively strong chemicals used to prevent unwanted contamination, not that I think there is something like a wanted contamination.

In essence, we are made to believe that chemicals are used to disinfect surfaces and, in this case, a hospital floor. We never give it another thought, but our belief is correct. There's also a saying indicating a pig will stay a pig regardless of the makeup you apply. The uglier the pig, the more makeup is needed, *but it still stays a pig*. Allow me to put this into perspective if I may.

The amount of blood a healthy human has is about 10% of their body weight, which comes down to about 1.2 to 1.5 gallons, or ten units, of which a unit is around 450ml if you are a person like me who compares everything to a pint of beer. Blood consists of 4 basic components that keep you alive and healthy: Plasma, Erythrocytes, Leukocytes, and Thrombocytes.

If you wondered, these four components are also better known as Plasma, Red blood cells, White blood cells, and Platelets. Only 45% of a healthy male's blood consists of Erythrocytes, which we call Hematocrit; for a healthy woman, it's around 40%, whereas less than 1% of our blood consists of Leukocytes and Thrombocytes. Plasma, therefore, makes up the rest of those components that flow through your veins and arteries.

Red blood cell and platelet volumes can be calculated even though they are extremely tiny, emphasizing extremely. The volume is given in something called Mean Volume, for which red blood cell volume is called Mean Corpuscular Volume, and Platelet volume is

MPV. The typical healthy man will have an MCV of between 60 and 120 femtoliter with an ideal of 80 femtoliter.

If you had to write that down, it would be depicted as 80fL, 80 x, or even 0.000000000000080L, which is 1E+15 times smaller than a liter of a well-aged bottle of brandy. That means it's one quadrillionth of a liter, with you having between 4.35 and 5.65 million red blood cells per microliter of blood. Also, a healthy human being's red blood cells typically have a diameter of between 5 and 8µm, which can also be described as 5 to 8 micrometers, more or less, which makes them impossible to see without a microscope.

To think about it, the amount of white blood cells in your body is less than 1% of your blood content: they are the military, the ones that keep you safe, with a typical diameter of between 12 and 15µm, which can only be seen through a microscope. The amount of white blood cells per microliter of blood is between 4,500 and 11,000, substantially less than the amount of red blood cells in your blood. Viruses, or most, vary in diameter from 20 nanometers to the largest of about 500nm with a maximum length of 1000nm. A nanometer is one billion times smaller than a meter and one thousand times smaller than a micrometer, understood as "what the hell" in upper case.

So, just what am I getting at here, you ask? Do you believe having your little pigtailed daughter or future quarterback visit granny in the hospital is a good idea? Sure, white blood cells are larger than viruses, but their numbers don't favor a certain victory. We can compare this to a mass of fire ants engaging in warfare against a foot that accidentally rested on their nest, with the foot being the white blood cell and the ants being the virus. I rest my case… I would rather lick wet paint on walls for a living and go with God than take my little snot nose to visit whoever is in the hospital, where sick people are concentrated under one roof with four walls.

A friend, now a well-respected and successful medical specialist, once took a smear sample from the floor in a hospital and sent it to the microbiology department, where they incubated the sample to see what it could grow. I shit you not; even though the chemicals did their job of keeping the floors shiny, there was a kind of growth that may cause you to grow an extra eye or perhaps a horn associated with some mythical creature.

Sure, you believe your child needs to be exposed to build a healthy immune system, but this is not a place where you let them touch surfaces regardless of the findings of the infectious disease department. If that still concerns you, I can refer you to another friend who takes all medical insurance for performing a snip-snip.

Allow me to share another interesting medical fact that may make you come across as Asclepius, the Greek and Roman god of medicine and healing: Antibiotics don't do shit to a virus, but they can help to treat bacterial infections. And by the way, bacteria can build resilience against antibiotics—just get the snip-snip already.

Humans, for whatever reason, also thought it good to concentrate toilet seats and urinals into a small box called a restroom, also referred to as a bathroom, even though it doesn't have a bath or a shower where a warm toilet seat shouldn't be appealing and appreciated like a warm bar stool. Feel free to visit any male restroom while breathing deeply with your partially open mouth like the sophisticated wine connoisseur.

You may conclude that the storyteller, me, has a foul mouth after reading the previous. Oh no, sir or madam, you will realize the hidden message once you do some intense research into what some antibiotics contain. No, I'm not suggesting that you consult Wikipedia or Barbara, the skinny ex of Uncle Fred, who has seen all the CSI episodes, but rather a proper library or online medical journal platform where you can truly grasp why I used "shit" instead of a more sociably acceptable word.

As for the wet paint licking, how much do you know about yourself if you've never licked wet paint anyway? You can't say you lived if you've never licked wet paint… Add that to your bucket list, along with using a public restroom in Japan, where squatting requires good aim…

It's early in the morning in a busy intensive care unit filled with holiday decorations and exhausted staff getting ready to do the handover to the day crew. Family and friends are usually allowed to decorate the private rooms of patients spending their holidays clinging to hope while battling the uncertainty of the next life. Gnomes and ornaments populate small bedside tables specially placed next to each bed by a thoughtful facilities manager and her elves.

This unit has quite a variety of guests, ranging from those who survived the scalpel, those knocking on heaven's door, and the miscellaneous. Please don't judge for using the word miscellaneous since your opinion about being offended will be in vain when you realize they all, or most of them, are on their way out and won't be able to raise their concerns about being offended. Perhaps you should not jump to conclusions but rather contemplate what "on their way out" means.

Ventilators silently compete for the annual preventative maintenance interval while vital sign monitors display graphs, and stacked infusion pumps deliver medicine to those needing cocktails for supporting organ functions.

Jacob lies with a slightly raised head, taped eyes, life subvention units connected, and a tube extruding below the blankets into an almost full catheter bag. The movement of his chest is barely noticeable, while his ventilator fills his lungs with a specific calculated amount of oxygen for an exact amount of time. He looks peaceful even though his body is fighting a battle known for his treating medical professionals as Jacob's Ladder. No, I'm not referring to penis piercings but to Jacob in the Bible, the man who dreamed about a ladder with angelical beings ascending and descending from it. Some of his medical team believes Jacob is about to climb that ladder step by step into the unknown, but we should ask him what he thinks about it.

A nurse enters Jacob's unornamented cubical to check on him and empty his catheter bag. She spends a few moments recording his vital signs and changes his bag. She is the 24-year-old Cassandra, the daughter of Anna-Maria, and a hardworking student on her way to making something with her life even though her mother sees her as the "prophet of disaster" as rooted in Greek mythology. Regardless, her blue eyes can lighten up a room just as much as her pearly white teeth hiding behind her full and soft lips when she smiles from ear to ear like she always does.

For some reason or another, she has stuck with Chinese bob since she was 16 and has never considered wearing her soft blonde hair in any different style, regardless of her mom's will to have her follow in the footsteps of a boring ponytail and the occasional perm. Cassandra is the black sheep with an inquisitive brain, which tends to leave Anna-Maria lost in a maze created by 24-year-old confusion and hormonal instability.

It's almost universal, don't you think, when realizing that some moms and daughters have this hidden thing living inside them that wants to make them scratch each other's eyes out? In all fairness, I may be exaggerating and neglecting that the same applies to some dads and sons. Establishing dominance comes in all forms and genders, just like you will typically notice when getting a Rottweiler.

Believe it or not, I think she's a perfect match for Jacob, at least in my opinion. He does fancy a little bit of craziness and unpre-dictability. But then again, even though I know him quite well, we can't play matchmakers based on my opinion, and not my dear friend's. Heck, I have arranged multiple blind dates in the past, of which several resulted in beautiful families and one being on some dodgy show where men wear diapers to openly express their hidden fetish, also known as "The Springer Show". As mentioned before, way back at the beginning of this journey, you may see him as an enigma whose brain is in a completely different category.

If you know Jacob as well as I do, you'll understand that he is fully aware of his surroundings and digging deep into his subconscious. He is most likely trying to change the past, present, or future with the aim of getting an understanding of how he even got here to start off with. He may have the ability to do weird stuff with his brain, but certain things, like moving your mouth and tongue to speak when you are intubated, are physically impossible. It's almost like filling your complete oral cavity with a cup of sugar or whatever amount you can insert and then trying to speak. In all likelihood, he is frustrated by not being able to communicate with you like a normal human being. Let's let him "talk" for a few, as he shared with me.

Jacob's subconscious thoughts with a raspy voice, "Welcome to my station. There are many like it, but this is mine, or shall I say, my bed. I bet you found the previous two chapters entertaining, even though it is quite disturbing to those who may have lost someone in such a bizarre way.

I stand by what my dear friend said about not wanting to confuse you at any point. He is rather trying to give you a look into the life of a man who's 38, successful, and has no idea what he wants to do for a living. What happened to me, you ask? I guess you'll have to wait till the end."

Cassandra draws blood from Jacob's arterial line using a small heparin syringe connected to a three-way stopcock, disconnects the blood-filled syringe, and places a small rubber cap on the tip. She walks to a Bloodgas machine located at the central monitoring station while gently rolling the syringe between the palms of her hands. She removes the rubber cap, expelling the blood in the tip onto a small gauze by gently pushing the plunger, followed by inserting the tip into the machine's inlet port and pressing the start button. A small built-in peristaltic pump transfers the blood over tiny iron-selective electrodes and pauses to have analyses performed.

The touchscreen displays the results about a minute later, and an automatic printout delivers a needed copy. Cassandra takes the copy and phones the treating cardiologist using the ward's mobile phone. She returns to Jacob's bed, his ventilator, and is still on the phone.

Jacob's subconscious thoughts with a raspy voice, "As my friend said, she is Cassandra, who works the day shift. She'll be adjusting my ventilator, yes, MINE; the other ventilators are connected to other people—duh. It's almost like saying I spoke to MY lawyer or went for lunch with MY broker, which are all useless when you're lying where I am. The mattress doesn't care if I defecate on it, but poor Cassandra does. Ultimately, this may be my last MINES, so let's pretend its MINE! I bet a *Lord of the Rings* character would've said that way better.

I've been here so often, not in this specific room, but connected to all these devices. I can tell you precisely what they are and what they do. Let's start with Cassandra's actions, shall we? In all fairness, you didn't choose to read this book to be educated on medical devices but rather on something more mental. We'll get there, I promise, just like my dear friend did."

Cassandra adjusts the ventilator while on the ward's mobile phone. A ventilator is a highly sophisticated device that keeps you alive; hence, it's called a life subvention unit, which can pull you through respiratory failure. This state-of-the-art device isn't just connected and left running but must be adjusted depending on various factors. There's even a qualified engineer appointed to take care of the ventilator's maintenance and potential troubleshooting scenarios, which aren't limited to ICU usage but may be required during surgeries.

Occasionally, a qualified engineer would need to replace parts during surgery, such as an oxygen cell, when needed. However, a standalone ventilator isn't used during surgery but rather an anesthetic machine, also known as a Boyles' machine, which is a more complex system that an anesthetist will use to keep you sedated while ventilated via intubation.

You may think the surgeon is the most crucial person in a theatre. Still, it would be a combination of highly skilled medical professionals such as an anesthetist, perhaps a cardiovascular perfusionist, and those who need to know every tool by name to support the surgeon. Since I'm the one sharing Jacob's life story, I get to choose the more important person during the surgery: the anesthetist.

Any person walking this planet can kill someone. Though not every person can keep you alive and calculate how much nitrous oxide, halothane, isoflurane, desflurane, or sevoflurane can be or should be used during a surgical procedure, which is also dependent on the length of the surgery. If your lungs collapse, you are at the mercy of the person responsible for running the anesthetic machine, just like a disc jockey is responsible for ensuring a hell of a good party for one-legged people high on nitrous while on a high beam crossing from the Empire State Building onto the top of the Brooklyn bridge.

So why did I choose to use the word theatre and not something most acquainted with, such as a surgery room? No, I'm not referring to the popcorn, soda, and making out setting but to something you can experience horror in person instead of on the big screen. Several centuries ago, surgeons performed cutting and gutting with numerous spectators, not just for studying medical professionals but also for those with the stomach to handle blood, guts, and the occasional rib sheers. Back then, medicine was still relatively in a kind of infancy, and all kinds of solutions were applied just to be seen as the best surgeons of their time. It was, and still is, common practice to have medical professionals attend a procedure never seen before to gain the knowledge required to apply it themselves.

Certain procedures, closer to our time, represent something done by someone closer to being a witchdoctor than a doctor, such as the famous Lobotomy, which, believe it or not, was developed not so long ago, therefore bringing forth a reasonable question: if this was a medical solution, what on earth did they do prior?

In 1936, this barbaric procedure was performed by its "inventor," Walter Freeman, who believed he'd found a way to diminish the pain and distress of the emotionally ill. The first procedure, the one in 1936, was performed on a woman who suffered from agitated depression and sleeplessness. According to him, it was a great success. Still, I bet President John F Kennedy strongly disagreed after his sister Rosemary underwent this procedure, ending up with the need for full-time care.

So, just what did this procedure entail? It originally started with drilling holes in the top of his patients' skulls to sever the connections between the frontal lobes and the thalamus. The procedure then evolved into hammering, not inserting, an ice pick-like tool through their eye sockets with a mortality rate of around 15%, give or take.

My question, however, is simple: Did Freeman face the firing squad, or did he get a slap on the wrist like several practitioners get when they've messed up? Perhaps this is also a solution Anna-Maria and her beautiful daughter Cassandra should look into if they can't settle the unrest among them. Rest assured, this horrific procedure ended in 1967 when a housewife in the City of Berkley, California, died due to the imbecile severing a blood vessel, resulting in death caused by a brain hemorrhage.

I say this with the utmost respect and gratitude: God save the Queen and California, the place known for solutions. Why is it that none of the theatre spectators intervened during the first procedure? Is it because they were keen on having a photo opportunity, or were they perhaps as dumb as rocks, too?

If not shocked by this, the following may just do the trick. It is the year 2024, and artificial intelligence is the hot topic of the day, rocket boosters land safely on earth, and Magnetic Resonance

Imaging (MRI) has more to offer than what we could have imagined centuries ago. Still, some medical "professionals" continue a theatre procedure called ECT (Electroconvulsive Therapy), where a certain number of Watts is used to induce a seizure to have chemical changes in an area of your brain, leading to improvements in how those areas of the brain work, or so they say.

All you need to do is bite down hard on a mouthpiece while two dildo size electrodes are pressed against your temples. I'm sure Randle McMurphy from "One Flew Over the Cuckoo's Nest" will vouch for the experience, all thanks to Nurse Ratched. Don't get me wrong, I'm no neurologist or psychiatrist, but the two patients I saw who had it done to them had memory issues, and one urinated in a bathroom sink, resulting in a nurse bursting into tears. Freeman also claimed great success until 1967, and Old Sparky, the electric chair formerly used at Huntsville Unit prison, Texas, proved its success.

I don't dispute the effectiveness of ECT, but I kindly ask the medical professional to do a "self" demonstration. Perhaps Dr. Jimmy Cooper could've tested this approach prior to turning to drastic measures. Again, I'm not a neurologist or psychiatrist but only someone telling a story with a history shared by my friend and some healthy questions you can ask during trivia at the pub. Technology has come a long way, allowing students or professionals to view the surgery remotely simply because there isn't enough room in a surgery room.

Also, the world is moving to virtual training. Imagine having a surgeon performing a highly complex procedure on you that they only saw during a virtual broadcast. Don't stress too much about that; they have good insurance. After all, it's called practicing medicine *with an emphasis on practicing*. Make sure you thoroughly read the fine print before you go ahead and sign permission for surgery. It's not exactly a car you are about to buy, or is it?

Jacob's subconscious thoughts with a raspy voice, "What Cassandra's doing is quite important, to be frank. You see, she can't adjust my ventilator going on RTFM, which stands for "Read The Freaking Manual," better known by engineers as "Read The Fucking Manual." Oh no, she can only do so, and if needed, with the guidance of the treating physician, who, in my case, is a cardiologist. And even then, they have to have something to go by: the results obtained from a state-of-the-art instrument called a Bloodgas machine.

Fuckit, and excuse my French, but this will take way too long to explain everything, but let's make a deal: you keep on reading, and my friend will explain a bit as we go along. To make it worthwhile, you can choose whether I live or die at the end. Nah, I'm just teasing you, just like she said at the beginning. Someone will murder me, but it's your job to figure out who did it and why."

5

"...MALE AND FEMALE HE CREATED THEM". #127

16 years, three months, and seven days ago, one of my exes broke up with me, which truly came as a surprise and a shock at the same time. She was beautiful and had a smile that could light up a room exceptionally fast. She also had a distinct smell, unique to each woman, just like all humans have fingerprints.

This made me think of Jacob's condition, Hyperosmia, which is the term for having a superior sense of smell. He is a connoisseur when it comes to recognizing all the notes and chords a perfume has, and he uses this skill to select or have his favorite elixir crafted.

In perfumery, there are several essential ingredients that we refer to as notes. The different types of notes may include citrus, green, leather, woody, lavender, and more, all chosen by a professional called a Nose. When you mix two or more notes, you'll create a chord, almost like a symphonic sound.

There is even a perfume pyramid depicting three kinds of notes and the amount of time each will present itself. The Head notes, the ones representing the tip of the pyramid, will last around 5 to 15 minutes. The Heart notes, the middle section, will last between 20 to

60 minutes, and lastly, we have the Base notes which typically last longer than 6 hours, as shared by Jacob.

He also recognizes less pleasant smells, which prevents him from visiting certain areas around a hospital, such as the unit where people are about to meet their maker and, more precisely, the morgue. He has the ability to smell death, however, not all the time, due to strong chemicals that may hide this unique smell, such as Formaldehyde, Xylene, and Ammonia.

Whatever you do, show respect to laboratory staff once you've visited the histology department, where xylene is used to ensure tissue removed from a patient is transparent for the sake of making the specimen easier to "read." You don't have to have Hyperosmia to recognize that smell, but rather a firm footing since high concentrations of this chemical can make you high and induce confusion accompanied by slurred speech.

No, you can't craft a signature perfume using Xylene unless you want to smell like cat piss during mating season, almost like the perfume one of my exes wore. Jacob can walk past a woman and tell if they would be a good match, almost like a Tomcat can smell a cat in estrus from a distance. Okay, okay, I chose a shitty analogy, but I'm sure you will get the picture that will eventually end with: Hello, Kitty!

Weird, right? There was this girl he dated who drove his hormones toward being a bunny, not only because he found her intellectually stimulating but because her smell reminded him of something pleasant with a sexual appeal only Debbie had when she did Dallas in the 1978 movie. Please don't Google that with your better half around, like one of the characters you are about to meet, Anny, would say. They, however, didn't last long. Her family was farmers who indulged in everything a freshly butchered animal had to offer, not because they were financially challenged but because of their culture. He had to make the tough call to walk away, given that it didn't sit right with him to eat a sheep's face. The eyes and brains were truly seen as a delegacy.

Just imagine biting down on an eyeball that may or may not explode, just like when you were to bite down on a Kyoho, which translates from Japanese as a giant mountain grape. For the sake of fucks and broomsticks, there is no way I would ever want to portray being the modern animal flesh-eating version of Hannibal Lecter.

Times have changed where just one piece of the brain is for entry-level, and the whole brain is for veterans. If they truly ate it or not, I couldn't give a damn, it's simply weird. People tend to think that the brain is almost like a rubber ball, but little do they know it comes across as such since the consistency is due to the brain being fixed in Formaldehyde.

In reality, our brain's texture is more toward a very soft piece of blubber weighing around 3 pounds, which makes it squishy. Its density makes it much softer than most pieces of meat at your local butcher. When removed during a post-mortem and placed on a flat surface, your brain will disform due to its weight pressing down and the blubber's viscosity.

Brains are fixed in Formaldehyde to denature the protein and, at the same time, harden it. Doing so allows the medical student to study a more solid piece of matter than you can spread on toast accompanied by an egg with a moderate amount of cheese, which you can patent as a replacement for beefsteak Tartare.

Believe it or not, surgeons can even suck some of that grey matter out during surgery using a meager amount of vacuum measured in mmHg or negative pressure, of which some use the latter to describe vacuum when they didn't pay attention during physics.

Poiseuille introduced the mercury hydrodynometer and the mmHg units back in the eighteen hundreds, not the formula for developing an Iron Lung. Therefore, please educate your pig-tailed daughter and future quarterback that some words, such as negative pressure, shouldn't be used unless they are about to design a technique to avoid contaminating outside areas using a left-hand screwdriver.

The human brain is by far the most complex supercomputer we know of, excluding your previous boss' brain, by all means. Your brain consumes around a fifth of your body's energy. It contains about one hundred billion neurons, each having ten thousand connections, making a brain network of a thousand trillion connections.

Not only are these numbers truly remarkable, but your brain even contains twenty Watts of electricity, which any electric car manufacturer can use to power the interior roof lights for a moment or two.

A neuron consists of several parts that allow information, or pulses, to be sent throughout the central and peripheral nervous systems. Every neuron has an Axon terminal, the most distal portion of a neuron's Axon and critical for neural communication. Electrical signals are sent between each neuron's Axon terminals and the receiving neuron's cell body, also known as the Soma.

The catch here is that the Axon terminal of the neuron sending the signal, also known as the neurotransmitter, isn't connected to the Soma of the receiving neuron. A tiny area known as a Synapse has a gap between the Axon terminal and the Soma with an approximate width of twenty to forty nanometers.

A normal metric ruler is divided into centimeters with a total length of thirty centimeters, equal to roughly twelve inches, with one inch being just about twenty-five million nanometers long. The gap itself is called the Synaptic cleft, which relies on particular chemicals, such as Serotonin.

In essence, Serotonin is the chemical through which the electric signal travels from the Axon terminal to the Soma. Around ninety percent of Serotonin can be found in the intestines, leaving ten percent being formed in the brain. Lowering Serotonin levels usually has more than one cause; therefore, it would be an uneducated decision if I had to attribute it to one specific reason. Without further ado, allow me to introduce those created in His image, which you may find well acquainted, yet you can't recognize their scars left by life…

Twelve patients are gathered in a sizeable group therapy room with art covering the walls created during arts and crafts by those eagerly awaiting the group therapist. They are the 39-year-old Anna-Maria, a single mother to a brilliant yet black sheep daughter. Anna-Maria always chooses the seat closest to the door, leading everyone else to claim their spot in the half-moon circle.

A large water dispenser and firm friend to a snack bar is proximal to an arrangement of exotic plants in the corner to the left of the entry, just opposite Anna-Maria, where the possibility exists of an imaginary mid-size orangutan helping itself to mints while peaking from behind the large leaves. Soft music can be heard between the faint water dripping caused by vaporizer mist against the leaves and into a circulation bowl. This light blue painted room with bright color art has several high-end tablets needly stacked on the other side of the entry tangent to the infant Amazone and adjacent to Anna-Maria.

Sitting next to her is Jana, the impatient, foul-mouthed, 22-year-old youngster whose life was ruined by a purple bastard, as she claims. To paint a picture of Jana will take a very skilled artist like Dali with the aim of portraying something Kafkaesque. Whether or not, you don't want to walk a day in her shoes.

Her life at this stage resembles several tumbleweeds tossed around on an endless dried-up Salt Lake surrounded by infinitely high dust walls with no possible escape and with something to quench her thirst. To her left is the legend himself, Dean, a man with a snow-white beard and a history of racial prejudice. He may resemble a wizard who had a staff and a pointy hat, which is my closest description. All I can add is that his pointy hat had no ability to point toward wind direction but had two holes for eyes. Then we have the much shorter 16-year-old James, not because he is truly short, but because the 6'9 Dean dwarfs him.

James is the one who lives behind closed doors where the devil rules with an iron fist. He has not had much exposure to love, but that doesn't mean he lacks the longing. All you need is at least one parent who loves you. William Makepeace Thackeray said it well in his 1848 novel *Vanity Fair*: "Mother is the name for God." Love, nurture, and the protection of God are understood through the image of a mom unless you are The Wolverine Killer.

James might be seen as a pushover, but at least he has enough savvy to realize the need for chair separation between Dean and Cathy, the 63-year-old African American woman, also known as Evangelical Cathy. She will lay hands on you like any good Christian should, followed by a "May I get an Amen!? Jeeeesus!" Perhaps you are embarking on a journey to find a purpose for your life, and if so, refer to Exodus 20:7 and Deuteronomy 5:11, which I personally see as the greatest of the Ten Commandments.

Alicia, an African American young girl, 18 years old to be precise, who relies heavily on emotional support from Cathy, is seated with legs crossed on her egg-shaped chair next to the woman obsessed with the greatness of God. The frail Alicia has no friends except her loving companion and half-blind dog, Charlie. Every group has an upstanding gentleman; in this setting, it's Bram, a successful businessman who recently celebrated his 47th birthday. You can turn to him if your past taunts you during your stay at this modern clinic.

We all know that soft-spoken woman in our close-knit group of friends, if you have friends, who have never truly had to deal with an emotional setback. They will try to hide it as best possible, just like

32-year-old Hanna, who justifies her 3-week visit to her goldfish Jimmy who went missing. Sad, but true. She keeps to herself not because she is shy but because she is ashamed of herself and her failure to have the perfect marriage.

Our next guest is one of those guys you only get to see in a "Dirty Harry" movie or perhaps on top of an alleyway thug while he beats the living shit out of him. He isn't the one you want to piss off when this 50-year-old officer with Elephant tusks for arms and a neck the thickness of an African rhino has access to cuffs and a service pistol. He will either pump you full of lead or perhaps hammer you to death with his stakeout sandwich container. Feel free to call him Stephen or Steve for short, but that depends on his mood.

Some strategically choose their seats, hoping they will reap the benefits of flirting, such as the sexually driven Anny, who has a thing for Bram even though she knows he is married. She seniors Bram with one year and outweighs him with a sex drive benchmark of 7 times daily. She reminds me of the woman I dated who would wake up at 3 in the morning to have a dance inspired by the animal kingdom.

You can't truly call it having intercourse, especially when she's on top while displaying her body on a four-dimensional canvas created by the illusion of continuous orgasms resulting in several demons making their appearance. You would beg her to stop when you realize she's into post-ejaculation torture but with the hope that it will happen again, which will, once you make peace with the fact that the restraints around your wrists and ankles weren't made from plastic or elastics. Don't google that shit unless you intend to make a grown man cry while taking pleasure in milking him drier than the Atacama Desert.

Bob, the 26-year-old prodigy, enjoys sitting next to our hormone-driven princess. I can't truly describe Bob in a singular sentence, but if I had to, it would be something like this: this kid isn't scared of death and would gladly end it all to get the opportunity to explore the unknown. Last but not least, we have the 25-year-old version of Jacob Van Der Linde, our unofficial jester who is a man of few words when sharing his private life. There is truth behind the understanding of broken people using comedy to hide their daily tragedy and trauma.

What all these people have in common is the question to which the answer is relatively complex. They all struggle with the most basic things in life, or at least that which is basic to them individually. None of them can be placed in a box like no other person.

Ask yourself this: when did you last visit a stranger in the hospital? When did you last look in the mirror before heading to work? Does it make you a narcissist lacking empathy if you admire your appearance while neglecting strangers' loneliness while lying in the hospital? Perhaps an ex would describe you as a megalomaniac, making you judge your personality while focusing on your shortcomings.

Remember this: they most likely were deeply hurt, and still are, when they made that diagnosis of who they think you are. Just so you are aware, the ICD-10 code for narcissistic personality disorder is F60.81, as listed by the WHO (World Health Organization), which I believe should be scrapped and banned from being used, just like several countries have banned HIV as the cause of death by medical practitioners.

No one, and I mean no one, except serial killers and pedophiles, should be placed in a box regardless of whether they ate your neighbor's dog; remember that. Sitting in this room may give you the answers to the riddles life has to offer. Still, it can also provoke Polyuria and imaginary sightings of a four-legged friend with a strange condition of shyness if you were ever left alone and alienated.

Some of our patients show signs of agitation, but at the same time, a few radiate the positivity they found during the first two weeks of a three-week luxurious stay in this privately owned medical clinic.

The young, skinny version of Jacob with nails chewed off to the bone decides to entertain the group with a joke he heard back in school. He's wearing Billabong boardshorts, flip flops, and a neon-colored shirt with the Quicksilver logo silkscreened. His short, wet-looking hair makes him appear like a surfer who just stepped out of a shower, accompanied by a subtle smell from Davidoff Cool Water. He may come across as a kid set in wealth, but the opposite is true. Everything he owns and wears is earned by three part-time jobs while attending full-time classes in engineering.

"Anyone ever heard the joke of Saddam Hussein planning to visit the sun?" he asks, luring the crowd with his symmetrical dimples, blue eyes, and shiny teeth. With a perfect mob haircut, dressed in hand-me-down punk rock attire, James peaks beneath his fringe while breaking the silence, "Who is Saddam Husein?" With historical accuracy, Jacob replies, "A Middle Eastern Dictator".

"Continue," replies James while sitting on the rim of the designer chair with tremor legs and clenched fists, clearly showing discomfort and angst.

Jacob, with a well-pulled-off British accent and Colgate smile, continues the joke and uses his impersonation skills to represent the words from the famous three.

"Barack Obama, Vladimir Putin, and Saddam Hussein attended a Space X launch. Putin addresses the crowd."

Jacob, as Putin, in a thick Russian accent, "We put man first in space."

The 50-year-old Stephen, in anticipation, softly utters, "I hate motherfucker commies," even though everything he owns results from indulging in fortunes of war secured by the advantage of being a corrupt police officer.

"Barack steps up to the Mic and laughingly says: That's nothing, we were the first on the moon!" impersonates Jacob with a Midwest

American accent. "Saddam rudely interrupts as he steps up to the Mic with a clenched fist and laughter. That's nothing, you infidels. We will be the first man on Sun," loudly impersonates Jacob, the voice of a madman with a broken Middle Eastern accent.

"May the good lord help this crazy lost soul," adds Evangelical Cathy, who has heard of Saddam, yet she always confuses him with some rogue Chinese leader. Jacob exclaims, "That's preposterous, says Barack!" With an assertive Russian accent, "No man can go to Sun! Man burn like Eastern War."

Most can feel the punchline approach and gather at the edges of the expensive egg-shaped chairs designed by none other than a world-renowned Danish architect. Jacob boldly represents the Middle Eastern madman using true dictator confidence and charisma, "Barack and you are stupid! We go to Sun when dark!"

Stephen launches out of his chair, "That was freaking brilliant, Aussie! You should be a stand-up comedian!" Most of the group breaks out with laughter, except a few who are more anxious by the challenge of partaking in a group session than anything else, even though this is their last week with multiple previous group sessions and "whoosah" moments. Have you ever experienced stage fright regardless of the number of times you practiced "I quit" in the mirror? The same applies here.

Getting back to Stephen, the man who has seen it all on the streets of Chicago, an ex-copper still waiting for his disability till they realize he shot himself in the leg for disability. As the story goes, he entered a crack house with the intent to confront some dealers who owed him protection money. The cockroach on the cork floating in his brain fell off, and he saw it as an opportunity to shoot himself in the leg, hence the disability claim. Once the cockroach climbed back on the cork, he realized the possibility of having forensics determine the round came from his service pistol. He then tried hanging himself while intoxicated but comprehended yet again that he wouldn't get disability once that's done—bourbon is a bitch! He ended up here thanks to the fine folk from EMS after his wife found his unresponsive body below the noose about half an hour after gulping a copious number of analgesics using his favorite distilled alcoholic beverage made from corn. As the saying goes: "Self-destruction will find you."

By the way, google the difference between Whiskey and Whisky, as you may be seen as a liquor omniscient at a friend's divorce party. You don't want to start a liquor war after all, even if both the Scottish and the Irish agree to "uisce breatha, " which is the Gaelic phrase that means "water of life."

As to the actual intent, the one I just shared, it would be better to keep to his original version of wanting to confront some badass people if you want to be considerate of him being here. But then again, he is an ex-copper with a questionable reputation. At the peak of laughter, the group therapist enters the room, fills a paper cup with water, and finds her dedicated egg-shaped chair.

She is 29-year-old Helga, a clinical psychologist who not only has a love for people, antiques, and animals but who has more psychology experience than anyone brave enough to host their own clinical YouTube channel, or shall we say dumb enough. She softly greets the group despite the laughter as she settles into her chair, "Morning, everyone," with only a few respectfully paying attention and replying.

Helga, also known as Beautiful Helga by her peers, can recognize scars left by life in the troubled souls of those equally created in His image. She would be any male patient's fantasy if she didn't have a slight resemblance to your sister, your mother, or perhaps God herself, which goes against any endorphin and oxytocin delivery when trying to fantasize about someone so perfect.

You feel an immediate emotional connection when in her presence with the reassurance that everything will be all right. You will quickly forget that something was wrong to begin with. Her calm voice doesn't portray weakness but something entirely the opposite, which only a few people have as part of their DNA. It's not precisely comfort nor discomfort, but only something Angelical beings ascending and descending Jacob's Ladder have.

Call her an angel if you want, as long as you understand that she can't truly be defined by your understanding of what an angel actually is or isn't, even if she reminds you of Frank Duval's "Angel of Mine" or perhaps Rammstein's "Engel". You get to choose, but let's leave it there. Ultimately, this zoo, which includes the mythical orangutan hiding behind exotic plants, has a keeper, Helga, the psychologist responsible for normalizing thoughts.

The 32-year-old Hanna, still confused, says, "Still don't know who Saddam is, but that was hilarious, Jacob! Your accents were original."

Hanna, oh dear Hanna, lost her goldfish, or so she claims, but we all know Nemo had no part in her decision to stop her life. Morbid, isn't it? She even gave it a name, Jimmy Rose, instead of Nemo, which in Latin means "Nobody," as if the fish would ever respond to her calls. And whom the hack chooses a name so specific anyway when not being able to verify if the fish has a pistol or a vagina if that is how it works? She ended up here after EMS filled her with activated charcoal to neutralize the ant poison, which she got hold of in their garage just after she and hubby had a massive argument, with him leaving the house with a door slamming and her tympanic membranes ringing from the loud sound difference. White-bearded Dean turns toward Helga, opposite the patients' half-moon circle.

Dean, the man God blessed with many more, bad health and no one to love or appreciate him. In my opinion, his name should've been Job and his last Methuselah. He is the father of tall tales and the inventor of folklore. His family got tired of all his suicide attempts and alcohol abuse. He lost his wife to cancer at a young age and raised his daughter alone with little to no help from the community or church.

Do you blame them, knowing that he was a Grand Wizard at the Klan? His first suicide attempt was around the kitchen table years after his daughter left the nest, with him enjoying ten beers and downing around 50 potent analgesics with the last two. EMS did pull him through after receiving an anonymous phone call, which some claimed to be the work of the White Klan Angel, that is if you were to believe in that kind of bullshit.

He returned home to redo it all over. While intoxicated and wearing his Grand Wizard mantle, he found his way to a local church where an African American priest read him his last rights moments after he collapsed in front of the altar. Neither his daughter nor his biracial granddaughter wants anything to do with him and his racial past. An overly excited Dean, who pays little attention to details, asks Helga, "Did you enjoy that Nurse Ratchet?" Even though she didn't hear the joke, she replies kindly, "That was a good one, Dean."

"The Nurse Ratchet part or the joke part?" asks Dean, unintentionally creating confusion for the psychologist. "I'm not sure who Nurse Ratchet is, Dean."

Shit, I didn't think of that, to be honest; search *One Flew Over the Cuckoo's Nest* and read it, then reread this book. There are no similarities, yet it would be entertaining if I could share my opinion, chief.

Before I forget, it is always good practice to clear your browsing history, especially after you previously searched the meaning of post-ejaculation torture.

The group is settling down as the awareness of a soft-spoken psychologist fills the room with kindness, patience, and empathy. "Thank you for bringing laughter to the group, Jacob," Helga gently says with a subtle smile. With energy and excitement, Dean asks, "Can I quickly tell one about pedophiles?"

"Let's wait till the end of the session. Is that okay with you, Dean?" she kindly asks without brushing him off. His question about telling a joke, which comes across as inappropriate, doesn't shock her in the least since she believes Dean should be allowed to express himself with limitations, though. With a slightly raised lip, not truly resembling a sneer but rather holding onto air he was about to waste on his joke, he replies, "Sure, Nurse Ratchet."

"How's everyone feeling this morning?" she asks. Most hesitate to answer, making Helga recall that laughter is a mask we wear to hide our sorrow and pain.

"Let's start at Anna-Maria and go in our famous circle. Remember to give each other the time they need. Anna-Maria…"

The consistent thought of her daughter's well-being is in the back of her head. With what seems to be tears forming in her eyes, Anna-Maria uneasily responds. "I'm feeling anxious, but I did sleep okay, thanks. I can't stop worrying about my daughter and whether I'll have money for her final years in college. The stress of losing my job is bearing down on me more than I can handle!" Anna-Maria recently had the bad luck of discovering money regularly going missing from her register at a large supermarket chain, which added to the stress caused by her and Cassandra's constant yelling and arguments.

She is a gentle and warm mother who lost her job due to accusations of stealing from the register, which ultimately led to a nervous breakdown, a hot bath, and an ice-cold razor. Turns out the manager's wife got a new ring, a car, and the list goes on. Helga recognizes the sheer pain of uncertainty Anna-Maria faces and responds kindly with words of assurance, "We'll make sure our team assists you in getting something new, Anna-Maria. Don't worry about it for now. Are you still doing your breathing exercises?" Anna-Maria nods, confirming that she practices the breathing exercise, also known as diaphragmatic breathing, taught by the highly skilled psychologist. "How about you, Jana?"

"I slept like saggy balls in a warn-out leather handbag neatly laid to rest on the backseat of a busted-ass Rolls Royce. I keep on getting the nightmares—fucking purple bastard!" Jana, with her messed up hair and asymmetrical pigtails, represents the kind of girl who doesn't care too much for shampoo or foundation but rather where her next fix will come from: cigarettes or weed due to angst.

Interestingly enough, pot affects people differently, with some chilling and thinking deeply about their work while others are more likely to chase car tires or spring clean the house, so I was told. Then you get those, like Jana, whose senses become so open to what they usually can't perceive, resulting in them feeling trapped in a body that doesn't have the natural ability to sense that which makes the world sensible.

Unfortunately, this world doesn't always make sense to most of us seeking meaning in life, but it is even worse for others, such as Jana. She has been clean for several months now, all thanks to the loving support from an anonymous source who knows the unhealthiness of traveling with pot for the same reasons people pack extra underwear and socks; you don't want to be stranded directly after Thanksgiving when flights got canceled without clean underwear, socks or weed. Intriguingly, 39 out of our 50 states legalized cannabis for medical use, such as for pain or PTSD, at the time this book was written.

Being cured of a drug is by far the biggest blessing you can imagine, especially if you intend to reset your dependence to re-experience the high that your body got used to, with no true aim of being entirely free at all. Sadly, neither your organs nor your brain gives a shit until you build enough courage to pursue a clean life before permanent damage. "Would you like me to ask your provider regarding your medication?" softly asks Helga, which promises action instead of barren pledges.

Jana's innocence was stolen at a very early age, five years if I recall correctly, and she never got the treatment she needed. Her memories go back to watching a purple dinosaur while singing along to the famous theme, which most kids her age did growing up. Sadly, those memories married the memories of her being undressed by a kindergarten teacher. She cannot recall the events with clarity, all thanks to a very cool mechanism we are all equipped with called Dissociative Amnesia.

Not that it was his fault, but please feel free to sing along to the melody of Barney and Friends —I Hate You, You Hate Me, let's Team Up and Kill Barney. With a big sharp knife and Barney on the floor, no more purple dinosaur!

Jana quickly adds, "And also mention I'm out of smokes. My goddam ex didn't bring me any." No shit, he most likely got pulled while snorting lines from the steering wheel doing 140 in a 65 zone. "I will mention it, Jana. Is there perhaps someone we can call to bring you anything?" asks Helga. Jacob quickly responds, "You can have some of my fags".

Energetic Dean, the man who spent time in some imaginary army back in the day, is just as quick to add, "Suck on that!" Certain words can trigger a quick response from him just like different car tires can provoke a response from a respectable Jack Russel Terrier trying to bring a car down like a cheetah on his way to the hunting planes of the deep Sahara.

Helga realizes Dean may have the wrong context with the reference to fags and quickly intervenes, "Calm down, Dean. Jacob is referring to his cigarettes."

"When I was in Nam—"

"—Namibia," Evangelical Cathy quickly interrupts Dean's effort to share a lengthy story.

"We had to kill for fags, and now we can't call them fags. Life used to have interesting stories," continues Dean. The quick-thinking Bob responds, "Paronomasia at its best!"

Confusion besets Dean as he realizes he has no idea what the hell Bob said. "Parona-whatta?" he asks while stroking his long bushy beard. "A pun, Uncle Dean, a pun!" replies Bob. Bob may sometimes be seen as an asshole but not as someone who would disrespect an elder. Dean, on the other hand, doesn't truly understand finesse while he mumbles from below his mustache, "Fucking kids these days with their fancy words!"

Bob smirks, knowing that Dean wasn't offended by the fancy word and would most likely start using the word too when telling tall tales about when he discovered the only living proof of a Jackalope. Whatever you do, don't ever believe that Dean invented the surfboard.

"Let's get back to the circle, ok?" kindly asks Helga.

Even though scarred from a very early age, Jana understands how to put a man in his place by looking Bob straight in the face as she mimics giving fellatio. To add, fellatio isn't the kind of word you would want to use during intimacy since it's reserved for medical explanations and not to arouse your partner.

Dean's excitement builds up since he knows he'll be next and ready to tell his joke.

"Dean, it's now your turn. How are you this morning? Any concerns you have or perhaps something you want to share?" There's no time for hesitation, he thought, and he quickly contributes to laughter, "Y'all can say what you want about pedophiles! At least they drive slowly around schools!" The group burst out with laughter except for Alicia, who stares downward toward the floor. They notice and refrain from laughing. Dean realizes he may have screwed up and quickly becomes the lord of the flies from the Hebrew Bible.

"I'm sorry if I offended you, Alicia. I didn't mean to hurt your feelings", he quickly adds, hoping his joke could be forgotten by a dear Alicia, who only has a dog as a friend.

Oh, dear God, the fire is boiling in Evangelical Cathy, "That was super inappropriate! What an idiot you are, Dean! You never pay any attention in the group!" This is just where Dean realizes his joke is now seen as a crucifix he'll have to carry for the remainder of the day or perhaps the rest of the week. "I'm genuinely sorry every-one…I'm sorry, Alicia."

Alicia isn't even looking up as her eyes are locked onto the carpet, which, within a second, becomes a focal point of disappointment. "Alicia, are you okay?" asks Helga with great concern. It's not as if she could've predicted the outcome, but then again, this is the outcome that needs to be placed in a room with ample space for an elephant to join the mythical orangutan.

It is sometimes needed that we are confronted with a deep cut while among friends in a trusted zone, therefore allowing us to understand that the outside world, also known as you, the reader, can say things that will cut deep into their souls. This will allow them to deal with such a situation and, simultaneously, prepare for a response to satisfy the social acceptance among you, the ordinary people.

No one wants to see someone run away crying at a party after a joke was made, do you? Cathy reaches for Alicia's shoulder to give her comfort. Alicia suddenly looks up and removes two small earphones.

"Huh—is it my turn?" asks Alicia with surprise. Dean breathes a sigh of relief, knowing he couldn't have offended her while she was listening to music. He is off the hook but still gets the evil eye from Cathy while Jesus removes the crucifix he had to carry for a short time.

"Not yet, Alicia. We're just checking to see if you're okay. Let's all try to be more considerate of each other. Is that okay?" asks Helga, expecting everyone to take those in mind who didn't come prepared with an energetic sense of humor. Dean nods in agreement.

"Coming back to you, Dean, I assume you're still doing well, or is my assumption way off?"

"I tried calling my granddaughter, but no one answered. I left a voice message—if only I can turn back time." You can be as tough as sixteen-penny nails, but when you are in the situation he is in, you'll rethink your reason to live, especially when you are the one staring up at a hammer ready to bury you among rotten wood, also referred to as your darkest memories. Helga wrote several books on this matter and is well-educated on how a lamb can become a beast yet still carry the soft soul of a lamb.

"We can't turn back time, but we can learn how to accept the faults we made. There'll always be guilt, which can completely consume us if we don't care for our health". Tears slowly run from his eyes into his white beard when he realizes the genuinely caring psychologist's emotional words.

"I'm 73 with absolutely nothing but a cat, poor health, and a granddaughter who doesn't want to speak to me. I hate myself for waiting so long."

"I'll see if our team can perhaps look into arranging a meeting with them." Dean softly wipes his tears, "I would really appreciate that." He retrieves a worn-out handkerchief from his pocket and wipes his nose like your grandfather did when he helped you bury your first goldfish. Emotion is what makes us human, and showing it is what the media doesn't want to see when you face the death penalty. Shit, you can only cry so much during your trial extending over several weeks, months, and perhaps years.

"How about you, James?" she asks.

Angst is one of those things you can't magically disappear with fags, especially before entering the auditorium for your clinical exam. It's one of the only things we share regardless of your background, financial status, or training at SAS.

In fact, nicotine can make anxiety worse and doesn't address the underlying cause. Anxiety can be caused by several factors, such as brain structure, brain chemistry, genetics, environmental factors, and many more.

Multiple neurotransmitters and hormones can contribute significantly to anxiety. In his case, his father made it very clear to his pregnant mom that he didn't want that thing, that thing being James. A friend of mine proved that a child in the womb could clearly hear what you are saying when he decided to read scientific books to his unborn. This resulted in his beautiful child being the top achiever at 7 in primary school.

In essence, anything, human or not, that has a brain should always be brought up with love. Like the fictional character Ali G created by Sasha Baron Cohen known for mispronunciation, said: "Life is the most precious gift Jual has given us." Damn, this book may just have turned into a self-help book, which isn't the intent. "I feel like a man on the edge, to be honest. I don't know what my life will hold once I leave here. The doc said I have bipolar disorder caused by trauma as a child, and I'll need meds," responds James with an uncertain and trembling voice.

James is the only one in this group who has, and still is, living with an axe above his head. His fists are permanently clenched, which is a sign of angst, and his trembling will remind you of a dog scared of its owner.

This kid has a hard time at school with children making fun of his hand-me-down clothes and the torn lip he had with compliments of his abusive father. Social workers were even made aware that his father tried to drown him in the toilet while blood flowed down his legs after meeting the switch specially crafted by Satan himself. His father even assaulted him in public, where bystanders hesitated to intervene.

This is James, the 16-year-old kid who swallowed over a hundred pills one late evening after he had to mow the lawn using a flashlight for guidance. James didn't wake up one morning at a bipolar assigning line jumping up and down while shouting: "Pick me, pick me!" His father made him bipolar, and will one day have to face the wrath of God. Romans 12:19-21 makes this very clear. My only question regarding this specific passage is: "Will only Christians enjoy this benefit?"

Just when you thought you grew up shitty. James has done nothing to the world to deserve this kind of abuse and treatment. He has been in a cocoon where he only had an English Bible, which never came to his rescue. If only he could read properly, he would have understood Isaiah 55:8-11 or so the local priest would've argued. After all, God works in mysterious ways, doesn't he?

The whole group is "kind" of aware of his situation and truly cares for his well-being, but not as much as Helga does. How could life be so unfair, and how could humans turn their back on a child who doesn't know what it is to be normal, she angrily thought. She pauses for a few seconds before replying, "I'll make sure our team gets you a safe place to stay, James, and all the support you need, I promise. You are safe and among friends who care about you dearly. I can't promise life will be easy, but I can promise you'll be ok."

"We love you, James. We're all here for you," adds Cathy caringly. Cathy, the woman leading the choir from the back row, would always want to bestow encouragement and unconditional love, not because it's her duty toward God, but because that is something she longs for. Do to others what you want done to yourself, the famous saying goes. Almost like an eye for an eye if you were to get on her wrong side. "Thank you, Miss Cathy," responds James appreciatively and with assurance in his heart.

Should you still search for your perfectly tailored Goal Driven Life book? Ask James if he wants a copy, which will make you feel better about yourself when you give it to him, but please remember that he has trouble reading. "Cathy, how are you this morning?" asks Helga while trying to overcome the emotions caused by James's concerns. Cathy always responds thoughtfully when given the chance to speak, "God is truly good to me, and I have so much to be thankful for. I slept well and did some yoga with the ladies this morning."

"And we got to watch, didn't we, Bram?" asks Dean with what seems to be a smile about to turn into laughter. Even though he is a gentleman, Bram would never let his compadre Dean be left hanging when he responds with a smirk, "I can't confirm or deny the whispering."

"Be respectful of my turn! As I said, I had a good morning and expect to do some crafts today," responds Cathy, clearly annoyed. Bob gets up and helps himself to a snack, knowing that the possibility of a mythical creature taking him hostage from within the pseudo-rainforest is rubbish. "Look for the truth" is his motto. He unselfishly assigns the name Orangutan Joe to the mythical creature on behalf of the all-knowing Cathy, who is driven by religion even though she has never read the Bible from the beginning to where "The grace of the Lord Jesus be with all. Amen" is written as the last sentence. He also believes he has the skills required to communicate with even the less intelligent primate walking this spherical rock, namely the Mandrill. He pauses for a moment just before he retakes his seat, which resembles the sinbinning of a captain who miserably failed in his duties to protect the nation from alien invaders, not that he believes in Aliens.

Bob may be a clever cat, but his intriguing question shows the opposite, "What did you mean with whispering, Bram?" To make it clear, Bob's focus has never been on the opposite gender, or any other gender for that matter, nor is he a guy who ever tried masturbating with a household vacuum machine, as most men walking this planet have, except those who believe a woman should sweep the floors and those who have access to Donkeys and trees with hip-height holes. "You can see the lips move but can't hear a word…" quickly answers Dean. Even more confused than a Tumbler pigeon instructed to ascend vertically with its trademark tumbling, "Huh?" responds Bob.

"Yoga pants—Y O G A pants—get it?" adds a smirking Bram. Cathy almost throws up in her mouth moments before aggressively responding, "YOU ALL NEED JESUS! JUDGEMENT OF HEAVEN WILL BE YOUR FATE!". Cathy has been in and out of clinics more than a squirrel running the race for hibernation. As to what her story is, I may not have the full rundown, but I know she has the hots for Dean. Some people have it wrong—all with the blessing of the Almighty. All went wrong after she sought God with the help of the unscented bottle of Vodka, which alcoholics prefer, followed by an emotional fallout with her fiancé. Her roller coaster booze addiction also introduced two men into her bedroom shortly after she and her fiancé decided to part. She quickly realized Vodka was the culprit and switched to a silver-foiled bag of red while flushing down a copious amount of Paracetamol.

Patients who decide to take the route of Paracetamol and survive will wish they were dead. Such an overdose may cause liver failure with a risk of one in a million, with her almost being that 1 in a million. Around 7.8 billion people walk this planet, which can also be denoted as 7800 million, thus statistically increasing your chances of liver failure due to an overdose of Paracetamol.

However, the figures don't point to a global, equally distributed possibility since paracetamol isn't available in every country. You will wake up with a very advanced hang-over compared to your student days of gasping from the devil's udders, also revered as the devil's tits.

This kind of hangover, due to Paracetamol, can result in Jaundice, vomiting blood, and much more. Still, here she sits after discovering God through the Bible. May I get an Amen, brothers and sisters? Your Amen will be short-lived once you realize she ended up here from a nervous breakdown shortly after touching the almighty's index finger from the top of a very tall building.

Just to clarify, her obsession with God does not make her a crazy person but merely a person longing for true love, like most of us. Who gets to define crazy anyway? "Gentlemen, may I ask that we kindly be respectful of the ladies in the room? Is that okay with you?" asks Helga. The men nod in agreement even though they know the presence of a perfect Moose knuckle, also known as a cameltoe, represents the perfectly wrapped birthday present, which you need to share or selfishly admire. Men are visual creatures if you haven't noticed by now, and I'm not referring to what I have shared so far.

"Alicia, do you care to share?" thoughtfully asks the psychologist with gold-plated credentials. Alicia looks up and removes her earbuds just as Cathy softly and with consideration touches her shoulder. "Huh, my turn?" asks the emotionally confused Alicia. With a warm, soft tone, Cathy responds, "Yes, sweetie pie," a sentence reserved for people down South and those within your inner circle. The girl who only has a dog as a friend concernedly responds with the heaven's flood gates about to open through her eyes, "I miss my dog so much!"

Bob knows she wants to say she misses her friend but respects the fact that she can control her emotions by refraining from having her seen as someone dependent on the love of a being that has a life expectancy of 7 years or so. Regardless, if you are in a private psychiatric clinic, you still don't want to come across as someone lost in a world where a mythical orangutan keeps the key to the next world. Helga inquisitively asks, "What's her name?" even though everyone, including Helga, knows the pup's name by now since this isn't the first time for group therapy. Bram understands that Helga is giving Alicia the right to refer to her dog as a friend by repeating his name, hoping she can contribute to the session confidently and, at the same time, giving her an understanding that her concerns are just as important as the rest's. Alicia smiles confidently, "His name is Charlie Figs—an English bulldog."

"Awe—they are adorable! My sister had one called Bella Milano!" contributes Anny with excitement. "That means beautiful Milan, right?" asks Bob to Anny. "Something like that, I guess," replies Anny with a mischievous smile.

"How did you sleep, Alicia?" Now fully engaged, Alicia responds with the knowledge that no one will judge her, "I didn't sleep much

—I'm worried about Charlie. He is pretty old and has become hard of hearing and night-blind. He's all the love I have."

"And where is Charlie now?"

"He's at my sister's place."

I know that feeling quite well having a cat who has no idea how to catch a mouse, thought Dean. Helga doesn't record the patients' responses but relies solely on a memory that can compete with an Elephant's or a whale's, "And did you call your sister this morning?" Poor Alicia just realized that her lack of attention in certain aspects made her miss an essential part of a patient living in this fine establishment. "Can we call from here?" asks a confused Alicia.

"Absolutely darling—as often as you want, and she can call you," confirms Cathy.

Alicia's synapses are firing throughout her central nervous system and into the peripheral, resulting in her sitting upright in her chicklet egg-shaped chair. "That's awesome!" excitedly responds Alicia just before she fully leaps from her chair toward the door, almost like a grasshopper realizing the window to escape. "Wait a moment, Alicia, we have to finish the circle first," intervenes Helga without raising her voice in any form. She half-heartedly returns to her chair, disappointed yet with less angst than she portrayed in previous sessions, "Sorry."

Alicia wasn't always like this, depending on a dog for love, but she allowed a wannabe gangster boyfriend who was more of a player than anything else into her life. Steve knew this gangster by name and was one of the crack house's punks.

At some point in your life, you will face the inevitable: heartbreak. That pain can tear your sole apart but add rejection to this pain, and the foundation on which you tried to build a beautiful home will crack and, in the worst cases, completely disintegrate.

You will never, and I mean never, become accustomed to emotional rejection. But despite that, time may bring healing, or so I was asked to add to the story. She still recalls the pain caused by heartbreak tearing her sole to pieces and the comfort her puppy gave her by licking the tears from her face just before her family discovered her unresponsive body next to Charlie, who safeguarded her. She had no access to alcohol or grass (weed) in her moment of desperation. Yet, she did manage to empty a bottle of her sister's prescription drug, which assured three consecutive days of being hooked up to a vital sign monitor, a Foley catheter, an arterial line, and a ventilator. Not to scare you, but you don't want to be awake when they connect the last three mentioned.

Alicia never drank, nor could she stand the smell of THC (Tetrahydrocannabinol), but moments of despair led her to consider it. Suicide, as mentioned way earlier, results from exposure to a very dark place where the emotional pain becomes so unbearable you simply lose control of your actions.

You want to stop the emotional overload using any means possible. Some gather their thoughts and take the time to say their goodbyes before stepping into the unknown, but those are exceedingly rare.

I am aware of several people who took their time and came across as they ordinarily do, but again, it is not that common. The mind is indeed a very strange place that we will never master, regardless of whether you believe in the application of shocks, lobotomies, isolation, bloodletting and purging, trephination, and even cocaine. Read up by yourself if you want to learn about some of the "medical treatments" I just mentioned; you'll be amazed.

People will always argue that it's a selfish act, leaving their loved ones behind in mourning. Still, those who have been there understand it's a selfish expectation from others to have you deal with an experience created by Beelzebub himself since God can't possibly be held responsible for anything but goodness, as Bob would say.

Have you ever had an animal you'd do anything for? This is one of those situations where the bond between a human, Alicia, and a dog, Charlie, can't be broken. Animals are the only ones who show unconditional love if you treat them with kindness and love. "And how are you this morning, Bram? Anything you would like to share with the circle?"

"I'm doing truly well, thanks for asking. These three weeks were tailored for a person like me," answers the cleanshaven Bram with St. Michel glasses and slight grey hair. Bram isn't the kind that will display his riches, but he is the kind of natural leader who will go out of his way to help you carry your cross. "And what makes you say that?" curiously asks Helga.

"We're free to visit the beautiful grounds and gardens with no one pressuring us into a confined area like those prison-type clinics throughout the States. I've also learned quite a lot from the other therapy classes and am getting the rest I need. I feel like a changed man indeed! If I may speak words of hope to all of us—God is good, and He is great!"

"All the time!" supports Anny, realizing Bram is a dead end to her sexual endeavors. Cathy realizes this is her queue, "Amen! Praise Jesus!" What is it with these worshippers of a man in the sky, thought Jana questionably. I would so much like to have Jacob right now, thought Anny, with her focus shifted from Bram. It seems like Bram is a changed man! Cameltoe watching will make you a changed man! In all seriousness, he is a successful businessman, husband, father, and the proud owner of a shit load of stress.

Not only was he on suicide watch a few days ago, but he has also become a true inspiration to the group—and an emotional support to Dean. Anna-Maria bravely retrieves a snack from Orangutan Joe's snack bar. "Does anyone like something?" she thoughtfully asks with genuine motherly kindness coming from within. "I'll have a packet of Goldfish, please—they are to die for," indicates Hanna. Anna-Maria hands her two packets and returns to her seat with a banana and a packet of Haribo Lakritz.

Bram has had it rough not only because a client canceled a mega deal after his late-night hard work stretching into the early hours but also because his hero father passed away, resulting in his foundation being ripped from beneath his feet. His father, who I haven't had the pleasure of meeting, was his rock and personal hero.

Remember that day the teacher asked all of us to write an essay about our hero? Bram didn't hold back as he described in detail who his father was and what made him more powerful than Superman. I even recall vividly from my kindergarten days how two kids during recess had a go at each other to settle their differences concerning whose dad was more powerful, almost like comparing Norris with Lee. They did beat the living crap out of each other, with both fathers bragging about their son's fighting skills, almost like parents bragging about their children being able to log into a computer. It doesn't make sense.

Bram had the most beautiful memories about his father, the kind every child should have. One evening, it all became too much when he browsed a family album with him and his father posing next to a car they rebuilt together. Some traumatic events such as these can trigger a horrible response when staring at a photo of a dearly loved one suddenly ripped from the world the same way Enoch was no more. Bram turned to rat poison and an old bayonet to damage a major organ, hoping to stop the pain he endured.

Bram and Dean have become quite good friends, and I don't foresee their friendship ever dissolving unless Dean decides to join Meatloaf and Sean Connery upstairs. It has become quite common for the two of them to share a hug with words of encouragement. Jana, very annoyed with this whole goodness of God and the man who supposedly fed 5000 people with two fish and five loaves of bread, doesn't hesitate to voice her frustration and opinion, "Not to be a mood killer, but I simply don't get it! Here we sit, all pretty fucked up, yet you see a God?! I am sorry, but I don't get it! Where the fuck was he when a teacher decided to do all kindS of shit to me in KINDERGARTEN?! The joke about pedophiles driving slow around schools was funny, but only to those with no fucking idea what scars that leave on a person, man, or woman! Am I the only one it this room who has enough sense to ask an imaginary man in the sky not to keep me alive!?"

She gets up and runs from the room. Everyone goes silent. Cathy indicates to follow Jana, and the psychologist approves. "Let's give her the space and time she needs. Is that okay?" suggests the psychologist. Everyone nods in agreement. Allowing a patient to raise her opinion is the right all of them have, even with anger and resentment, as long as the situation is controlled and the patient refrains from harming those around.

Jana did her best, yet she stayed in control, which is of cardinal significance. You may beg to differ, but remember, this is a special place where you can be who you truly are. Pull such a stunt at work, and you'll be asked to enroll in a particular communication course, that is, if you don't get sacked. We don't all need to follow like sheep, which is perfectly acceptable. Just ask Joe, the fictitious orangutan about climbing the water dispenser like Kong did with the Empire State.

We create and believe things, yet we have no tangible proof to back our claims.

"GOD, I HATE CHILDREN!" says Bob scornfully, representing his true feelings toward things out of his control. "Remember Bob, you used to be a child once," responds a caring Anna-Maria. Not impressed, he ends the discussion just as quickly as it presented itself, "With emphasis on WAS Anna-Maria." Helga thoughtfully directs the tension toward the session, "How about you, Hanna? Are you feeling good this morning?"

"I am, yes. I asked my provider to change my meds a bit—I struggle to focus in the mornings due to the sleeping pills. Besides that, I'm doing quite well and looking forward to my husband visiting."

"Thank you for sharing, Hanna, and remember to let us know if anything else needs to change." Hanna, shamefully yet hopeful, responds with a smile.

"Stephen, how are you this morning?"

"Living the life, doc!" The only reason why Stephen uses doc instead of ma'am, madam, or Miss is that he wants to come across as an alpha who has his shit together, especially when you understand his reckless behavior. "Would you like to share something, Stephen?"

"I spoke to my lawyer, and it seems we have a strong case! Can't wait for this ordeal to be over and done with—have my eyes on Florida," he confidently replies with a slightly raised right shoulder and his finger scratching the fibrofatty tissue slightly below his Maxillary sinus and beside the opening of his right nostril. Everyone lies. It's not a question of whether we are lying but rather why, which only he and his conscience know. "I'm glad you feel positive. How are you sleeping?"

"Alone…," responds Stephen with a smile. "I hear you, brother," contributes the A-sexual Bob, whose father withheld his sixteenth birthday present because he was convinced his son had intercourse with his then-girlfriend, Bob's girlfriend, which he didn't. Let me put it into perspective if I may.

Bob did dry-humping, the thing you do which can be compared to a lap dance, resulting in a rude awakening when he took it one step further to explore the inside of a vagina, as fingering was quite normal and perhaps still is. Ladies and gents, that is pretty much on the bucket list of most adolescent men, but I'm not generalizing since I have no accurate statistics to back it up. Perhaps this is where the 12.8% mentioned at the beginning applies.

Still, I base my opinion here on "locker room" talk. He expected a smooth tube which made him conclude that he'll never put any body part, his Antenna, which is a euphemism for a penis, into a hole that demolished his expectation. No one ever teaches that in sex-ed, do they? Maybe that is too much of an advanced topic not suitable for sex ed, considering that we don't want adolescent men to think it is encouraged.

Allow me to answer a question frequently searched for on the internet, which I believe should be shouted from the top of the Eifel Tower: YES, pre-ejaculation fluid, also known as precum, can cause pregnancy! Teach your children that and the world will be a better place. Please don't hate me for being candid, and don't think for one moment that I'm trying to tell you how to raise your children; rather, cherish the free advice. Essentially, this will also prevent weird-ass internet searches.

Bob's dry-humping experience also resulted in a more traumatic "outcome" when a white substance shot from his Gear-shifter, which made him believe he had just broken something inside his body. Sure, the feeling was out of this world. Still, it laid the foundation for feeling guilty and ashamed whenever he gathered enough braveness to lust at whoever's vulva is displayed in a porn magazine resulting in sticky pages, almost like that cookbook with that favorite recipe.

Strange, don't you think, that men are visual to the extent of having a vertical eye with lips, hanging or tight, making them harder than a baseball bat... Needless to say, his feelings of being ashamed and guilty finally led him to become celibate and an abstainer from having the smell of bleach on his hands, making his shirts slightly stained, or bush styled by someone who never perfected the application of gel to something supposed to be waxed. "Let me know how we can assist you in getting the support you need with the disability application."

"Ten-Four doc, Ten-Four."

"Anny, care to tell us how you feel?" How should I answer this question, Anny thought, knowing she needs to come across as normal as possible in the presence of the younger Jacob,

"Ok, I guess…"

"Would you like to share something with the group?"

"Is my medication supposed to make me horny?" asks Anny with her perception of normal. Dean realizes that she might have painted a target on her forehead, "Yeah, mine does that too. I feel like that pink thing at the end of a dog's pistol!"

"GROSS!" responds Alicia with laughter as she immediately remembers Charlie as a male dog with such a device.

Anny confidently moves to the edge of her chair while making quick eye contact with Jacob, followed by a wink. "I'm being serious! It feels like I want to mount something. But besides that, I'm not too bad—enjoyed the yoga this morning."

"I didn't know you do yoga, Anny," replies Helga with surprise. "I don't—I watched…"

"As for a high libido, I suggest you ask your provider. It may be something hormonal, which she can run tests for."

"I'll make sure I ask her," naughtily replies Anny, while faintly running her tongue on the inner sides of her lips. The erotic adventurous Anny got tired of a husband who believed missionary style was the answer to intercourse and denied several of her requests to go down on her, which ended in a divorce when she discovered a generous secretary at work.

They had no issue doing the horizontal monkey dance, nor does Anny have any problems masturbating while she drives, in the back of a cinema, or the back of a bus. Her libido seeks adventure wherever she goes, and her battery orders from Amazon are scheduled to be delivered once a month. Unfortunately, the relationship between Any and the secretary didn't last long, adding to the disappointments of rejection she faced throughout her life.

EMS revived her shortly after they pulled her from the car she drove into the lake. She managed to get her life back on track and convinced her eighty-eight-year-old sugar daddy to take her back, even though she preferred the erotic sensation of a tongue exploring her inner thighs. If only she could find the man willing to explore her deepest desires while keeping her standing as a trophy wife.

This circle is based on trust and respect—it's not as if any of the men will take whatever she says to their advantage. She's currently not into men if I have it right—but that may change when the session ends. They share pretty much everything—a knitted family.

Masturbation and high libido don't make you bonkers. It just makes you human. Every person masturbates, and those who claim they don't, just don't know how to, or if you're Bob. Embrace your sexuality, but please do so responsibly. Using a vacuum machine, as previously mentioned, isn't the ideal toy when you constantly have to toggle the on/off switch, nor is the Zucchini you were about to cook. Cathy will tell you that we were apparently made in someone's image, which means…EVERYONE masturbates or masturbated at some point, perhaps the white-cloaked guy too who smelled like "fresh flowers and honey" when he was around, since nowhere in the Bible is it seen as a sin, nor is it a strange sight in an N.I.C.U. (Neonatal Intensive Care Unit).

Some men prefer a small amount of lotion, and some a lot, whereas some ladies like the low while others love the high setting. Think about it and do your own internet searches where the truth goes undisputed.

Also, is this still blasphemy once you realize that your religion should never be put above any other person's belief system? Will this result in you making the world burn while behaving completely differently than what your book says, or are you wise enough to light a candle just before you ask whichever creator you worship to have Bob or this storyteller join whatever system you believe in?

By the way, feel free to also pray for the millions, individually by name, who were born into something else and don't follow your creator, and who also refrain from seeing their creator being the only one to follow instead of burning in a fiery pit created using a vivid imagination, referred to as a Seir, Soothsayer, or Oracle who lived thousands of years ago. Or perhaps there are bigger things to worry about in the world, like children in certain African countries who don't even have H_2O or soap to wash their hands; even if they did, who is supposed to teach them?

Then, there are even regular people who have to walk on stumps while others move around on their buttocks. What about the wars that flare up historically often between nations whose citizens have to reap what they didn't sow? If you can solve all these issues, we can start talking about your unhappiness against something just said.

Bob knows he's up next and isn't waiting for the psychologist to ask the same boring questions. He quickly lays down his thoughts just like a professional hitman will lay down a map of your dwelling next to photos of your family before you give him whatever he asks for. He rapidly shares his thoughts with little to no air inhaling, "Before you ask, I'm chilling and enjoying this circle of sex, drugs, and God servicing our needs—our deepest desires! I slept well and intend to do so for the rest of my days in this fine establishment we call home. Screw it—let's start a cult and get it over with!

Did you know a golf ball has 336 dimples, there's a company that turns dead bodies into ocean reefs, dolphins sleep with one eye open, vacuum cleaners were originally horse-drawn, Alfred Hitchcock was frightened of eggs, Saddam Hussein wants to go to the sun even though the surface temperature is 5778 Kelvin, and pigs don't sweat?" Everyone's silent and astonished.

Bob carries on with his fountain of knowledge without blinking once, "And that's not all ladies and gentlemen—for 20 years, a cat served as mayor of an Alaskan town, and Anny masturbates seven times a day while squirrels are behind most power outages in the US? And to make it more interesting—Shakespeare's epitaph contains a curse for grave robbers…"

"Jesus! I didn't know horses drew vacuum cleaners," says the astonished Stephen. "How do you know Bob?" inquires Anny. "A cat told me," he replies with a hint of sarcasm. "Son of Sam's ass!" says Bram. Bob got here because he overdosed on his concoction of Norpseudoephedrine and several other junk, which legally forced him into a mandatory medical vacation. His brain can be compared to a nuclear submarine embarking on its maiden voyage, repeating 365, steered by a crazy skipper heading to start a war. According to him, his whole life is based on the aftermath of religious lies, which were force-fed since he was a kid.

After leaving the nest, he took it upon himself to study the Bible in detail to find evidence for the sign of the cross, which led him to conclude that God can't be love since he never experienced that between his mother and father. I shit you not; the last time his parents were intimate was nine months before Bob appeared in a world where religious differences fuel every major war. He isn't uncaring, as proved by his sincere representation of students who voted him in as chairman for the school of engineering, with no knowledge of his desire to explore life after death. He doesn't own a Bible, nor will he try to retrieve the burnt pages from the backyard burn barrel at the frat house for damaged goods.

Most people tend to believe that brilliant people have an obsession with calculus and a brain filled with facts—sure, they do, but what makes them different is that they don't follow the rules of this world. They get bored and seek understanding from the lies they've been told. He searched for an answer, which ultimately drove him bonkers—who made God if a God actually exists? My only question is, how does he know dolphins sleep with one eye open?

"Thanks for sharing, Bob. So, you are doing well, I can assume?" asks Helga, still impressed by his quick thinking and awareness. "Per definition, yes," he responds, resilient to his dosage of whatever his provider prescribed.

"Jacob, how do you feel this morning?" she asks with kindness. "Not too bad, I'll say—slept well, thanks."

"Perhaps anything you want to share?" asks Helga, concerned since he started the session jokingly and responded with little effort. "Nah, not really. I'm just glad to be part of this awesome group and the treatment I'm getting," hoping her attention will be shifted to his jolly persona.

Psychologists may see him as an ICD-10 code F44.81, but she isn't the kind to jump to conclusions classified by the WHO. Oh no, she has more than enough knowledge to refrain from assigning a code, just like a butcher will when grading a piece of meat. Her respect for everyone is driven by compassion and alternative solutions to a pharmaceutical approach. "I'm glad to hear that, Jacob." Anny realizes the sudden awkwardness and places Jacob back in control, hoping that his demeanor will shift from being in the doghouse to someone willing to eat her out like a Sir, "Tell us another joke—love the accent." He realizes her rescue and quickly searches his databank of humor. "How do you mess with a blind person?" he asks with a rictus. Realizing that she may have scored brownie points, "Tell us!"

"You move his furniture," while staring her down, knowing her intentions. "On that note, let's adjourn for the morning. Remember to attend as many of your therapy sessions as possible, and I'll see you tomorrow morning," concludes Helga. Everyone gets up and leaves the room except Jacob at the psychologist's request, "Jacob, can you stay for a bit?"

She chooses her words carefully, not coming across as demanding his presence but instead giving him the option of staying. After all, there is a vast difference between "will you stay" and "can you stay," with the latter being the free choice. "I can—I'm in trouble?". She replies with genuine concern and care, " You know we are here for you, right? I'm worried about you, Jacob." He tries to assure her while touching his nose as blood quickly rushes into his nose's erectile tissue, "Thanks for the reassurance. There's no need to be worried about me—I'm doing quite well." She understands just as quickly that his micro expression indicated the opposite of his reply, "I understand." The 25-year-old Jacob leaves the room and goes into a hallway leading to the grounds and lush green gardens.

6

DINER, BOBBLEHEAD JESUS, AND A LETTER

August 2023

The history of diners can be traced back to the late 1800s, but coffee, orange juice, and chicken eggs can be traced centuries before the famous Austrian Tyrolean hat. What do all of these things have in common, you may ask? Absolutely nothing, just like people in a diner, have nothing in common except hunger or thirst for a drug that stimulates your brain and nervous system, also called caffeine, which most of us have in common anyway.

Building a diner from scratch takes quite some planning, not only to realize your lifelong dream of selling Nanna's famous pancakes, but predominantly because you'll have to get permissions and licenses for highly skilled professionals to erect the building itself.

Let's imagine you identify a spot across from Giovani De Luca and on the corner. You first must get his blessing and that of our sponsor, which you'll meet much later during this journey. Once the cutter and sponsor approve, you'll have to secure the land by paying 1.1 million simoleons to the seller, which isn't necessarily the easiest thing to do regardless of how many children's piggy banks you empty. You'll also need to consult with an architect who typically has strong relations with engineers to redo your Microsoft Paint drawings.

The fees associated may add up to around 150k, 15% of the money you set aside for the physical building, which is, in your case, 1 million Bones. Next, you'll have to apply for permits, which will be around 50k but worth every penny. Permits allow you to start building that empire you've dreamed about since you gave up working for that slave driver, whom a very generous yet dangerous Tyrolean hat-wearing German took care of.

The next step in the process is to get a team consisting of builders, contractors, electricians, plumbers, and the list goes on, to have your building erected by someone other than Jacob's Uncle Fred, who boasts about building the Empire State Building using a teaspoon, tampons, and duct tape while banging a bearded prostitute named Phillis.

Whatever you do, don't let Uncle Fred know your venture, as he has the reputation for making building materials disappear—ever wondered why Home Depot secures their electrical wire with locks? There's no need to search for the reason once you've met Uncle Fred. Your building will need a solid 4" concrete floor. Still, before you get there, you'll have to have rough grading done, which requires the use of large earth-moving equipment and a few shovels, while a ditch, also known as footings, will be dug either by hard-working "shovel engineers" or with the help of another machine. Footing should, at minimum, go as deep as twelve inches into previously undisturbed soil, which isn't enough to hide a body. Besides feeding the deceased to swine, it is better to leave them sitting upright on a Central Park bench closest to the Ritz. Why? Fuckit, don't ask me. I heard it from a German.

Once the rough grading and footings have been dug, an inspection will follow, after which the plumbers and electricians will lay the pipes and conduits, followed by yet another inspection. Now that these items have been checked from your list, the concrete can be poured for the footings, followed by the main slab itself. I don't know much about bricks and mortar, but this is where the internal and external building starts using the plan submitted by the architect, not the one you did using whatever comes free with Windows.

Their first goal is to ensure the building has a roof, two doors, and two large windows, which is perfectly suitable for a diner on a corner. One door shall be the entry for patrons, the other for deliveries at the rear, which also serves as the occasional late-night hookup spot for an overpaid young chef obsessed with hairy women and bacterial vaginosis. Our entry door will be positioned at the side next to one of the large windows, with the other window facing the street overlooking De Luca Sartoria.

The outer walls will be built using cinder blocks, rebar, and lots of cement, followed by the outside completion with sandstone cladding imported from Oorlogskloof, South Africa, in the province of the Northern Cape, which isn't just renowned for their high quality but also their precision cutting. After all, you want to be the best diner; hence, you need to be displayed as such. The internal structure, or walls, will be done using two-by-fours, sheetrock, and a few Mexicans recently dropped off by a bus with the compliments of Florida.

Once that is done, it will be time for, wait for it…, another inspection. Let's assume everything went according to plan, excluding Carlos's nail gun incident; it will be time to finish the walls. "Hold on," you say with confusion. Didn't I just mention an inspection for the interior walls being done before finishing the walls? Shouldn't we first finish the walls followed by an inspection instead of inspecting and then finishing? I definitely did, but that was for the internal skeleton part, which consists of cheap American wood finished with one side of sheetrock.

See it like this: you have a back and a stomach, which can give you a view of the intestines when dissected from your body. You don't need to remove your back and beer belly to see the intestines, but one side will do. That is exactly what an inspector is looking for: the insides of what you would call a wall. I know it does come across as complex, but please don't see it as such since the complexity lies with everyone in it for the money. Hell, just how many inspectors do you need to approve of something?

Okay, we passed the inspections, and the walls look like a new prison: white, clean, and without any Samantha Fox posters. It's time to use your imagination with what you want inside the diner beside the boring white walls. The solution is to get hold of the rich and famous Anny, who has a libido bigger than that of a rabbit, the reigning champ in procreation. Not only does Anny lust for life and something just as hard as rebar, but she also has a taste for fancy things.

Let's start with the bathroom, not because it's where you can bathe, but because it's where a deep breath with a partially open mouth can be shared by the connoisseur and the humble pedestrian making their way toward Times Square. We need two bathrooms, one for the gunslinger and one for those who prefer sitting while browsing Facebook updates, just like many German men do when taking a tingle, as shared by a foreigner who's dated quite a few.

Each bathroom, or shall we say restroom, needs at least two toilets, which this storyteller, me, had to clean growing up. Every restroom, by law, has to have two or three grab bars as set forth by the Americans with Disabilities Act, also known by general contractors as ADA. Grab bars unsettle me more than escalator handrails, knowing that everyone walking this planet at some point or the other wiped their intergluteal clefts, ending up with feces on their fingers, especially their thumbs, which doesn't turn out to be a finger due to the medical fact that it only has two phalanges.

There is no need to deny it; embrace it! Once you realize the possible odor that engulfs itself upon your hands, it will be the right time to wash them in either of the two fancy basins Anny had imported from Italy. Since we already understand the setbacks of using air hand driers, it would be ideal to have an automated paper-fed dispenser installed accompanied by a bin compacting the paper you wasted drying your hands, which is manufactured by none other than the man who invented a Rain Collecting device back in 2010. Soap dispensers are a must. They should be activated using built-in proximity sensors, the same kind of sensors built into your robot vacuum machine for it to turn around just before it flattens its face like the English bulldog Alicia has.

Before I forget, the toilet handle must be on the opposite side of the diagonal grab bar. I shit you not, but drowning in a restroom is highly likely if you were to grab onto the toilet's handle instead of the diagonal bar. It's time to start focusing on the kitchen, shall we? In all fairness, I'll point out only a few requirements besides the ones already mentioned. We need a kitchen hood, also known as the dragon's breath to the outside world, which must be interconnected with the heating-ventilation-air conditioning, also known as the HVAC system.

An ANSUL system must be installed to prevent large, hazardous fires without human intervention, not that I believe fires can't be hazardous. When we check this from your list, we can start furnishing your dream kitchen with the essentials. This is where Anny works her magic, considering she has had a few rounds with a wealthy restauranteur.

Let's start with the oven, the versatile piece of equipment needed for baking and braising, and the list grows. We also need a range that can be gas or electric, a deep frier for those with a good cardiologist, a grill for those who fancy the smoky flavor, and griddles that may be confused with a grill even though it has a flat metal surface. Holding equipment is required to keep the food about to be served at a specific temperature since most of us prefer a fresh and warm meal, even if it's your grandmother's bunion served on French toast.

Anny will suggest a salamander or broiler, which are perfect for melting cheese and toasting bread, even though we'll add a Star Holman toaster with a conveyor. No one likes a cold bagel except for the bachelorette trying to get rid of the saggy ball gentlemen she hooked up with after indulging in the art of Mixology by a Russian named Dave. Why do people go to a diner instead of indulging in expensive food? Think about it if you want but know this: people visit a diner for coffee, and if you believe differently, you should buy into owning a diner.

We can't have a diner with shitty coffee. That's out of the question. Anny hooked us up with a La Marzocco Strada electronic paddle, which happens to be the most expensive expresso machine, coming in at 50k. Still, she also managed to secure a killer deal of 11k for a Nuova Simonelli Prontobar Super Automatic Machine, all in the name of waking up with a semi-flaccid morning wood while regretting the previous night or the shitty job you have.

All we need now is furniture, an overweight cook, a few waiters or waitresses, and The Butcher of North Rhine-Westphalia, also known as Dangerous Dieter, among others. His girlfriend calls him Horsy because he has an abnormally large dingdong, which military men call a knee slapper. On the other hand, he also refers to her as Horsy, not because she has anything abnormally large, but simply because her bum represents the humble police horse that is always ready for a ride, or so I was told by a wealthy inventor who shared several bottles of red with them, imported from Sicily.

Before installing the fancy equipment, contractors must install a gas supply line, electrical hookups, water connections, and floors. The health department then gets to add an additional requirement for an arm and a leg because you didn't plan on having a handwashing sink. Once all these have been done, a final inspection will follow. We will ask the owner what she prefers for wall decorations. I was thinking along the lines of Tim Nyberg, Ryan Fowler, and Pela Studio…

The diner is as precise as you imagine: small and cozy with state-of-the-art equipment and walls decorated with surreal art as chosen by a surprised and grateful owner who received this beautiful place from an anonymous Samaritan. Jacob crosses the street and into this new cozy diner after visiting De Luca Sartoria and the letter he inserted in the USPS post box, where he is met by the proud new owner, Anna-Maria. She is pleasantly surprised and excited to see Jacob as she gives him an emotional hug, followed by them completing the formality by "La Bise."

"La Bise" is the greeting where people gently make contact with both cheeks while making the sound of a kiss. "Jacob! So good to see you! Where have you been all this time? Everything still okay with you?" greets and questions Anna-Maria with sincere excitement. Jacob smiles from ear to ear, exposing his symmetrical dimples while replying, "So good to be seen by you, Anna! Been busy as always—how's your daughter?" Anna-Maria's face lights up even more, "She's doing great! She got a job at a local hospital a few weeks ago, working in cardiac ICU."

Jacob, the man without kids, sees Cassandra as a go-getter and expresses his excitement, "That's freaking awesome! To think you worried about life several years back…" She settles down for a moment, realizing just how fortunate she truly is while placing her palms together with stretched fingers as if she's about to pray, "Exactly—God has been good to us, Jacob! Table?" she asks while making Jacob feel like a King who just entered a place reserved for high valued guests.

He scans the crowd sitting on matching light blue stools at the bar with elbows resting on the marble countertop supported by Amazon rosewood. They indulge in whatever the overweight chef flips while enjoying their coffee, espresso, or freshly squeezed orange juice. He doesn't immediately recognize whoever it is he's looking for while his eyes scan past businesswomen and men enjoying their breakfast in light blue matching booths while focusing on the front pages. At the same time, joggers boast about their latest times while being served orange juice and fruit salads by a beautiful and tall waitress doing the rounds.

He suddenly recognizes who he is looking for, like a Kalahari Meerkat would recognize an edible scorpion lost to nature. He points toward a booth directly at the large window overlooking De Luca Sartoria. "Aha, the man with the funny hat gave me a bag of Lakritz. Want to try one? I absolutely love it!" exclaims Anna-Maria while retrieving a small packet from her apron's pocket. "I won't say no. The first time I had Lakritz was when I visited Hamburg during the 2006 World Cup Soccer", he replies as he retrieves a piece from the Haribo packet. "Enjoy your breakfast—I'll send the coffee over right away," says Anna-Maria with assurance. "Thank you, Anna," replies a grateful and sincere Jacob with his trademark smile while giving her a wink.

He makes his way toward the booth, taking care not to bump into someone accidentally. There is nothing that can ruin someone's day like spilled coffee or juice on a designer suit or a jogger's crotch. He approaches the booth, a man and woman get up, and they greet each other with kisses on both cheeks.

The man is Dieter, a middle-aged German with a yellow stained toothbrush mustache, a Tyrolean hat, undersized chino shorts, flip-flops, and a t-shirt with a cartoon character. She is Alegria Cruz, a professionally dressed C.I.A agent of Hispanic descent with curves only a snake has during mating season and bosoms with pancake size areolas, which any respectable man has wanted to explore since he was brought into this world. Her olive skin face is that of an angel, and his, Dieter's, is that of a man who has had a brush with a blind sculptor using a very blunt chisel. I believe there's a word for that— fugly. They shovel back into the booth. "Hell, it's been too long!" says Jacob, with pupils fully dilated and excited. "Look at you! All dressed to impress and with a refreshing smell! I'm sure the ladies throw themselves at you!" replies Alegria while gently moving her black fringe to the left side of her head.

Jacob knows she is trying to flirt but quickly dismisses that thought, knowing Dieter's ability to read micro-expressions. "Not for me, thanks. Having someone is way too much drama," he replies with a hint of sarcasm. "What happened to that beautiful girlfriend you had?" curiously asks Alegria. "The one with the funny nose?" asks Dieter with a serious face and with a thick Bavarian accent. The only time you'll see Dieter smile is when Alegria buys donuts with oversized holes and when he sees anything with a bobblehead. "Benimm dich, mein Pferd," she demands in German with her Spanish accent. "It's true—her nose was so pointy she could kill a cockroach in a corner," replies Dieter while trying to extrude his own nose with his hand, hoping to express his observation of a woman with a pointy nose. "She was way too nosy for me, Alegria—started sniffing around," assures Jacob, complimenting Dieter's opinion. "I'm so sorry to learn that, Jacob. And what about the one you met in Spain?" she asks, hoping to get an exciting answer. "You mean the one with that gap in her front teeth—a Boeing 737 can make a U-turn in between..." adds Dieter. She is getting agitated by his comments and responds in Spanish, "No podrás ver mi trasero durante un mes si segues insultando a sus mujeres!"

Dieter, also known as The Butcher of North Rhine-Westphalia, is not the kind of man who would ever apologize for anything other than eliminating the wrong target on behalf of whoever paid him. Still, with Alegria, he has to put his pride in his pocket, knowing her feistiness can result in a serious international incident. "Tut mir leid, meine Liebste," responds Dieter while slightly turning his head away like a dog, knowing he had messed up. A waitress carrying a full pot makes her rounds toward the trio. "May I fill your cups— compliments of the owner," says the waitress, realizing she froze for a bit when her eyes locked onto Jacob's.

Jacob notices her attraction but doesn't see the need to do anything about their few seconds of soul-searching. The last thing he wants is complications at the place across from the De Luca Sartoria. "Do you sell Mezzo Mix?" asks Dieter, knowing the answer. My father used to point out that there is no need to ask a question if you know what the answer will be. It's evident we didn't have the same father, but I'm sure there were similarities.

The Butcher of North Rhine-Westphalia didn't get his name by his own selection but managed to build up a ruthless reputation for slaughtering top-ranking Russian war criminals on behalf of whoever paid him.

Some refer to him as the German Ghost, while those who have crossed his path refer to him as a man only the devil answers to. He owns more LLCs than a comic bookstore has comics, not because he is wealthy, which he is, but because he believes in paying taxes. He lives his life governed by Mark 12:17, where Jesus said, "Give back to Caesar what is Caesar's and to God what is God's."

Is Dieter a devoted whatever? No, he isn't religious at all, but he doesn't want to be pushed into a tiny cell for neglecting his taxes. He is okay with being locked up for his heinous past, but not for tax reasons.

He saves every single receipt and every bullet casing to ensure he can be seen as a respectable businessman. It doesn't sit right with him to have any god forgive his past and approve the sward he lives by. He doesn't believe one should wait for the good Sheppard to bestow His wrath on those who should be cut down. He established his businesses to do the work on whatever god's behalf, even if it means he has to ride his fire-breathing dark horse alone into the abyss, consequently paying his debts.

Rain or shine, I know with certainty he will ensure he has a rope to hoist himself out of hell's bottomless pit. Men like him simply has a way confirming the existence of the "Der Kopflose Reiter" in German folklore. Some of his businesses hide in plain sight, not because he is reckless but as a form of communication, allowing his clientele to disappear whenever they realize one of his LLCs has been shut down, even though it sounds bizarre.

Several questions will arise from a business being closed by the government, and Dieter is no stranger to keeping his supporters' info confidential till death do them part. Listing a few will give you a better understanding of who or what he is. Let's start with Driving Dieter.llc, his taxi service consisting of only one taxi. He never takes a penny nor a pound for a fare since the ride will be for a particular purpose, such as taking an abused mother to safety or dropping an elderly off at an assisted living accompanied by a cheque, which secures a restful life and a peaceful funeral. He occasionally uses the taxi to get rid of body parts, or so rumor has it, but that doesn't happen that often because he got a new white van just like the ones seen on TV.

Then there is Dirty Dieter.llc, where he sells high-end adult toys to those who believe Germans make the best porn. He also uses this llc as the opportunity to hunt down snuff film producers, which he then carefully spreads all over the US in some form of hamburger or liquid. His third is Dangerous Dieter.llc, which he uses to sell weapons to those who want to inflict as much destruction as possible, and finally is Demolition Dieter.llc, which is known by a few as a business that sells fireworks, or so they claim.

To make it even simpler, don't be alarmed when a taxi with a Tyrolean hat-wearing German shows up at your house, for he's either there to take you to safety, hit you to death with a dildo, or blow you to kingdom come just before he pushes the "meet Jesus" red button on his keychain. However, he has a bobblehead Jesus on his dashboard, which may give you some comfort.

Dieter respects only two people: Jacob, the man who created him, and pancake size areola Alegria, the woman he dearly loves. "Remind me again why you call Dieter your Horsy?" asks an enter-tained Jacob with curiosity. "Let's not go there..." replies a blushing

Alegria with a smirk while grabbing Dieter's crotch below the table. "I actually started calling her my Horsy," Dieter says, his head held high as if he invented the word. "I rather not ask," remarks Jacob. "I'll tell you someday," utters Dieter while realizing he won't be able to stand up for a few.

"How's business?" asks Jacob, with a slightly raised hand trying to get the waitress's attention. "Business is good, my friend!" assures Dieter while trying to shift his focus from Alegria's hand to Jacob's presence. Alegria lets go of Dieter and adds with concern and disappointment, "Wish I could say the same— the agency might be closing my station in Havana." Jacob is intrigued and tempted to enquire, "Why's that, if I may ask—not sure what C.I.A officers may share."

"Budget cuts, I guess," she responds with a hint of confusion and concern in her voice. "Yes sir, how can I help?" asked the waitress, who noticed Jacob's hand slightly raised. "May I please order a cappuccino?" he asks, knowing that cappuccino will only be served up to 11 a.m. as rooted in Italian tradition. The waitress looks toward the beautiful Regent Street Metal Analog Clock next to the Salvador Dalí Figura en una finestra and replies pleasantly surprised by the time of day, "I'll have one ready in about ten." The waitress leaves toward the kitchen with confirmation from Jacob. "So, what is your plan Alegria? Thinking of leaving the Agency?"

"At least she has the experience to help me with my business," Dieter assures. Jacob lowers his voice to whisper, "Training contract killers isn't exactly a business, Dieter."

"Female assassins too…" responds Alegria excitedly, just like a little girl who successfully made her first cupcake. "As I said, business is good, my friend…" Alegria realizes that chit-chat isn't the reason why they are all here, "So why this mysterious breakfast meeting?" Jacob reaches into his pocket and hands Alegria an envelope with a South African address written on it. He looks Dieter straight in the eyes, "Remember that day you promised to pay me back?" Dieter recognizes the look in Jacob's eyes and responds with the same level of integrity the question was asked, "And I am still keeping that promise…"

"All I want is for you to post this letter if something were to happen to me," he whispers with anticipation. "What do you mean —someone after you?" asks Alegria as she grabs Jacob's hand. He realizes he may have caused more concern than intended, "Not at all, all I want is this favor." Dieter reaches for his hat, removes it, and places it against his chest, which is a sign that he cherishes the request. "You have my word, friend," assures the wealthy yet humble Dieter. Confused, Alegria lets go of his hand, "But how will we know?" Dieter, the man who has stared death in the eyes too many times, realizes the seriousness of Alegria's concern and takes control as an alpha, "We will know, my love, don't you worry."

7

FAGS, ENGINEERS, AND A SAFE WORD

Happy hair, also known as Maybe hair or Bed License hair, plays a phenomenal role during the development of boys, not to mention "Stoneys," which is also called Gynecomastia. Two of the most concerning issues among adolescent men are having hair down there and the possibility of developing breasts when Stoneys presents itself, which is a small lump forming behind the nipples due to a hormonal imbalance, just like the exaggerated case of Bob's bitch tits in the movie adaptation of *Fight Club*.

Not only is Stoneys an intimidating event, but it's quite sensitive and painful at times, especially during physical activities. However, these developments have several advantages that most aren't aware of. Still, unfortunately, they are limited to certain unofficial organizations referred to as High School Cigarette Clubs or High School Fag Clubs. No, I'm not referring to a term you chose to associate with homosexuals but rather to slang for a cigarette.

Cigarettes, the most addictive drug since the beginning of time, or since your teens, can be purchased in any country where people have lungs except from Bhutan, which is a Buddhist kingdom on the Himalayas' eastern edge with a population of approximately

727000. Several other countries, such as England, Germany, and France per example, take a firm stand against sucking on the devil's stick, referred to as a rocket, bine, blem, cancerette, and the list goes on with only your imagination limiting you to creating your own synonym associated with coughing like a cannon. Germany, for instance, sells packets of twenty cigarettes containing only seventeen because three are removed for taxation purposes, or so Jacob shared.

Not only do these countries take a firm stance, but they also require cigarette manufacturers to include pictures of dissected lungs, amputated legs, and other graphic medical images on the packets to deter people from procuring that which is associated with having a chill moment or several while consuming your favorite Pills, Lager or that shitty beer known as IPA.

Believe it or not, some high schools, such as the one Jacob attended, have an unofficial license program among students governed by an age-old tradition set forth by someone's grandfather or great-grandfather. Jacob's uncle, Fred, smoked a pack of thirty a day, which was impressive and the benchmark everyone strived toward. He had a continuous cloud of smoke gently leaving his mouth while sharing a tale from the good old days, even when he killed his cigarette two minutes ago. He was the man who managed to ash the tip of his cigarette four feet away from his boots and against the wind without having ash all over the place, as the legend goes.

Not only was he well-respected but also an admired smoke-breathing dragon who made smoking more appealing than Paul Newman on the back of a flatbed with ankles chained together. Sadly, Uncle Fred died the next year just after increasing his daily consumption from thirty to thirty-one and a half, next to a six-pack of shitty IPA. It is heartbreaking yet legendary, knowing that teens still mention his name more than Beetlejuice's, preventing his soul from getting rest.

How did he and so many others obtain their licenses? There are, in fact, several kinds of licenses depending on who you ask, of course. According to Jacob, there were only three kinds of which he obtained all three throughout his high school career. He is a fervent smoker who manages to go undetected among those with whom he has little interaction. He smokes not only because he is addicted but also to mask certain smells due to Hyperosmia. He also mentioned preferring to work with engineers who smoke, especially those who can step away from a sophisticated problem to have a soda and a rocket.

According to him, it allows the engineer to process the problem with a possible solution when not directly confronted by the sheer size of the issue. He has done this multiple times with success, even if it took a bit longer than anticipated, and can back his approach with several technological developments, which he is known for.

The first kind of license, referred to as the Bare-Frog and Bare-Pears, or BF and BP Card, is for entry-level smokers who don't have any hair down there yet. No one actually verifies the presence of hair as that is reserved for the second license requirements and also because of the honesty system.

Regardless of the presence of a bush, you'll still have to complete the official certification, where you must lie on your back with a lit cigarette. Your goal, while having the smoke in your mouth and a fireball candy within your oral cavity, is to suck on the rocket, inhale and then exhale until the cigarette is finished.

Sounds easy, right, but there is a catch. You must fully finish the cigarette without having any ash over your face and have the ash stacked, therefore representing the Leaning Tower of Pisa. Then, and only then, will you be allowed to enjoy two vomit-tasting sticks per day among fellow first-license holders and in the presence of two or three second-level license-holder ladies, referred to in their singular as My Lady. As a freshman, you were never allowed to make eye contact with any senior, especially not a My Lady.

The second license is a bit more challenging, with several

requirements. You must be sixteen, have Happy hair, Stoneys should be in your past, and you should partake in any recognized sport, which excludes Chess and anything requiring the wear of a helmet. The presence of Happy hair, also known as the happy ending trail, will be verified by a My Lady, which should run from your naval to the top button of your pants. To put your mind at ease, no genitalia are exposed during this certification process.

The more challenging requirement offered two options: either eat five cigarettes, without the filter, of course, or get branded on the shoulder with the tip of a flaming hot lighter, known as a Smiley. The latter reminds me of branding cattle and wasn't the option to go with unless you fancy walking around with a mark older people associate with the occult. Hiding such a painful scar from your parents was impossible anyway, and that's why he didn't take that as an option.

Your success in obtaining this second license, known as a 20-Pack Card Holder and PCH20 for short, will be communicated to the senior smokers. You will then be allowed to carry 20 cigarettes if you manage to buy a packet from the local mom-and-pop store, managed by none other than Bullhorn Margret, the 69-year-old aunt of Piears, spinster and queen gossiper who enthusiastically shares the "youth of today" inadequacies. The solution to this obstacle is to procure such contraband with the help of Piears, a very tall and slender 20-year-old who got his nickname with reference to his extremely long pistol, known as a knee-slapper, and his satellite dish-like ears.

Another issue when obtaining the second license is the crosshair it comes with. Senior smokers will pester you to support their smoking habits, therefore leaving you with only two cigarettes a day, which is the same amount you're allowed as a BF and BP Card Holder.

The only real advantage of having a PCH20 license is one step closer to obtaining the senior license, known by various names such as The Old Dog, The Meerkat, and the officially recognized King of Ladies Card. By now, you'll be seventeen with more bush than the imaginary Orangutan Joe, complimented by a ripped body obtained from sports, and you'll most likely know a few English words.

Obtaining the final license is no bloody joke but worth the success, consequently giving you access to a surplus number of cigarettes carried by PCH20 license holders. Don't, for whatever reason, try the following at home!

The applicant must run a set distance between two garbage bin lids placed on the ground within a cut-off time. Once he reaches the distant lid, he has to consume a glass of lukewarm water mixed with lemon drops, pull on a pre-lit smoke three times while inhaling and holding his breath for a few seconds between every puff, followed by squatting down with his hand on the lid and turning three times around it, almost like Jacob's cousin did when he burned tires on the school's front lawn in protest for failing his Happy hair measurement, using a corrupt cop's motorcycle.

The applicant will then have to run towards the lid he started off at and repeat the process. He has to go back and forth within a two-and-a-half-minute window, which happens to be when Piears, the ding-dong king, makes his final pull on an unfiltered stick. You will most likely vomit in the process, but that shouldn't be seen as a setback but rather as a step closer to leaving a town with buried dark secrets in the middle of nowhere and attending the Kanamara Matsuri in Japan once you have mastered English, which may take another decade.

Cigarettes aren't the only culprit in the franchise of tobacco products, but so are chewing bakka, dip, snuff, sniff, and the list goes on. No, I didn't misspell tobacco when I mentioned chewing bakka. People down South, or at least those who grew up there, commonly refer to bakka instead of tobacco. Also, those who dip, the shit you put behind your bottom lip accompanied by spitting into an empty plastic bottle, refer to dipping as snuff, as printed, even though it's physically impossible to snort due to the consistency. Remember this, even if it's the only thing you take away from this adventure: spitters are quitters doesn't apply here.

Sniff or snuff, as referred to by your great-great-grandparents, is a tobacco powder that can be snorted, therefore giving you the nicotine fix craved by nicotine receptors in combination with the habit itself, also known as *the little monster inside*. It isn't a strange movie scene where the interrogated, the almost dead cowboy or soldier asks for something to calm their nerves or perhaps have the last piece of pleasure just before meeting their maker, which Bob and some of the fellows tried to portray in the school play with James managing the school's newly acquired sets of lights. Another interesting topic, which I won't get into, is that of non-smokers loving the smell of smoke without craving a rocket.

College and Varsity students who smoke will suck through several just before entering the auditorium for a test, believing it will calm their nerves and settle them down. Still, to the contrary, it lowers your SpO2 levels, which is the oxygen saturation level within your blood. Jacob once shared his love for indulging in this habit just before attempting to complete several tests during his engineering student days, which resulted in lower grades.

Cigarettes contain the following, according to trusted medical institutions, which aren't just harmful in the short run but can be deadly when consumed for an extended period: Nicotine, Hydrogen Cyanide, Formaldehyde, Lead, Arsenic, Ammonia, Benzene, Tar, Carbon monoxide and so forth and any additional fluids Anny laced the filters with. Stephen discovered her dirty little secret, with Dean knowing very well this erotic surreptitious, which Bob eventually shared while addressing the high school freshmen, resulting in him securing a monopoly in the "underworld" of selling single sticks.

Formaldehyde, as previously mentioned, is used to denature protein and, at the same time, harden a medical specimen such as the human brain, lungs, limbs, and pretty much everything you can cut hanging from a human body. Benzene is a chemical that is a light yellow or colorless liquid at room temperature, which has a sweet odor and is highly flammable.

Tar, for instance, can be produced from various materials such as coal, wood, petroleum, or peat, but regardless, it's a brown or black viscous liquid. At some point, I believe it was used to waterproof Noah's Ark and the shingles he used for the roof. These were only three chemicals I mentioned, driven by no intention to shock or deter you from sucking on your favorite pastime.

One thing I do like to share with the hope of putting the destruction caused by these chemicals into perspective is the unbearable smell once a Y incision has been made from your clavicles down to your happy hair, followed by breaking your thoracic cavity apart using bulky rib sheers to reveal your fucked-up lungs which resulted in you drowning in your own fluids. That smell is just as horrible as that of nose cancer, lip cancer, and anything used to suck on, which resulted in Jacob's uncle getting to hang with Jim Reeves and Sinatra. A post-mortem isn't interesting in the least once you've seen how a loved one was taken apart like you would a sheep, with the only difference being respect for the dead…

It's a beautiful hot afternoon outside the Psychiatric clinic, where patients stroll through the lovely flower gardens with birds chirping among the lushness of ten-year-old trees. A visiting family member accompanies some, while only a few enjoy the solitude of benches around the large pond and below the trees, with several others engaging in philosophical discussions with their noses dissecting the scent of a freshly picked flower.

Most patients are still attending group sessions and individual consultations with their psychiatrists. At the same time, Jacob relaxes under the shade of the trees while on a distant bench overlooking the painting progress made by men in white dungarees as they apply only the best paint to the frontal face of this large and modern building.

Psychologist Helga can be seen through a window staring at a smoking Jacob without noticing her emotional concern from a distance. James is slowly making his way from the main door, down the steps, and past the large water fountain toward Jacob, where he arrives with a fake smile and clenched fists as he approaches the bench. "May I join you?" asks a frail and confused James. Jacob knows this sight quite well and has no intention of adding to whatever James is facing as he responds with kindness and assurance, "Absolutely, take a seat mate." He offers James a smoke, which he hesitantly takes from him, sitting on the edge of the bench, his right leg bouncing up and down from angst, unknowingly mimicking a man sitting on the edge of darkness.

This is where the license system for smoking doesn't apply, and Jacob knows that James has always been treated like shit. By offering him a smoke, he made him feel like a human being and a friend he could turn to. Jacob lights the cigarette using a Zippo engraved with his family crest and initials. "Thanks," says James while understandably coughing as he tries to fit in.

He has never thought of smoking, knowing the words his father always said just before punishing him with a switch, which is not just contained somewhere in the Bible but also preached by Jamaicans as: "Bend di tree while it young, cause when it ole it will bruck." James's father is everything but Jamaican, but rather that which represents the beliefs of a Middle Eastern Tyron with a hunger for blood inspired by his own demons of frustration toward raising a rebellious teenager.

"A beautiful day, don't you think?" remarks Jacob, with smoke symmetrically rushing from his nose as he exhales. James realizes his lack of confidence can be described in a single sentence while he softly replies, "Just another day for me." A teenager like him will eventually come to terms with realizing the blood on the world's hands for not preventing his misery. He will see straight through tears and good intentions to dismiss love as nothing that can exist. His scars have started shaping him toward someone who would never know how to show love, just like Bob, who has never experienced what is much needed in a healthy family.

It's not a question of whether or not they are heading in a sociopathic direction but rather how to go about showing their burning desire to love. James will eventually end up having no true friends at all, which should not be confused with borderline personality disorder, ICD-10 code F60.3, but should be understood as a result of something most parents neglect to teach their children: it's okay for friends to disagree on topics. "Truly," agrees Jacob to just another day. "May I ask you a question?" inquires James with enough courage to overcome his fear of being seen as benighted. "Shoot…"

"What brought you here?"

"That's an excellent question, James," replies Jacob, using his name instead of "kid," making James a valued individual who no longer needs to go by as a failed number in a society driven by stature and statistics. "Needed a break from reality…" continues Jacob. "What do you do for a living?"

"I'm still in university—studying engineering."

"May I ask another question?"

"Feel free to ask whatever you want, whenever you want," assures Van der Linde while lighting a Lucky. A Lucky is a cigarette you turn upside down when opening a fresh pack of rockets, which is a tradition with a history lost in time but is the last cigarette you'll smoke from a deformed pack pulled from your pocket. "Is life supposed to be this shit?" asks James while flicking the tip of his index finger in an attempt to master the displacement of ash from the cigarette. "At your age?"

"In general…" How do I answer a question without any hope for

James, questionably thought Jacob. "I honestly can't tell my friend, but I can assure you that you'll get through whatever you're going."

"If I may ask, why are you here, James?" James is experiencing a nicotine headrush when pausing to answer, portraying him as a deep thinker, followed by an honest self-assessment, "I'm a failure—I guess. My father beats the shit out of me and pretty much my sister and brother too. Kids make fun of us, but no one knows what happens in our house. I have nowhere to go and don't know what will happen next."

"I know exactly what you're talking about," sympathizes Jacob, who also has had a brush with a devilish personality hidden deep in a father figure. Helga, as seen through the window, is observing the interactions and taking notes.

"You grew up like that too?"

"Pretty much the same."

"And how did you get through it?"

"I made friends with people like you, like us. We understand each other's circumstances regardless of how you perceive it now. The only way to successfully get through what you're going through is to adapt and build."

"Adapt and build?" asks a confused James, who just killed his Happy Stick.

"You need to steel with your eyes and your ears. How old are you now?"

"Sixteen."

"Two more years to go, buddy, till freedom presents itself. I know that's not what you want to hear, but that's the only way you'll pull through. I also know that if you get back home, you'll feel like you're back in hell, but hang in there," encourages Jacob, knowing that words can't change the past but can give comfort, especially coming from someone seen as an inspiration or friend. Anny approaches and joins the conversation with a baby pacifier in her mouth and a colorful dress containing flower arrangements. She removes the dummy and asks charmingly, "May I join you, fine gentlemen?"

James gets up and offers his seat, but she decides to sit on the lawn. "No need to get up, James. I'll sit on this beautiful, soft lawn. My tush needs to cool down anyway, I believe there is even a saying for this kind of heat—something about crows."

"Yep, it's so hot even the crows are yawning. What's up with the Dummy?" asks Jacob, knowing the possibility of an interesting story presenting itself. "Pacifier Jay, a pacifier. I filled it with honey," she says while intentionally licking her lips with the tip of her tongue, followed by a wink. "Tomayto, Tomahto, same thing." This woman is full of surprises, thought Jacob, realizing she is flirting with him. James never had the opportunity to obtain a PCH20 license and is unaware of the chemistry caused either by sucking on something or having his Happy hair checked which a hopelessly horny Anny strives for when looking at Jacob. He opens a new pack, turns one upside down, and offers her a smoke, "Care for a fag?"

"She removes one, and he offers her a flame."

"Thanks. We had a fruitful morning, don't you think?" she asks while holding the smoke like a lady from the early sixties. "It was fun indeed. What do you think, James?"

"Seems like it."

It feels like someone is staring at my soul, thought Jacob, unaware of the psychologist's studying methods but with the assumption that there may be a connection between him and Anny. She knows the history of child neglect quite well and tries to add hope to James, "You'll be fine, James—look at us, we turned out quite respectable."

"And still building our empires," compliments Jacob with a light fist bump on James' shoulder. "What would you like to do after high school, James?" she asks with sincere interest, almost like a doctor would directly after diagnosing you with having an Urk in your navel, which Bob will elaborate on later.

"Not sure yet."

She lays slightly backward with her palms resting on the lawn and her cigarette perfectly in the middle of her lips if you had to draw an imaginary vertical line running straight from her crown to her BF just before she removes it to encourage James, "You look like you can become whatever you want!" A nurse wearing a typical white dress approaches and asks James to join her, "May I steal James for his provider appointment?"

"Sure thing, but bring him back in one piece," eagerly responds Anny, knowing she and Jacob will get a chance to be alone. James and the nurse leave toward the building. Anny shouts toward James, resulting in him slightly turning his ear towards her, "Don't bang her, James! You have your whole life ahead of you!" Anny turns towards Jacob, spreads her legs, revealing a clean-shaven BF, which may be mistaken for a vertical-shaped eye, removes something from her bra, and throws it towards him. Anny, with an erotic voice, "My thong—just for you. Even though we have an age gap, I so want to ride you right now— how about you?"

"Not sure if you've noticed, but there's quite a lot of people around, and to be honest, I don't have what it takes to please a woman right now—meds," replies a pleasantly surprised Van Der Linde with a slight blush. Helga's notes show concern knowing the possibility of disastrous romantic relationships that can form in a place where broken people rely on each other for comfort. "So let me blow you!"

"Don't get me wrong, Anny—I find you quite attractive, but this will be a major fuckup for both of us. One, we will get caught, and two, it would be pretty messed up and awkward knowing I couldn't reciprocate," says Jacob with hidden hope before lighting another stick.

"May just be, but perhaps we can do the horizontal monkey dance?"

With never hearing that saying, Jacob replies with interest, "The what?"

"You know…69."

"Sounds fun…"

"Can't wait till we get out! I want to do all kinds of things to you."

"I thought you were into women?"

"At times…but nothing compares to a good explosion in the back of my mouth, almost like biting down on a large grape."

"You never know—the pool table in the entertainment room?" A bell sounds from the building, indicating the afternoon therapy group. Both get up, and he hands her back her pink lace thong as they leave toward the building, "I appreciate the gesture, but I'm sure you may need this while here."

"I'll make sure I keep it moist."

"Not exactly the word I was expecting." Fuck, I so would like to have her from behind, thought Jacob, even though his medication is suppressing his libido.

"Mam nadzieję,że lubisz sok z cipek," mentions Anny in perfect Polish.

"More than a fat kid likes cake," responds Jacob, presuming she would most likely strap him to a bed to inflict as much erotic post-ejaculation torture as she sees fit.

To conclude this chapter, I would like to share the psychology behind men sharing "dick pics" and the obsession most have with being blessed like Piears, the man with the knee slapper. It isn't uncommon for men to purchase penis pumps or stretching devices with the hope of increasing length and girth, almost like the standards for a magic wand. Hell, some would even use the tube from a vacuum machine, especially when uneducated about the various options that can be found on the internet.

Why, oh why, are they obsessed, you ask? Men are hunters, visual, and sometimes territorial, but most importantly, an animal that walks on two legs. Lions, for instance, will display their mane and strong-sharp fangs, while antelopes typically display their antlers, all with the hope of securing a mate willing to be dominated by the certainty of security. Several birds, including the peacock, will display their beautiful colors to secure a mate that can produce offspring. Canadian geese, for instance, will mate for life unless they see it fit to part ways. It is sporadic to see a female animal with these characteristics, which doesn't truly add any value to what the male is looking for.

That is precisely why men do what they do, showing off their "antlers" even though it comes across as weird and inconsiderate. Adding to the reason is the fact that it is a rush, doing something frowned upon because we are truly distant from what we used to be. I do not intend to crucify men here alone on a cross.

Ladies, why do we wear push-up bras with foam or gel cups? Gotcha! We do that to make ourselves appear to have the perfect set for the ultimate pleasure, either to be played with or serve as the launching valley for something warm. The shitty thing is that we will eventually have to remove the push-up revealing some of us to be part of an itty-bitty titty committee. At least men are honest upfront with the size of their disco sticks.

If you are a man reading this, don't think for one moment that I am suggesting you start sending selfies all over. For the sake of fucks and broomsticks, keep it classy, even if you have to buy it a miniature cowboy or Santa hat. Get a sharpy while you're at it and give it some eyes as long as you understand that we'll share that selfie wide and far with a hell of a laugh while having a glass of wine and listening to "Short Dick Man" while one of us post your .22 caliber on a very specific website next to your profile picture. If you are engaged or married, we'll send all the details to your father and mother-in-law.

The history of lipstick, perfume, and studded condoms is a result of what we used to be and how we went about doing our perfect dance to lure a mate into experiencing ultimate pleasure when procreating. Smell used to be how cavemen went about finding a partner who is ready to chisel and engrave, yet we saw it fit to replace pheromones with something more appropriate, such as whatever a perfume house can come up with when relying on the sought-after skills of a Nose, even though it remains an uncertainty since adults have no functioning vomeronasal organ which can be attributed to evolution.

What makes us different from animals is the understanding that animals don't have intercourse for fun but for procreation. Nonetheless, humans get to choose. That, my friend, is how we get hooked on cigarettes. There is absolutely nothing tasteful about cigarettes, it tastes like crap, but we get hooked on the original rush caused by doing something we aren't supposed to, just like Anny with her thong and her assurance being moist, which is any snarfs wet dream. You can be an unbeliever. Still, it won't change the fact that you've just read this with concurring, even with the slightest.

8

JACOB'S COCOON AND A WORD FROM OUR SPONSOR, PART II

December 2023

Queen, the famous British rock band known for various successful songs for which several received accolades, making them one of the most well-known bands since the seventies. One such song, Bohemian Rhapsody, sold over six million copies worldwide and over 2.5 million in Britain. These numbers don't truly reflect the song's success but merely the copies legally obtained. In 1986, they recorded and released a six-track album, "A Kind of Magic," of which one specific song, "Who Wants to Live Forever," written by their lead guitarist, was for the movie "Highlander" starring Christopher Lambert. The song falls under the ballad genre, which not only makes it great for making out and dry humping but also one to force tears from your eyes when your grandfather's dog, Rufus, dies. One of the phrases, "This world has only one sweet moment set aside for us," describes one inevitable thing: death and the loss that comes with it.

We are obsessed with our bodily representation, resulting in some getting implants, liposuction, tummy tucks, and even rhinoplasties with the hope of looking at our younger selves again. We hunt down the best plastic surgeons and spend thousands hoping we won't end up looking like some 60-year-old Hollywood actor or actress who will have no problem with makeup and special effects when auditioning for a new wizard movie depicting trolls and goblins.

We no longer focus on loving ourselves but rather admiring ourselves, hoping to preserve something that can't be preserved: life itself. Yes, you will eventually end up looking fugly, like Martha the Mastiff, who won the 2017 title of the world's ugliest dog since your implants can't mimic cell degeneration in perfect synchronization with that which your body naturally does. Your body may possibly develop an immunity to the poison you inject into your face, therefore requiring more and more. I don't judge since my wife and I enjoy looking a bit younger, but eventually, we'll have to stop, which you should perhaps also consider.

Many books and screenplays discuss the possibility of living forever, but only if we can find the Elixir of Life, created by either using unicorn blood or by finding a hidden fountain somewhere in an imaginary world ruled by pirates or ghouls, which contains tears from a mystical creature.

That said, none of those books or screenplays depicts success, or at least the few I have seen. It always starts out with some expedition where a whole company of explorers and soldiers set out to find the solution and stake their claim to living forever. Unfortunately, most die on their way there, with perhaps only one seeing the elixir.

I personally view these movies as a lesson, conveying one message: You will die trying to find it. Everyone will die trying to find it regardless of the number of implants or poison you inject into your body. Worms will find their way around your artificial implants, and not all men or women enjoy something looking unnatural, regardless of what porn movies may want you to think. In the end, you will fall short of gaining access to an elixir, six feet to be precise.

Finding such an elixir is not only impossible but also preposterous since there is no such wonder backed by science. For some reason or another, we believe that death will find us at a ripe old age, but I hate to break it to you; it can be tonight, tomorrow, or the day you were born…bummer.

This doesn't mean you should give up hope but rather look at medical history to appreciate the failures in creating such a magical potion, as tried by Johann Conrad Dippel, who was born in 1673. Johann, also known as the original Frankenstein, claimed to have discovered both the Elixir of Life and the means to exorcise demons. His potion, referred to as Dippel's Oil after its inventor, was made of a distillation of horns, blood, leather, and ivory, which is not surprising as he frequently experimented with animal cadavers.

As might be expected, his potion was short-lived when he was laid to rest in 1734. But let's imagine we had access to such a potion; what good would it do if none of your friends or family members could afford such a black concoction? Will you be able to process laying future loved ones to rest, over and over, until you are the last? Think about it, but again, not for too long. People die all the time, with heart disease and cancer being the top two in the United States.

Your heart is the primary organ for blood circulation and is seen as a pump, a pump within your thoracic cavity referred to as your chest. The location of your heart is between your lungs in the middle of your chest and slightly left to your sternum, otherwise referred to as your breastbone. A sac with a double-layered membrane surrounds this pump called the pericardium, and the pump itself comprises four chambers: the left atrium, the left ventricle, the right atrium, and the right ventricle.

The left atrium will receive oxygenated blood and direct it into the left ventricle, where the blood will then be carried to your body via the aorta. The right atrium will receive oxygen-poor blood via the vena cava and direct it into the right ventricle, where the blood will be pushed via the pulmonary artery into the lungs.

By the way, most people believe arteries carry oxygenated blood, which most do, except the pulmonary artery. Consequently, we don't distinguish between veins and arteries as having oxygen-poor or oxygenated blood. Remember this as something you can share with your local phlebotomist since the possibility of them not knowing is likely high. Any pump, excluding penis pumps or breast pumps, need electricity the work, and the heart is no exception.

The heart's electrical system is called the cardiac conduction system and is quite unique. In a nutshell, this system controls not only the heart's rhythm but also its beat. With every heartbeat, an electrical pulse travels from the top of your heart to the bottom, which causes contractions, resulting in your heart pumping, with 2.32 psi systolic and 1.55 psi diastolic for a healthy patient, based on what Jacob shared years ago. Germans refer to a heart as "Herz," and interestingly enough, a healthy person's "Herz" has a Hertz of one, consequently having a rate of sixty beats per minute, on which I'll elaborate later.

Fibrillation is not only a word that needs dictionary verification but is also associated with risk, especially when combined with atrial, which may be a bad choice of words when posting your biography on Bumble or the likes, where women get to choose their potential partner.

To keep it basic, fibrillation is the uncontrolled twitching or quivering of muscle fibers, and when married with atrial, it indicates a potential setback that may result in deviled eggs and club sandwiches being served in your memory after your sudden death.

Unfortunately, you won't be able to indulge since your sister's fat kid, Timmy, will help himself to several servings with the hope of outliving you. Atrial fibrillation, also referred to as AF or AFib, is a condition in which your heart doesn't beat normally. The two upper chambers, the left and right atrium known as atria, beat out of rhythm with the lower chambers, the left and right ventricles, resulting in the heart not being able to be efficient because it has to work harder, resulting in blood not properly circulating throughout your body, which may result in having a stroke or heart failure when not treated correctly. Trust me, you don't want to neglect your heart, bearing in mind the possibility of failure during your 2 a.m. sporadic intercourse session.

James Prescott Joule, a well-known brewer, mathematician, and physicist born in 1818 and died in 1898 at the age of 70, created something represented by J or Joule. That specific something, Joule, represents energy as per the International System of Units (SI), which states that 1 Joule is the amount of work done when a force of 1 Newton displaces a mass through a distance of 1 meter in the direction of the force applied.

Not only is this formula applicable to physical displacement but it's also used in electricity, referring to the energy dissipated as heat when an electric current of one ampere passes through a resistance of one ohm for one second. Joule unknowingly laid the foundation for several technological marvels, such as the modern-day defibrillator.

Defibrillators, with alias Joule's machines, are equipment found throughout any respectable medical facility and have also become quite visible in businesses, not only because all businesses should have one but because some businesses must have one. Those found in businesses are securely stowed behind a transparent box with A.E.D written on the front, which stands for Automated External Defibrillator, revealing the existence of internal defibrillators, which are small implants for those suffering from fibrillation, or so I was taught.

When will an external defibrillator be used, you ask? In our case, as below, cardiac failure resulted from atrial fibrillation. It is also relevant to understand that not all defibrillators are automated since some do require manual interaction, portrayed in several movies by the word "Clear" associated with cardiac failure and synonymous with "DO NOT FUCKING TOUCH THE PATIENT" unless it's your intention to test the power Thor's hammer will have on your body with no possibility of you not pissing your pants. Regardless, this is definitely not a BDSM toy, nor can you persuade Dirty Dieter.llc to source one. Before I forget, a defibrillator's success is monitored on an ECG screen which in the US is called an EKG even though ECG is English and EKG German...

It's late at night, with instruments suddenly alarming and lights blinking. Staff scrambles toward Jacob's bed as a result of uncontrollable jerks in response to cardiac infarction. The ICU staff, led by the Charge nurse, rushes to his bed and starts performing CPR while one of the nurses, a junior, rushes toward the emergency trolley.

"Coding, bed 11! Where's the defib?!" shouts the Charge toward supporting staff.

"I'm coming!" responds a young and less experienced nurse. The Charge performs chest compressions while loudly counting out, "1,2,3,4,5,6,7,8,9,10..."

"Make way!" instructs the junior nurse as she bumps into another nurse assisting. The Charge removes the paddles from the defibrillator and quickly applies electro-conductive gel. She sets the dial to 120 Joule to initiate defibrillation. She then places the interior paddle to the right of the sternum below the clavicle and the lateral paddle below his left nipple just medial to the anterior axillary line. "CLEAR!" loudly says the Charge while simultaneously pressing both buttons, one on each paddle. His body responds with an extensive convulsion whilst an excessive amount of energy enters his body. With eyes on the vital signs monitors, specifically the 12-lead ECG screen, with the hope of seeing a graph vaguely resembling a QRS complex. There is no time to waste as she instructs the assisting nurse to increase the dial to 200 Joule.

The assistant's amygdala responds by sending signals to her

hypothalamus, which stimulates the autonomic nervous system, which consists of the sympathetic and parasympathetic nervous systems. Whether the assistant will freeze depends on which system dominates the response at the time, complimented by the release of adrenaline and cortisol throughout her body. Her extensive training results in the sympathetic nervous system dominating, resulting in her setting the dial to 200 J.

Being a Cardiac ICU nurse isn't a walk in the park, especially when God and Beelzebub decide to play ping pong with a soul, Jacob's soul. "CLEAR!" shouts the Charge, followed by the synchronized pressing of the buttons. There are still no visible signs of a complex, prompting continuing defibrillation in combination with chest compressions. Please, God, don't let this happen, not now, not like this, thought the Charge in desperation as hope decreases with every compression. A faint complex presents itself on the screen, followed by several trailing.

Jacob's subconscious thoughts with a raspy voice, "Remember I told you to google Dissociative amnesia? A defibrillator is the mother of all medical devices—not a toy for the masochist! Did it hurt? Not a bit, due to Dissociative amnesia, but I'll definitely feel the chest compressions once awake— intercostal muscles tend to tear from the ribs, which can be illustrated when separating ribs like troglodytes indulging in the rack you smoked since 3 a.m.—hurts like a bitch for two weeks or so!

That's not nearly the worst pain you can experience—try having a medical professional feed a catheter through your urethra and into your bladder, otherwise known as indwelling urinary catheters. Frederic Foley, a Boston, Massachusetts surgeon, developed the Foley Catheter, which comes in various diameters but is denoted as Fr, with 1 Fr being 0.013 inches. Fr refers to French units that range from 6 to 26, with 26 representing a diameter of 8.7 millimeters or 0.34 inches.

People who overdose on medicine, like our patients in the clinic assisted by Helga, would've most likely experienced urinary retention at some point, resulting in the insertion of a Foley catheter at the entry of the urethra and into the bladder, where it will be locked in place by an inflatable retention balloon.

Medical professionals, in general, excluding forensic pathologists, prefer working with people who want to live than those with a morbid outlook on life. A solution to remind someone not to overdose is using a large catheter, which will painfully stretch the urethra with an inner epithelial lining, a spongy submucosa, a middle smooth muscle layer, and an outer fibroelastic connective-tissue layer. By the way, Every ICU has an emergency trolley, which is used for situations I just experienced—nothing magical to it except for the defibrillator with a capacitor the size of a brick."

Regardless of whether you decide to quit on life or smoke yourself to death, we will all face the uncertainty of what comes next. We tend to be scared of the only place no one has ever entered and report back on how to navigate through a possible endless blackness regardless of the claims of individuals visiting death, which led them to believe that they have an answer.

We get carried away when philosophizing on what the possibilities are to return to reality with no progress on creating a viable solution to cheat death.

9

PEANUT BUTTER, A PERFECT MAN, AND A FRENULUM MASSAGE

Dogs have become man's best friend not only through companionship but also due to the endless amount of fun we, as pet owners, have with our four-legged friend. One thing most pet owners tried at least once is to treat them with peanut butter, either directly from the spoon, our fingers, or on a complimenting treat purchased from nobody but the best, seeing that the dog enjoys the treat while extending their tongue in all possible directions to conquer the tacky-like liquid with a very high viscosity. Jacob once shared a video depicting one of his dogs indulging in what seemed to be a dog cookie covered with peanut butter lying on the kitchen floor.

Under normal circumstances, this would be a short video if the dog had a protruding muzzle. Still, both his dogs are brachycephalic, which makes for hours of recording since lifting a treat from the floor using their snouts in combination with their tongues and teeth isn't an option for them.

In 1884, Marcellus Gilmore Edson, a Canadian, patented the peanut taste from milling roasted peanuts between heated plates.

Shortly after, in 1895, Dr John Harvey Kellogg patented a process for creating this unique butter from raw peanuts.

Peanut butter is one of the more well-known spreads, except in some European, Asian, and African countries. According to Jacob, he had to visit particular stores for foreigners in Germany and Japan to add some familiarity to his dietary needs. After all, one can only eat so much "Mettbrötchen" and quail eggs before turning to your dog's food or accepting a dinner invitation from a lonely Dieter, the man Jacob created.

America, the House of Peanut Butter, has quite a variety of peanut butter-containing products, such as peanut butter cups, peanut butter-flavored candy bars, and cheese-flavored sandwich crackers with peanut butter filling in between two crackers, to mention a few. The latter, sandwich crackers, can be obtained from Walmart for below $20 per 40 packs when this book was written, bringing the price to fifty cents per pack. This snack might be nice to have around the house for when you become pecky but should never be seen as a dietary supplement, considering the lack of nutritional value to sustain a healthy body and mind.

One of Jacob's ex-girlfriends, the thoroughbred redhead whose head slightly turned with eyes changing color when she lost her shit, refused to add the crackers to her monthly shopping list, for she believed fresh fruit to be the answer to a small spot that needed to be filled. I can't blame her, to be frank, for it is Jacob who enjoyed endless entertainment watching her enjoy a fresh banana.

I also concluded that peanut butter snacks are the choice for airlines throughout the States, not only because they are cheap skates but mainly because they are, after occupying several flights from coast to coast and island to island.

Where are the days of butchering a goat while cruising at 35000 feet? Some prisons throughout our civilized world still produce their own fresh produce and manage their delis regardless of the possibility of creating a cholera outbreak, blamed on the sinful behavior of whole population groups and the just wrath of an angry God, and regardless of everyone contracting the human version of mad cow disease called variant Creutzfeldt-Jakob disease.

Visiting a prison and not as an inmate can be quite the eye-opener to a world where privileges are controlled by nine-to-five employees who are possibly unhappily married and underpaid. Visitor benches are bolted down to concrete floors, and you are under the eagle eyes of guards carefully scanning each movement. Contact between visitors and inmates is kept to a minimum to prevent the possible exchange of contraband. Your time spent with a loved one is limited, and visiting rights aren't open 24/7, 365.

You may argue the prisoners had their time to be part of society. Let me remind you that what makes us human is the same attributes they share regardless of their past. I have met several "normal" people who should be in the same institution, but judgment isn't mine to cast. High fences, heavy doors, cameras, and security officers, alias guards not only intimidate but make you realize just how futile a system can be when it induces angst and depression in an inmate who is confined to a volatile environment without having a second or a third serving of peanut butter flavored sandwich crackers.

Luxuries aren't benefits inmates will enjoy, and their food is the same kind your kid will bitch and moan about.

Prison reform programs are designed around structure and discipline as their backbone to ensure the progression of becoming a respectable citizen, excluding those who ate the pastor's wife. With the utmost love, I suggest looking into having your kids try a bit of structure and discipline without demanding money for taking the trash out. No, you aren't doing them a favor, but just the opposite.

Entitlement is not a healthy approach, considering they will eventually have to enter the world of wolves, your and my world. By now, you are most likely to believe that I'm not a big fan of kids. You are right to an extent since they are more unpredictable in certain situations than hardcore criminals. Nonetheless, treat them with respect and love using guidance and leading by example.

"Criminals" have most likely never had that opportunity, nor am I trying to justify some of their actions, but rather, I'm trying to highlight the possible outcomes for your little clone. A typical day in medium-security prisons begins with breakfast around 4:30 a.m., more or less the same time you are supposed to sleep at your deepest, followed by reporting to work assignments at around 6 a.m.

Between waking up and getting ready for the day, they also need to comply with grooming standards unless they want to face disciplinary action. In South Carolina, convicted murderers must keep their hair short and be cleanly shaven. Everywhere they are expected to arrive, they'll do so in a single line. Privacy in a prison system is non-existent, which may be a result of previous unwanted events.

When they have no work assignments, they may have a class to attend or spend time in their bunks reading, writing letters, or listening to the latest remix of Queen's "I Want to Break Free" done by the in-house disk jockey named Alberta. Lunch will be served around 11 a.m., followed by gym or rec yard exercise. The last meal, supper or tea, depending on where in the world you find yourself locked up, will be served at 4 p.m., allowing the inmate to attend evening classes, watch television, or play dominos. Lights out is still a mystery, but my assumption is around 10 or 11 p.m., two hours after returning to their cells.

Everything in prisons should be closely monitored to ensure safety among the inmates and simultaneously track riots or prevent a probable escape attempt. If an inmate becomes aggressive toward themself, or if an act of aggression has been carried out toward a fellow inmate, the inmate may be committed to solitude since torture was part of the Dark Ages.

The Chinese realized the problem with physical bodily torture and introduced a faster yet mentally painful solution described by Hippolytus De Marsiliis in the 15th or 16th century. To understand the solution, we need to look at one of the things we dislike most: someone pretending to throw something toward your face repeatedly, taunting your reflexes.

Marsiliis describes the solution as a form of water torture where a restrained victim's forehead is exposed to the continuous dripping of water. The mental breaking part comes into perspective once you, as the victim, can't use your limbs or complete body as part of your natural fight or flight reflexes. All you can do is wait for the drop to hit your forehead, resulting in you giving up your firstborn rights to avoid another drop.

Another form of torture would be to access a busy arcade accompanied by a blindfolded subject. Strap the subject's neck in a brace, put them in a chair directed to a white wall containing a singular dot, and remove the blindfold. For some reason or another, we need to look around, evidenced by people taking a seat and immediately scanning their surroundings. Our subconscious relies on our conscious to gather information to feel safe, understand, process, and conclude.

By removing this possibility, we deprive the subject of much-needed information and create two possibilities: one will break you down to your core, and the other possibly evoke aggression. We see this all the time in prison systems when inmates are sent to solitary confinement, hoping to settle them down with a lonely lesson. Little do they know that solitary confinement should be avoided as far as possible, for it may create a higher form of aggression toward other inmates or staff members.

Prisons may argue against this as an uneducated opinion. Allow me to share an observation Jacob once made. A child was promised a toy, which also included physically seeing the toy, which was, at that stage, a popular toy with bright colors. The child's eagerness to have the toy increased linearly with the promise of having it in combination with seeing it.

Frustration overtook the child, resulting in him tearing it apart once he did get the toy. It may not make sense, but depriving someone repeatedly of something or over an extended period may result in elevated aggression. The child didn't end up hating the toy but rather the process and the person who held the toy.

The catch, however, is that children's reactions in specific environments, such as their environment, are much faster than that of a calculated offender who has all the time in the world to tear down a building brick by brick until the foundation is exposed. I can recommend "Law Abiding Citizen", even though it's just a movie, as it will support my argument.

The offender who has been exposed to solitary confinement may not end up hating themself since that is no longer a possibility once they are introduced into an environment on edge. Still, they will accumulate hatred not only toward the person who ordered the confinement but also toward the person who sealed their fate with the fall of a hammer.

I thank the lord almighty I never chose to study law. It would be way too much stress knowing I sent a person to an institution who will eventually be released or who has possible connections to the outside. The law on its own can be corrupt, and it brings forth the question: Does a judge or a prosecutor face prison time for sending an innocent to a cell and, more specifically, death row?

Blaming is considered part of a defense mechanism called projection. It should be taken into consideration when hosting human beings for an extended period, especially those in psychiatric clinics or hospitals, seeing that they are under severe stress, depressed, sad, lonely, hurt, and with feelings of being worthless.

Let me share what most psychiatric clinics or hospitals in a particular State have in common with some prisons throughout the US, which should be seen as a sample from a broader network stretching this fine country. When entering such a clinic, you will be expected to strip down to your bare in the presence of an unknown person, regardless of whether you voluntarily admitted yourself for seven days or if you were legally ordered to attend, even if you have violent tendencies.

Don't worry too much about violent outbursts in a confined building, seeing that those will be locked in an impenetrable sound-proof room known as a solitary confinement area. After your strip and search welcome, you will be issued with socks, toothpaste, a toothbrush, single serving shampoo and body wash, alcohol-free mouthwash, a towel, washcloth, and a bed in a room you'll share with people who are on edge caused by angst. You will be fed three times a day, at which you must align in a row and march toward the mess where you may or may not be confronted by someone who wants to swap portions. You will be allowed four 15-minute sessions daily to engage in outside activities, such as smoking or shooting a ball, while being observed by security personnel and video cameras, even though you are behind 15-foot fences with nothing but concrete below your feet.

By the way, not all clinics even have an outside area. Your daily activities are limited to group sessions, which adds no value to your life, seeing that no life skills or coping methods are shared. You will be allowed to spend time in your room, but you will be monitored every 15 minutes by a person taking notes. Night activities are limited to watching TV on devices behind metal bars, and your only option for a snack will be peanut butter-flavored sandwich crackers. In essence, psychiatric clinics in this beautiful and free country are nothing but prisons and, in some cases, worse than prisons.

You can't keep people confined to a small area for 23 hours a day without physical or mental stimulation, nor will it break your budget when offering healthier snacks such as fresh fruit instead of 50-cent packs of crackers. Also, it can't be a healthy environment when mixing moderately depressed people, who voluntarily check in with the hope of getting life skills and answers, with those who take plea-sure in creating havoc when they lose their tempers.

Some patients, or shall I say inmates, will be admitted with nothing but a hospital robe, which will be exchanged for either tent-size clothing or something only a stick man or woman can fit in. You will not get a replacement set if you decide to have your set washed until the washing is done. You will enter such a facility with hope but leave with more angst and no progress besides being able to bite down hard till the last day.

Can you leave earlier if you voluntarily check yourself in? It will take an act of God, but it is possible. Do your research and read the reviews, knowing that clinics and hospitals will market themselves as one of the best, if not the best.

The sad reality is that the management, including directors, is either disconnected from reality or takes pleasure in running an institution founded on prison principles. Their statistics, like the 80% made up on the spot, may give you a false perception of what happens behind closed doors, and it doesn't take a rocket scientist to figure that out, but rather a person who just spent thousands, realizing a poor investment and cut their losses.

After all, isn't a psychiatric facility supposed to be a place of tranquility where people are treated as humans with access to privacy and activities in large open space areas while taking full responsibility for their actions? Or is there such a massive difference across the globe in the mentality of humans living in civilized countries that you can't leave them alone for just a moment or two?

Whether they form romantic relationships or not, they should still be given the benefit of the doubt. Think about it, but longer than usual. Allow me to ask you just this one favor on behalf of my dear friend; stop eating shit that tastes like peanut butter, for that is reserved for people confined in small areas and for dogs about to be recorded. "Was der Bauer nicht kennt, das frisst er nicht," like Dieter would say…

All psychiatric clinics or hospitals should have a patient entertainment area such as the one our patients enjoy. Apart from being rigged with various entertainment options, this room also offers patient privacy, which is crucial to allow them to be themselves and luxuriate.

The room is 150' x 150' with washed brick walls lined with several canvas prints, each illuminated with a different color. The prints are those of icons such as James Dean enjoying a fag, Einstein with his tongue sticking out, Monroe with her skirt gently lifted by air, and Bill Murray as portrayed by The Chive entertainment channel, just to name a few. At the far end of the room, opposite the entry door, is a Venture 22' Monaco shuffleboard running parallel to the wall and internally illuminated by light blue LED strips.

To the left of the board are two coinless vending machines, of which one sells sodas and the other snacks. A patient can swipe their patient ID card and select their choice of refreshment, which will be added to the final invoice. To the right side of the board is where those without tennis elbow can compete against a fellow patient when trying to hit the Bullseye on either of the three Winmau Blade dartboards, each with its cabinet and with various color backgrounds. 6' away and parallel to the shuffleboard is a set of high-end leather sofas facing a custom-made tempered glass coffee table resting on an artificial lawn cut in such a manner to represent a green at a golf course.

Extruding from what seems to be the green's hole is a custom-made 3D-printed silver arm holding a pink chicken egg. Two 6' Great American Neon Lites pool tables give the room a proper arcade look, both positioned in the middle of the room, with internal LED strips illuminating the bumpers and industrial Steampunk-like lights illuminating the sleets. Except for the sofa area where the fake lawn is used, the entire floor consists of lightly colored screed sealed by epoxy paint, giving the room a quasi-industrial look.

A René Pierre 61-inch Foosball Table with telescopic rods is surrounded by several Super Pac-Man adjustable barstools, offering spectators an elevated position when following the tight competition between players who either favor Messi or Wimbledon's Jones as their leading player.

Empty spaces allow patients to freely move between the wall-mounted digital jukebox, several pinball machines from known rock bands, and giant bean bags scattered around and complimented with three randomly placed high bar tables with epoxied tops and chairs, of which one contains an anonymous suggestions book. A second set of high-end leather sofas, closer to the entry door and adjacent to a large water dispenser, adds alternative seating for those interested in reading a book or finishing level 15440 of Candy Crush. Dimmable light switches drive the ambient setting manually or automatically by audible activation, complimenting the relaxed mood from any of the Café del Mar albums or whatever Rammstein's controversial lyrics may represent.

Most are in the room except Bram, Dean, Jana, Bob, and Alicia, partaking in some form of entertainment. Anny is teaching Jacob how to play shuffleboard, Stephen and Hanna are engaged in a game of darts, and James is setting a new record on the Iron Maiden Pinball machine. At the same time, Cathy, dressed in pajamas and a robe with compliments from her church, reads a religious book. Bob, dressed in shorts, a "Pulp Fiction" t-shirt, and flip-flops, enters the room, proving our need for fraternizing as social beings just as he approaches her sofa.

"May I?" he asks, contemplating the possibility of choosing the sofa at the room's far end. Cathy looks up while keeping her current page with her right hand, preventing the book from misplacing her spot. "Sure," responds Cathy with a warm smile. Bob boards the religious train, positioning himself on the large cushion leather sofa, and crosses his legs, during which he breaks the ice for potential conversation, "Didn't know people still read books."

"I try to keep myself spiritually refreshed from time to time," responds Cathy, knowing that her religion isn't anything to be ashamed of but celebrated.

"What's it about?"

"It's about having a purpose for the life we live."

This specific book she is reading has truly changed countless people's lives, not only those who acquired the books themselves but also some that Jacob's mother shared the book with, all thanks to the donation of the American author himself. Jacob's mom is certainly one of the more inspirational people I have had the pleasure of meeting, considering her past and the lessons she shares during her free counseling sessions. "Heard about it—figured you more as a Mills & Boon fan. Is it any good?"

"If you believe in God, yes. Do you?"

"Do I what—believe in God?"

"Yes," responds Cathy with a burning desire to spread the "Good News."

With a raised left eyebrow and a bit of scorn, responds Bob, "That's a question only an illiterate can answer." Cathy knows quite well that only a fool will try to defend a religious point of view against an outspoken atheist who most likely knows the Bible better than a pastor in the suburbs. "Explain…" encourages Cathy without appearing desperate to defend a point. "I've never seen or heard him, nor do I think I ever will," he responds with slightly raised shoulders and hands turning with palms facing the almighty. "Trust me, he's all around and all-knowing," she responds with a faint smile and eagerness to continue the conversation. "And that's exactly why we are here… It's okay to say you have a relationship with God or Jesus, but don't mention you heard other voices—immediate ICD-10 code R44.0," he adds with a fervent knowledge of the international classification of diseases related to psychiatry.

"I'm afraid you lost me there."

"It's a code doctors use to diagnose a patient having auditory hallucinations," responds Bob with his right index finger making circular movements toward his right temple. "So what makes you skeptical of God's existence?"

"That's just the thing—I'm not skeptical at all. I believe you can only be skeptical if you have something to be skeptical about, such as being skeptical about something that may just be true or not."

"Then I can assume you don't believe in Jesus either?"

"It's possible he did exist, but people proclaiming him to be the son of God or God himself is ludicrous. Jesus never claimed to be God," replies Bob, knowing very well the general misperception people have toward what Jesus claimed versus what people assumed he claimed. "He did say: before Abraham came to be, I am…"

"Indeed he did because he knew the Old Testament well, especially the part where Moses wrote in Exodus: I am who I am. It's simple: Jesus knew he couldn't physically say he was God because he would be stoned, and he kept everything a guessing game for uneducated people who followed him. If he truly was the son of God or God himself, why did only one of the 12 apostles claim him to be God, as written in the gospels? It's also one thing to speak in circles claiming to be God, and it's an entirely different thing saying you are God—physically."

"Interesting argument you have. May I ask what led you down this path of thinking?"

"The older I get, the more I realize people who taught me religion aren't exactly the cleverest of cats. I find women to be devoted only because of their need for a perfect man and nothing more—perhaps daddy issues or failures they see in the men around them. Also, none of them ever read the Bible from page 1 to page 1200," responds a collected Bob.

"It sounds to me like you're angry at someone or something…" she responds calmly toward a man who set the benchmark for being calm. "Fairy tales shape a child to be nothing but a tool. Have you ever wondered why teenagers walk away from the church once they enter college? They realize no one prepared them for adult life."

"What's your take on the afterlife?" she asks intriguingly, knowing that Bob has vital points, even though she doesn't have to agree. I believe we simply come back," he proclaims, with the understanding that people may jump ship when presented with an option not part of their own culture. Cathy is open to new concepts backed by her sincere recognition of people's rights and opinions regardless of their heritage. "Reincarnation?"

Bob pauses momentarily, trying to gather words that would appeal to those who understand love toward not only Homo sapiens but also towards anything covered by the broad definition of life. "Have you ever studied the behavior of animals—really studied? They show emotion, love, anger, trust, distrust, and commitment," answers Bob while visually indicating the attributes using his fingers, just like someone would when counting. Cathy finds Bob's points more toward being plausible than philosophical. Still, she needs clarification to satisfy her interest in a topic only Bob and Ethologists appreciate, "Elaborate on the commitment part."

"Most Canadian geese usually pair for life starting as early as three and perhaps two years. The gander will protect his dame at all costs and fend for her and the goslings—more than what some humans do. Hell, they even divorce at times." Pleasantly surprised, Cathy smiles, "In that case, I would like to return as a black cat, preferably Persian."

"Mmmm, a Persian cat—interesting choice…Why's that?" asks Bob with intrigue.

"They are adorable," she answers with awe. "I'd rather choose an Abyssinian cat," he adds with an acute "1-UP" mentality. "A what?" Most people, including myself, aren't aware of the existence of such a living or mythical creature, given that neither Tolkien, Rowling, nor Herbert ever mentioned one. "A brilliant cat—not a lap cat at all but rather one that will kick Lassie's ass in an agility course," he assures with confidence. "Could see you as such…" she affirms with a twinkle in her eyes. I wish the world would give rise to a beautiful young lady for Bob, she thought, being mindful that men like him need an extraordinary woman without a doubt.

With a braided beard, thanks to Jana's talented hands, Dean enters the room alongside Bram, carrying a snack platter his wife dropped off. Dean's younger spirit reveals itself with a few cha-cha moves. "Ahoy, fellow party animals! Anyone up for doubles on pool?" he asks with the same enthusiasm your sister or brother may have once they've figured out how to tie their shoelaces, something we all do but never brag about. "I'm in!" responds Cathy as she closes her book after folding the corner of her current page inward as a position marker. Bram places the snack platter on a bar table, removes the plastic wrap, and visually indicates the availability of something to snack on. "Bob?" asks Bram, knowing that Bob most likely has a trophy cabinet containing proof of winning streaks for underground pool tournaments organized by nerdy exchange students or perhaps those obsessed with geometry.

The only stick Bob is used to holding in his hand is the same one he uses during flight simulator play and is referred to by many as a joystick, for a disco stick is something Anny would prefer to grab onto. "Cathy and I are about to kick your asses!" responds Bob knowing well that geometry isn't his strongest forte. Cathy places her hand on Bob's leg, looks him in the eye, and concludes, "All we can do is to search for meaning—you found yours in science." Dean is well aware time is not on his side as an elderly and, at the same time, knows the fun they have will end within this week as he eagerly and passionately instructs with clapping his hands, "Let's get going, ladies —chop-chop!" Pajama-wearing pigtailed Jana with a Superman cape, accompanied by Alicia, who's wearing pajamas with English bulldog prints, enters the room. Their faces are painted with all the colors known to clowns and street performers, representing their far-from-perfect influencer dreams. "We'll take the winners of round one," energetically adds Jana, who has the petiteness needed for trick shots.

"Want to play for smokes?" asks James to up the stakes, which have not yet been agreed on, as he leaves one of the pinball machines. Jana hesitates for a moment as she replies, "I don't have any except the few Jacob gave me." Bram hands her a full pack of Lucky Strikes, knowing there has been a time in his life when cigarettes were seen as an expensive commodity and most likely still are. "Hold on to this pack. We'll play you for the few Jacob gave you," suggests Bram. "That's to say you beat us," boldly adds Cathy with a well-hidden understanding that pool tables have never been part of her life besides that one evening she rather not openly acknowledge. "And we don't smoke," murmurs Bob. Cathy retrieves a soft pack of Camel filters from her pocket, which comes as a surprise not only to Bob but to the ex-Klan member Dean. "Now we do!" she says while throwing the pack onto the pool table's slate.

Alicia is tiptoeing around the table and eager to get the game going when she sees an opportunity to speak with the assumption of her and Jana stepping away victoriously, "You can keep them all, Jana, they taste horrible!" Cathy makes her way toward the table and starts packing the balls randomly. No one truly cares how it's packed but whether they'll have a good time, which they all have the energy to contribute. "Super Bitches is our team's name!" yells Jana while chalking the tip of a cue. The tall Dean is just as quick to invent a name complimenting his and Bram's vertical advantage above the rest. "We are the Midgets of Mordor!" boulders his gentle giant voice. "What shall we call ourselves, Bob?"

"The Kings of Babylonia," answers Bob to the motherly Cathy. Hanna and Stephen approach when they notice the possibility of joining an event everyone will carry with them long after they return home. "We're in," confirms Hanna on both her and Stephen's behalf. "You need a name to enter this tournament, young lady," says the braided beard giant. "Guns and Daisy," secures the limping Stephen with his right hand on his hip and index finger with thumb representing a pistol having a barrel and hammer, respectively, and several darts still in his left. "I welcome you all to the league of Fangs and Fags," says Bram, during which he initiates handshakes, followed by handing Cathy the white ball to get the tournament started.

"How many cigarettes does each team have to put up as stakes?" inquires Hanna. "Will four work?" questions Bob while surveying the faces representing each team, with each confirming the amount as being acceptable. "James, you ready to be the DJ?" he asks, knowing every social event should have a dedicated DJ to control the flow.

Not only did Bob ask this, knowing the need for flow, but he specifically asked James to give him some sense of belonging, a purpose he will cherish for the rest of his life. James reaches for a pen in his pocket as he goes to the book for suggestions lying on a bar table. He carefully tears out a page, leaving no evidence of a missing except the incrementing page numbers. "I'm ready," indicates an enthusiastic James. I can't believe actually having friends who don't judge me on my appearance or my social stature, thought James gratefully, who has now identified a possible occupation besides becoming a train driver as suggested by his father.

James's father's aspirations for a "difficult" son are driven by his inadequacies, as evidenced by his belief that his son will be able to experience the entire world once he secures a job as a train driver. Don't get me wrong, I don't see train drivers or associated staff as less of human beings, but I do believe James is destined for something completely different than doing the same thing over and over, therefore limiting his full potential, which to my understanding may be concurred to by Helga and may be a reason for his father not understanding his son.

Sadly, he will end up misplacing his personality due to trying to fit into a society driven by admiration. Steeling with your eyes and ears can result in a healthy person losing their uniqueness, but it can also be used as a coping mechanism. He starts recording the song requests on the blank paper with the heading, *"Die Buiter En Sy*

Bende," written in his mother tongue, and fellow countryman's "Rise Above This" as the first song. "Gotta Be Moving On Up," shouts the elderly Cathy, clearly ready to imitate the art of twerking, which she missed out on in her teens and early twenties. "Got it. Hanna, how about you?"

"And I'll have anything from Rammstein or perhaps Wu-Tang!" she requests, not only stunning the entire group who only know Rammstein for being associated with hardcore German music as represented by the well-known "Du Hast," but leaving Jacob and Anny dumbfounded. Anny turns toward Jacob, who is jointly seated on the leather sofa, most distant from the door and six feet away from the Shuffleboard. "I bet you she's secretly into hair pulling and shoulder biting," she whispers erotically into Jacob's right ear. Gentlemen, embrace the power of pleasure whenever your better half wants you to try taking a walk on the wild side, but remember the fruits of enjoying sexuality are contained in a bidirectional lane of which your priority should be to please and not to receive. "Please add "Human" from that stocky guy," requests Alicia just as she finishes up chalking the tip of a cue. "I'm only human after all," murmurs James, concurrently trying to spell. "Add "Bawitdaba"," adds Jana, paying more attention to correcting Dean's braided beard. "How do you spell that," he queries while battling with the previous request. "B A W I T D A B A," methodically spells Hanna, who has opened like a ten-thousand-year-old fountain of knowledge. Dean is no stranger to a good rhythm when he asks for "In the Air Tonight" ahead of Bram requesting Robby Williams' "Feel."

Stephen contemplates which song from his library of stakeout music he should choose and settles on requesting, by surprise, the well-known "Yes Sir, I Can Boogie" from Bacarra. He may come across as a bullshitter, which may be valid to an extent, but it doesn't change the fact that he is an overworked human who survives paycheck to paycheck. "Jacob—Anny!" shouts Bob toward the two, joking around with slight bites and gentle kisses, paying little attention to the song requests. Anny realizes her name has been called and responds just as quickly, "Play "Human" from Rag`n´Bone Man, please!" Alicia notices the affection between the two, who seem about to swallow each other whole. "Eeeww, that's disgusting! Choose another song we haven't chosen yet," playfully shouts Alicia toward Anny. "Don't hate the player, sister; hate the game," responds Anny with a smirk. "What should we choose?" she asks Jacob, who has his hand on her back and below her t-shirt, gently stroking her skin. Jacob turns his attention toward James, "I'll have Peaches by The Presidents of the United States of America!"

"Elle King's "My Neck, My back"!" adds Anny, whereafter she turns her attention back to Jacob's lips with her hand on his lap while slowly reaching for the top seam of his shorts.

Hanna realizes one song is still due and selfishly asks, "What about Bob?" Bob knows exactly when and when not to speak, but when he does, he may come across as being deadly direct or cocky. Regardless, he adds his "1-UP" song, which most people his age will acknowledge as the best song in the world and not just a tribute, "I saved the best for last regardless of your opinion on the Chinese rice crises or the bad weather which resulted in North Carolinian farmers facing large financial setbacks due to crop failures on trees bearing marshmallows. I would also dismiss claims you may or may not have when referring to Spaghetti farms facing the possibility of closing the doors on the age-old tradition with its origin in the Ticino valley of Switzerland. Regardless of your perfection in having the tip of a toilet roll hanging to the left or the right, up or down, it still doesn't change the fact that I would like to add Tenacious D's "Tribute" to our eclectic mix and also Rammstein's "Ich hasse kinder", please, James."

No one knows what just happened except James and Bob. To simplify it, Bob asked for a song called "Tribute" by Tenacious D, which James remarkably understood.

"We're all set then. Let the games begin!" instructs a laughing

Bram, who eventually grasps the intent behind Bob's sophisticated song request, which I'll leave you to figure out, along with the three little pigs' analogy used earlier in the chapter: Dr. Jimmy Cooper's house.

Still holding the white ball, Cathy places it on the slate opposite the triangle-shaped cluster of balls at the opposite end of the table. Hanna hands her a cue. "Thanks," she responds while leaning forward and aligning the cue tip in a straight line behind the white and toward the triangle cluster. Her cleavage slightly shows as she takes the opening shot, with Dean taking notice, resulting in him trying to compliment the Almighty's wonders, "When I was in Nam—"

"—you didn't get to see trenches so perfectly, did you?" responds Cathy by completing the sentence while tightening her robe a bit higher. Why are men, most of them attracted to breasts? The first thing a man reaches for after entering the world is an asymmetric set of cushions promising food and safety, or so I was told by someone else but Jacob. To think about it, it doesn't truly make sense, given that most women aren't attracted to other women's breasts even though breasts were the first thing they also sought once entering this world. But then again, I'm not familiar with whether such polls have ever been conducted to deliver statistics, which may or may not put curiosity to rest. "Your turn, Uncle D," says Bram when he hands a well-chalked cue to Dean. "Solids or stripes?" he asks, with his brain still wandering among the beautiful war trench he saw moments ago. Jana quickly responds to the gentle giant, "Either way, she hasn't sunk any yet."

Dean leans forward, aims, and delivers a power shot resembling the power a giant has when putting his shoulder behind it. He sinks two solids with one shot. Where the hell does he get that from, questionably thought Stephen, making him realize he hast to bring his A-game when it's their turn. The game goes back and forth, with Bob getting a go at the final shot. He aligns the cue with numbers and lines scrambling through his frontal and parietal lobe areas. He pulls back on the cue, steadies it, and shoots just as Anny dims the lights and exits toward the restrooms.

You would expect a man like Bob, a man without any true friends, to perhaps lose his shit for missing the shot due to someone dimming the light. On the contrary, he is grateful it happened the way it did since he never had a cue in his hand before today. Nobody needs to know as he responds like a true champ would, "Fuck, I shot like an Urk!"

"Like a what?" asks the intrigued Hanna. Stephen, the man who has seen and heard it all, yet not this one, "Yeah, like a what?"

"I shot like an Urk," confirms Bob with a serious, straight face. "Enlighten us…" requests Cathy. "An Urk is a small man living in a man's navel, which only comes out when it's a full moon, like tonight, at which he'll start barking at your testicles until they retract," elaborates Bob, waiting for the joke to kick in. "Is that even possible?" asks Hanna with confusion. Silence befalls the room, followed by an outburst of laughter. Stephen, barely able to stop laughing, responds with his version of something being messed up, "Now that, my friend, is what I call confuckulated!"

Anny is back next to Jacob after dimming the lights and visiting the restrooms. She has a small amount of lotion obtained from the bathroom in her hand. She reaches into the front of Jacob's shorts, past his boxers, and onto his penis, also referred to by many names depending on which woman you ask. She lubricates his rooster, whispering, "Blimey, your waxed disco stick is such a turn-on. I hope you can hold your composure…I'm about to milk you dry."

She always keeps to her word when presented with a hard-as-a-rock toothbrush with the possibility of keeping to the status quo, rejecting the thought of being a spitter like a quitter. Milking you dry shouldn't be seen as her most vital attribute because she can also suck you dry, which may result in the back of your head denting inward while giving it a go like a heifer being bottle-fed. By now, you most likely question the sexual content but let me remind you that this book is based on true events, as mentioned at the beginning.

By the way, gentlemen, there are plenty of ways to ensure a presentable love rocket, guaranteeing hygiene and preventing pubes from acting as dental floss whenever your better half decides to brush teeth using the one-eyed python or, in most cases, the Barbados snake. After all, we live in the twenty-first century, and you're also past the age of hoping for a bush.

Pleasantly surprised and conforming to a well-known song by ACDC, he replies, "Would be a first for me." Cigarettes are exchanged with Dean and Bram, who are now facing Hanna and limping Stephen. Ex-Klan member Dean breaks without sinking any balls, resulting in the mysterious Hanna entering each pocket with her selection of solids. Cigarettes are exchanged, balls sink, losers cuss, and winners celebrate their victories. James keeps the music going while toggling the room's lights, creating a feigned nightclub where it's okay for the cape-wearing Jana to facetiously kick balls toward the 3D-printed silver arm holding a pink chicken egg in protest of Dean and Bram's winning streak all to the beat of Limb Bizkit's "Break Stuff", which James added to the playlist. At the same time, Anny continues giving Jacob a frenulum massage with no one truly noticing to the beat of Incubus' "Wish You Were Here", which James also added to the playlist. Bob has Alicia over his shoulder while running through the room to celebrate life and happiness among friends who share something unique and whom only this lot of them have in common. Hanna mimics blowing kisses toward Dean to compliment the physical French he receives from Cathy.

The clock is ticking while they are making use of every second to be themselves without being in a world filled with misinformation and prejudice. This is not something most people will grasp, but judgment among ordinary people labeled as basket cases is seldom or perhaps non-existent, depending on whom you ask. Dean steals

Jana's cape, puts it around his neck, and runs through the room with Jana sitting on his shoulders.

It's a magical night that ends with Jana and Alicia claiming final victory with loads of cigarettes, which any inmate in a prison where wheeling and dealing is unofficially accepted as a form of trade can dream of. "Shit, don't you ever cum? I'm about to get carpal tunnel syndrome, and I don't even have my broom," laughingly asks Anny toward Jacob, still awaiting the explosion of oxytocin and dopamine, which he also doesn't want to have. "I guess I'm an all-nighter," responds Jacob, intentionally holding back since he's well aware of his meds' role and the regret followed by the shame he has directly after a climax. She has become a turned-on percolator in a room that only these two occupy after a magical evening of friends being free to be themselves. "Mind going down on me and eating me out like a Sir?" she asks, hoping to quench her lust toward a man not only well-built but with a smell crafted by Issey Miyake. "As long as you don't mind a bit of nibbling and small love bites," mentions Jacob. Helga's previously taken notes through a window while observing the two outside show concern, knowing the possibility of disastrous romantic relationships that can form in a place where broken people rely on each other for comfort, which doesn't apply to these two. Neither Anny nor Jacob intends to invest in a relationship driven by hormones, not only because they live thousands of miles apart but also because both of them are intelligent enough to understand the possible failure of a relationship formed in a clinic.

As previously mentioned, what makes us different from animals, excluding certain monkeys, is that animals have intercourse not for fun but to procreate, and we get to choose our reason for having a burst of oxytocin, the love drug, except for Jacob. Then again, I don't know of a dog or a male cat who has ever proposed. Did they do it for fun since they also have oxytocin?

Bob may see us as animals, but are we? Why do you think we get to choose whether to do it for fun or selfishly bring children into this world? Perhaps it is a mental advantage we have to allow us to enjoy that which your supercomputer wants as part of a reset or reboot, or there is no reason at all, and animals on all fours are deprived of this choice since they may have messed up in a previous life.

Think about it if you want as long as you realize it is what it is, and you would definitely not be the first to ponder, hence "Que sera sera". As Anny, a woman Jacob shared three weeks within a clinic, said: "I don't know why, but I love my addiction."

10

KEEP ME MORBID BUT FILL ME UP WITH HOPE

July 2010

Bubbles, bubbles, and more bubbles describe a refreshing drink poured into an ice-cold glass while awaiting your friends at a neighborhood grill, the strippers' bar, or the Wednesday art class at your hole-in-the-wall. Another universal characteristic, a sound, is associated with cracking a cold one when pulling on the tab or removing the lid from your favorite soda or beer. Suppose one were to ask people to describe that specific sound using a combination of alphabetical characters. In that case, one shouldn't be surprised by the differences, such as "krrkr-kok, chssh, chisck-awe, and even tcktukcyaaawhhh," to mention a few.

When observing the freshly poured content, you'll notice the size of the tongue-tickling gas bubbles increasing, which you also may find challenging to describe using pen and paper. Fortunately, this behavior can be described using a combination of scientific laws such as Boyles', Avogadro's, Archimedes' principle, and the Boltzmann constant. But then again, I'm no scientist, nor would I ever claim to be, not only because it's above my skill level but also since

129

these principles and laws were brought into the world by those who refrained from eating products containing Monosodium Glutamate prepared by a Japanese biochemist in 1908.

That being said, it doesn't change the fact that we all hear more or less the same sound, nor does it change the fact that I despise complex laws and formulas invented or developed to increase the amount of high school homework during my younger days. I would rather walk barefoot over the South African Drakensberg toward a distant African country, taking my chances not to be eaten by a laughing pack of Hyenas. Or perhaps that same pack can keep me from my scientific misery with a quick bite to the neck.

Jacob once traveled to the beautiful country of Malawi to assist in much-needed medical research. Still, he was flown into the wrong airport, Lilongwe Airport, in the capital city of Malawi, consequently resulting in him renting a busted ass rental to cover 196 miles as quickly as possible toward Blantyre.

When performing an internet map search, you'll notice the distance and the time needed to cover such a journey, estimated to be four and a half hours. On the contrary, it took him thirteen hours to cover a relatively short distance throughout a country with a developing infrastructure with only one or perhaps two tiny mom-and-pop stores along the tedious journey. When I say tiny, I mean approximately 132 square feet at most.

After several hours of driving in God's country, he came across one such shop, which had one twelve-ounce glass bottle of pop within a non-functional refrigerator, a few expired packets of chips and cookies, and bags of maize or corn flour, also known by the locals as Nsima, Ugali, Posho or Mielie meal in more Southern countries such as South Africa. Not only was he as hungry as a lion, but thirst started to dry his mouth, just like waking up with a sensation caused by a Poodle, which took a nap in your oral cavity.

He was hoping for a sealed bottle of a known water brand, knowing that sugar-containing products, such as the pop, would result in his blood-sugar levels spiking, resulting in body cells releasing water to restore the balance in his blood once the sugar reached his stomach, subsequent in flowing in his bloodstream. As the cells lose water, they send signals to your brain, urging you to consume water.

According to the U.S. Department of Agriculture, a twelve-ounce soda or pop consists of about 89% water and an equivalent of nine teaspoons of sugar; hence, you shouldn't shoot me, the messenger, but rather the one who came to the nine-spoon conclusion.

What if he was presented with an ice-cold beer, knowing he still had to cover several hours in a car having an Africon instead of an aircon? A massive migraine will force him to crawl next to the road on all fours, hoping for his head to explode. Alcohol contains a main ingredient chemical called ethanol that converts into another chemical once in your system that triggers migraines, especially when your body lacks what is genuinely needed to quench your thirst: water.

To answer your question about what an Africon is, it's when you drive with open windows with the hope of a breeze cooling you down. Alas, Jacob left empty-handed toward his destination, but he did purchase a few items, which he gave to some children outside the shop. Believe it or not, most children in Africa have never seen the sea, nor will they ever, let alone taste the flavor of that which drives possible obesity and diabetes, for which you'll eventually hate yourself.

Hate is a strong word, but when used right, you'll be able to allow people to concur with whatever the subject is, such as mathematics. Jacob hated math during high school because of his lack of concentration due to domestic issues and because it required 87.2% sitting on your rear, with 12.8% physically solving equations.

Another contributing factor, I believe, is the teacher's inability to convey information understandably, not because I knew her, but merely that it is a big issue in schools throughout the modern world. On the other hand, chemistry appealed to him from a young age, even though he only managed to pass each test with 5% at most. One of the most acquainted chemical symbols is water, regardless of whether it's in Japan, Sudan, or Timbuktu, which happens to be a city in Mali.

Not only does water promise the possibility of life whenever we scan the surfaces of planets with the hope of one day populating that which we can destroy, which is indeed a morbid approach, just like water can be seen as something morbid. Water is represented by the symbol H_2O, which I assume you are well aware of, consisting of two hydrogen (H_2) atoms joined by a single oxygen (O) atom. Heavens, it's so popular that even your body consists of around 60% water, not as if your body got to choose due to a popularity contest.

Each year, Jacob teaches himself a new skill, of which last year's one was to build a swimming pool from scratch using scrap pieces of wood, ample pressure-treated two-by-fours, and lots of fiberglass in combination with resins, or so he shared. Not only did he perfect something he could enjoy during the hot summer months, but it also attracted several species of birds with the hope of enjoying something cool to drink or perhaps take a bath. As always, it inspired Jacob to procure a birdbath to allow for these precious flying shitting beings to mess in their own source of H_2O.

So, just what makes H_2O morbid? The answer is Edward Teller, who was born in 1908. This Hungarian-born American theoretical physicist is often referred to as the father of the hydrogen bomb, alias, The H Bomb, who not only managed to convince then-president Truman to develop a crash program for the hydrogen bomb, which he believed was feasible but also successfully prove his beliefs by having such a device developed with the first workable thermonuclear device produced in 1951.

One year later, the USA tested this destructive device dubbed The Mike Shot in the South Pacific, which resulted in a blast roughly one thousand times more potent than the bomb dropped several years earlier on Hiroshima, resulting in the deaths of some 78000 people and shadows of those who perished burned into walls, sidewalks, and concrete.

Another morbid yet exciting fact is that Hydrogen gas is nontoxic but highly flammable, with an ignition temperature twenty times smaller than natural gas or gasoline. Not only does Hydrogen have a morbidity factor, but so does Oxygen. The air we breathe only contains 21% oxygen since the rest consists of 78% nitrogen, 0.9% argon, and 0.1% other gases.

Breathing pure Oxygen at higher-than-normal pressures can disadvantage your body, resulting in dizziness, nausea, convulsions, loss of consciousness, and even vision loss. Vision loss due to too much oxygen in infant incubators has also been noted throughout medical history. Birdbaths, like the one Jacob got, can also be seen as a "negative" object or experience, depending on how you look at it.

Having a birdbath is not just about having birds puddling or quenching their first, but it also entails regular cleaning, which isn't too challenging. Still, we typically postpone it since our brains believe it isn't a priority due to its simplicity. More important is to ensure fresh water, which will result in what the bath is supposed to do, which is visual gratification when viewing beautiful colors.

Returning to the universal sound of opening a beer or soda can make one realize the beautiful sounds unique to each bird species. All animal species sound different, such as dogs from cats, cats from lions, lions from elephants, etc. The deeper we delve into the uniqueness of each species' sounds, the more we realize the vast difference between the sounds a specific animal group has.

Anny is known for mastering the famous Afghan Hound experience referred to by many as the doggy style, which is not limited to a specific dog breed. Each bred sounds completely different, with smaller dogs barking with a high pitch, like the famous Yorkshire terrier, versus the deep bouldering sound associated with the African Boerboel, which is a hybrid of several large species of dogs bred to ensure safety, among others predominantly.

Not only do different animals sound different, but so do the different breeds of that specific kind of animal and the individual animal itself when comparing apples to apples. For instance, Jacob's male and female English bulldogs sound completely different, but so do they when comparing them to other English Bulldog males and females, respectively, based on his observations. But what if he is wrong? What if all bulldogs sound the same, and what if all dogs sound the same?

Who can honestly tell the difference or set the default for what a dog sounds like? Don't get me wrong; each sounds different, but that's the point. It's all about perception, regardless of how you perceive a cold can of beverage, mathematics, chemistry, a bird bath, or the level of satisfaction when viewing someone's lower back tattoo from a slightly elevated position. We get to choose how we see things based on our unique personalities.

Even though they come across as the same, humans are entirely different concerning our personalities and perceptions, evil versus good, morbid versus cheerful, and so forth. However, there should be a balance, just like the water bath serving its purpose while having the water level consumed, followed by replenishing something that can be broken down and compared to artificial forces of destruction and infant blindness.

If there is one thing I'm genuinely proud of, it would be that I teach my students, alias children, that we are ALL full of secrets and mystery. I specifically tell them that people don't know what they don't know, and they should use that to such an extent to learn by stealing with their eyes and ears.

No, I'm not teaching them to pretend, but rather how to learn more. Perhaps that's not the right thing to do, but regardless, I want to share a vital life lesson. When we are born, we learn lessons from life, such as when to give and when to take, accompanied by "thank you." The responsibility of parents is to teach vital life skills, not just the ones that will require a non-stick pan, a hammer, or a nail.

No, we as parents should also share the importance of getting up and trying again when we fall. I teach my children another fundamental lesson, especially my son, that we should be mindful of the emotional needs our partners long for. Regardless of gender, I truly believe it applies to both parties. I only mentioned my son because he conforms pretty close to the definition of a caveman.

Medical and psychological facts do make it clear that women are more emotional than men, but it surely doesn't mean that men are heartless beings. Our aim as humans should be to be like a fountain that gives and needs to be replenished from time to time. Somewhere in your life, you most likely heard the phrase "the season of giving," which shouldn't be limited to a specific time of year but rather to an entire year, forever and ever.

We need to give emotions, emotional support, an ear that listens, a shoulder to cry on, and hope, even when we doubt ourselves. Humans are indeed like fountains that don't have an endless supply but are just as vulnerable to drought if we don't take care. Men, it is okay if you stumble and fall as long as you don't expect your girlfriend, fiancé, wife, or life partner to keep picking up the pieces. Ladies, this also applies to you. Speak openly with one another, give what you can, and fight for your relationship to stay afloat.

Invest in all possible resources to assist. We are meant to maintain a healthy balance, which again can be compared to a fresh spring of water. It is not my intent to sound like a broken record. Still, we can't keep consuming thinking that the spring will last forever because the assumption is the mother of all fuckups resulting in you crawling the scorching desert seeking something which should have been maintained.

Just so is human psychology geared toward relationships and individualism. We can't keep taking from our partners, but we should also replenish them and ourselves; we can keep hammering ourselves about our weaknesses but should instead focus on our achievements and good qualities.

I once asked Uncle Fred why he got divorced all six times, and his answer was simple: "I wasn't aware of the different kinds of love languages." Invest in learning these languages or at least get yourself a freaking fridge magnet reminding you of a dried-up desert. I'm sure you'll have no problem getting one from Etsy or the like.

Sadly, people tend to judge, just like animals sometimes do among themselves, with no proper explanation for why we prefer to remember the bad things, which goes back as early as 1 Corinthians 13:5: "It does not dishonor others, it is not self-seeking, it is not easily angered, *it keeps no record of wrongs*," where "it," refers to love. We are all unique, just like fingerprints, and we all have our shortcomings, but we all have a candle of goodness that can shine among memories associated with failure, hurt, hate, and so much more. We tend to put love aside, which we exchange for admiration, as said in the chapter "Jacob's cocoon and a word from our sponsor, Part II".

The sooner you realize you have reasonable and even great qualities, the sooner you'll enjoy yourself with a balanced perception. George Bernard Shaw said, "The optimist invents the airplane, the pessimist the parachute." Both these qualities are needed in your life to maintain a healthy balance. Refrain from seeing H_2O as something that can be used for "good *or* bad" but rather something that can be used for "good *and* bad" since it limits the possibility of being naturally seen as bad.

People will see you as being a megalomaniac, but remember that it's driven by their perception of an incomprehensible tendency toward something that comes as natural. And those who bravely diagnose a family member, friend, or foe should understand that your words can cut to the bone. Leave that for someone or a team who spent years grasping psychology and psychiatry, knowing even they can be wrong at times, but at least your insurance will cover that. No one can fit into a box …

For complexity creates a hunger, a hunger for creating, solving, conquering, and perfection, all driven by a reward system called dopamine. For removing that, may result in an absolute void. Keep Me Hopeful but Empty Me with Morbidity

URK

It is early morning in the group room with everyone in their designer egg-shaped chairs, ready for what has become a formality with only a few days left, except for Jacob, who has an appointment with his psychiatrist, referred to by Americans as a provider. Fictive Orang-utan Joe and the Urk, who escaped someone's naval during a late-night frenulum massage, play hide and seek with those ready to replenish with a strong shot of caffeine. As usual, some are tense regardless of the excellent time they had last night. Helga, dressed in a pinstripe double-button suit grafted by no one else than the maestro himself, leads.

With her legs crossed, a straight-back posture, and a smile, she breaks the ice, "I heard the group had some fun last night—"

"—Fangs and Fags," boldly interrupts an overexcited Alicia with her pearly white teeth complimenting her flawless dark skin. "The official unofficial on the spur pool tournament—damn, that was fun!" adds Hanna, who finally managed to overcome her embarrassment toward what most people perceive as normal, that being ructions in the marriage. Cathy looks at Dean and winks, knowing very well what their future holds. It's a strange sight to imagine in your mind's eye, knowing that eventually, they'll end up bumping uglies, even if it's every other day. "Fun is what we had," adds Cathy with assurance. Helga, known by many as a possible angelic being, replies gently, "I'm glad all of you had fun last night—remember not to break the place down. Is that okay?"

"Ten-Four, ma'am," acknowledges Stephen, who decided to be who he was supposed to be. I believe "doc" will now be reserved for his provider. "We always behave appropriately," contributes Anny, who secretly enjoyed three consecutive orgasms, all thanks to Jacob, who indeed ate her out like a Sir while revealing her as a squirter. "Perfect. How's everyone this lovely morning?" You know that specific head nods and thumbs-ups everyone does during a Sunday morning's sermon after the pastor, priest, or reverend asks if they did a particular passage of scripture studying? Well, this is what they just did to keep the show rolling.

"I'm glad to learn. Jacob will be joining us a bit later—he has another appointment. We will do some challenging group therapy this morning, requiring you to share something personal. You can choose what you want to share, preferably something you are ashamed of or regret, and how much you want to share."

The group shows signs of excitement even though the promise of discomfort presents itself, just like an almost-ripe pimple where your Alar fibrofatty tissue and major Alar cartilage join with no possibility of you popping it with a needle when both your index and thumb was removed which led to dismissing you as an avid Freemason candidate. Call it entropy if you like.

"I'll go first as an example—I once accidentally walked out of a store and forgot to pay for an article. Needless to say, I was arrested for shoplifting even though I told the police it was an accident. The store owner didn't press charges, but I felt so embarrassed knowing I was seen as a bad person, even though just for a moment."

"Damn, that sucks!" remarks Stephen, who takes pleasure in cuffing punks, but not women who are perceived as angels and who can't possibly poop. "Who wants to go first?"

All thawed out and ready to grab her husband by the "horn," Hanna takes the first step on behalf of a group about to spill the beans, "I'll go first." What the fuck did she smoke, thought Bob with curiosity. It took him years to master the art of public speaking, yet she sidestepped all the mirror practice sessions as a result of playing darts and pool. Perhaps it was the "Back, back an' forth an' forth" lyrics from her song choice, which Bob always associated with his hot physics professor. "Go ahead, Hanna," confirms Helga with a voice able to turn chaos into a safe haven. "I've cheated on my husband with a new colleague after a night out with our office. I was head over hill for this guy but unfortunately blinded by lust. I still regret the pain I caused my husband, even though he can be an asshole at times. The strange thing about it all is that we never humped but only dry-humped until he shot his load." Bram almost spits his coffee as a result of a shocking surprise. Jesus, she swears, thought Bram laughingly. And the plot thickens, thought Stephen, who last dry-humped before he got invited by a woman with cuffs and a baton to taste the forbidden fruit.

"Thank you for sharing, Hanna."

"Yes, thank you," adds Steven, who just learned something about his pool partner, who doesn't disappoint while her beautiful self-courage takes to bloom.

Alicia eagerly indicates her interest in going next, "May I go next?"

"Please do, Alicia," confirms Helga, realizing the possibility of this session being genuinely successful yet again. "I once slapped my friend Charlie on his bum as a result of me losing my temper. I was studying for a math test, but he kept begging for attention. He then decided to lift his leg against my pot plant, and I completely lost it, which led me to yell and slap his bum."

"Who? Uncle Charlie?" asks an astonished Dean. Alicia hangs her head in shame, which Dean immediately notices, accompanied by a sudden improvisation, "That's perfectly okay, Alicia; we are just human, after all. I'm sure he forgave you just as quick as he directed his pistol toward your plant." Alicia burst into laughter, appreciating an ex-Klan member's care toward a black girl born innocent into this world relying on a dog with a piglet tail. "Thank you, Uncle D," she responds with a tear of happiness. "Thank you for sharing, Alicia. Who wants to go next?"

No God damn way I'm about to share my frequent prostitute visits, thought Steve. He might be as tough as a sixteen-penny nail used for framing, but the true reason for his emotional setback was a result of walking into the postmortem dissection hall when his sister's kid was taken apart the way you would gut a fish. Again, something is seriously wrong with you when you long to attend one. Sure, you have seen a few episodes covering the topic, but the episode doesn't include sound or smell, which will find a suitable home in your sinus cavities or hair, not to mention your clothing. "I will," says Stephen while getting from his chair and taking the posture of a cadet about to graduate with a $3000 graduation handshake.

This is the only time I've seen Steve nervous, thought Cathy. Perhaps he is defaulting to what he has been taught when placed on the spot: stand up straight, chest out, and keep it simple, thought Bob while trying to dissect whatever is going through Steven's head. I instead ride a porcupine bare ass than mess with his attempt to represent the brave men and women in the force. Sure, he has a history of doing dodgy shit, regardless, he still takes pride in being a super cop brave enough to shoot himself in the leg—in the fucking leg! "Hello, my name is Stephen, and I pick my nose in the cinema, behind people in elevators, and even when I'm driving." He breathes a sigh of relief, "Damn, that feels so good getting it from my chest, but I also punched someone in the goddam throat for forgetting my birthday—motherfucker," he adds with flaring nostrils and a slightly raised voice. "Take a deep breath, Stephen, and try to focus on where you are right now," suggests Helga. "I do, too, not punching someone but picking my nose. I sometimes wipe it against something nearby if I cannot chew on it," adds James, who dreams of becoming the only DJ in a small middle-of-nowhere town where KFC is only known by the rich. "It's one of the most natural things humans do," contributes Bob with reassurance after digging deep into his bank of knowledge and wisdom. "Enlighten us," says Anny. "Have you ever seen someone teaching a two-year-old to pick his or her nose followed by indulging in a salty snack that doesn't nearly taste like peanut butter?" Think about it, and you'll realize the truth behind his argument.

"Yeah, all kids do it regardless of nationality or geographic location. See it all the time on TV whenever some charity in Africa tries to catch you in a web of lies," adds Cathy. "Damn, that seems a bit racist, don't you think?" asks Alicia. Some shit can't be explained, such as two African Americans possibly facing a standoff around the definition of racism. The entire group burst out with laughter, realizing the irony behind this madness, including Alicia and Cathy. "And by the way, that's where children get styes from—picking their noses then touching their eyes," adds Bob again. "Been doing it 73 years now and still tastes like snot," contributes Uncle D while stroking that which used to be a beard after it recently turned into a braided work of art with compliments of a girl who has asymmetrical pigtails and a Superman cape.

"Anyone else?" asks Helga, who is suppressing her laughter. "How about you, Bob," queries Hanna while taking a bite from an apple from the fresh bowl of fruit next to Orangutan Joe and the newbie Urk's jungle. Collected and assertive, responds Bob, "I sometimes do weird shit just to feel alive or understand something better. I once took a shower and placed my wet hand against the coils on the inside of a toaster—shocked the shit out of me and tripped the electricity. My father was pissed as hell, which as a result, led him to tear down all my Hentai posters in my room! I sometimes also try to see how long I can keep my eyes closed when driving on a highway." Still sipping fresh orange juice, Anna-Maria responds with motherly shock, "Jesus, you can die, Bob!"

"Hold on, what is Hentai?" curiously asks Bram. "Japanese animation porn of which I don't own a single picture, but thank you for paying attention to my boring adventures and for asking 'What about you, Bob' instead of 'What about Bob' since that is driven by prejudice toward the severe lack of understanding toward those who favor Laplace while secretly fantasizing about the out-cum of solving that which only Fourier was able to do with his time in prison."

Silence befalls the room with no understanding of what he just said, nor did I in all fairness and sympathy. By the way, don't ever, and I mean NEVER, say Hentai out loud in Japan! You'll upset the Daruma cart. "Wait, did you wear clothes?" asks Anny in anticipation. "What do you think?" he responds. Anny hesitates momentarily, "Nah, I don't see you as someone walking on the wild side."

"Never judge a book by its cover," reprimands Evangelical Cathy. "That's very true, regardless of the topic being nude walking and touching the coils of a toaster. We humans rarely take the time to read the book jacket that contains the summary. It would be a good idea moving forward after your discharge to consider this because it would be fair toward other people and because you would like to be understood before being judged," suggests Helga. Bob takes his time as his brain computes the logic behind that madness. Suddenly, a light comes on, and he is home. "I concur," he confirms, with the whole group agreeing to this natural leader's assertiveness, who believes perfection can only be achieved if you are willing to keep updating, just like a computer's image, or perhaps toward the image of God. What is taking Jacob so long, thought Anny with genuine concern. "You want to go next, D?" suggestively asks his buddy Bram. Dean agrees to put his neck below a guillotine, or so he felt when building enough courage to share something worse than missing alimony court. "I did some pretty messed up stuff that I'm not proud of, which should be lifted from my chest. I'm sure I'm the devil in someone else's hell."

"You are among friends, Dean," assures Cathy, who surely has a few hidden gems of disappointment, or so would the police officer say who found her sucking instead of blowing the breathalyzer. "I still recall treating my late wife like shit when I was young and wet behind the ears. I gave her hell about silly crap like how to arrange the dishes in the washer, all thanks to my drinking. Since then, I also pretty much treated every girl like crap. My deceased wife was the only one who truly loved me for who I am. Man, o, man, do I regret fucking that up—bless her soul. It seems I intentionally sabotage relationships to see who's truly dedicated or not—almost like thinning out the herd."

"We can't change the past, like I said earlier. All we can do is accept that we can't change it and strive to be better versions of ourselves. Thank you for sharing, Dean. I realize and understand just how much pain this has caused not only your family but also yourself. Your commitment to taking responsibility moves me. You are a good man." comforts the psychologist. "And you have a beautiful big bushy beard," contributes Hanna with a smile and eyes an owl can be jealous of. I guess I neglected earlier on to describe Hanna's big, beautiful eyes—my bad. "Thanks, Y'all," humbly replies Dean. Jana is moved by Dean's courage and volunteers to go next with a tear running down her cheek. "Go ahead, Jana."

"I once tried jumping off a bridge as drunk as what that bottle of wine could make me."

"Into a lake—skinny dipping?" queries Anny, who still has concerns about Jacob being late.

"Into oncoming traffic…"

"Oh fuck, I'm sorry. I didn't mean to come across as being insensitive."

"No worries."

"What made you not jump, if I may ask?" probes Bob, who believes death should be embraced.

"An overweight female officer grabbed me from behind and pulled me to safety."

"Jesus almighty, I'm glad she wasn't as petite as you!" exclaims motherly Cathy.

I don't know Jana personally, but only what grown-up Jacob

shared, and I can vow that he would've taken the journey himself to the gates of hell to retrieve her soul if she ever made that jump, regardless of her not being his daughter and the fact that he doesn't believe in hell either. He sees something in her that only one other person sees: Helga. "Thanks for sharing, Jana. Who wants to go next?"

"Removing brain matter from a car's confuckulated windshield must suck," respond Bob with a wink toward Jana, who in return gives him the finger. "I once had a call to a scene like that—confuckulated indeed seeing how that man clinched onto life with regret in the one eye he had left, and before I forget to add, I like the smell of my own farts," says the man who lost empathy on the streets of Chicago three days before he shot himself. Hanna feels relieved knowing that someone else shares something some may perceive as weird, "Don't we all love that smell?" In all fairness, I realize I just messed up the view of a woman who can't possibly fart. "It's called habituate—liking the smell of your own farts—around half a liter each day. With a population of 7.888 billion in 2021, it is safe to conclude that we all, excluding animals, produce around three billion one hundred fifty-five million two hundred thousand liters daily. When converted for the sake of understanding among those not familiar with the metric system, it results in more or less eight hundred thirty-three million five hundred fifteen thousand six hundred fifty-nine gallons. Also, the possibility that Alicia like the smell of her dog's fart is highly likely because it's a familiar smell associated with the love she has for her dog," shares the only one who takes pleasure in numbers and random facts. Dean, as lost as someone trying to solve a complex Laplace transformation while chewing gum, asks, "What's habituate Bob?"

"To form a habit, also known as moreish." Uncle Dean still has no idea what Bob said and pretends to grasp whatever is supposed to be understood when using large numbers and words only Bob and a cross-eyed librarian with a slight mustache and perky breasts would know,

"Aha, that makes sense."

"I fart when in the bath—a funny feeling when bubbles run down the bottom of your legs and pop when reaching your feet," surprisingly continues Anny, who is more familiar with mastering the art of stimulation using the handheld shower's extension than adding numbers.

"Eeeww, that's gross," exclaims Alicia. You know that technique of saying something, hoping no one will pick up on it? Well, this is what Cathy is about to try, as she says in a soft tone, "I got fired from a job for trying to baptize people with the water dispenser." Anny has ears like a field mouse and didn't miss the attempt to conceal something, "How does that work?"

"I went up to our office's water dispenser, filled several cups, and emptied on colleagues' heads, followed `by going on my knees in loud prayer. I never thought it through before emptying it onto their heads. And I stole flip-flops from Walmart once, but I made sure I left my original pair of worn-out shoes for someone who may have a need," responds Cathy with her head hanging in shame. Human, after all. I enjoy this session of digging deep into our vulnerabilities, thought Bob. No laughter was expected from anyone in the group after the baptizing part. Don't ever mess with someone who just shared what they see as a severe mistake, regardless of your belief system, that even Bob understands. "Thank you for sharing, Cathy. Who wants to go next?" No one walking this ball is perfect when measured against what the world sees as "normal." After all, normality is determined by the uneducated majority, who believe that history can't possibly repeat itself. "Hello, my name is Bram, and I banged my secretary. I also subscribe to porn."

"Join the club—watching porno," bravely responds the mysterious Hanna. "Membership fees paid to me…" laughingly contributes Cathy, who most likely is into soft-porn subscriptions.

This is it, boys and girls! Just when you thought Uncle Dean didn't know shit… "Now that's called habituate—porn addiction!" he says while pointing his right-hand index resembling whatever confucku-lated speech Hitler ever gave. "Touché Uncle Dean. By the way, did you know it's physically impossible to get addicted to something without a brain?" asks Bob, rising to his feet. "You don't get addicted to masturbation or watching porn but rather to the chemicals released into your brain when aroused, known as the love drug."

He sits back down and waits for a response to break his random statement of awkwardness. Anny is a bit freaked out, not because of what he said but because of how he said it when he stood up straight and stared toward the door without blinking an eye. "Are you okay, Bob?" He turns his head slowly toward her as if he's a robot in a late 80s or early 90s movie, with his voice mimicking the speech pattern, "And that is why artificial intelligence will never be able to love or understand love—beedi-beedi." Alicia breaks out with laughter while Anny breathes a sigh of relief. "What is artificial intelligence," asks Hanna. "It's that thing your husbands' testicles do—you know… moving when not even touched," explains Cathy. "Gotcha."

"Anna-Maria, would you like to go next?" asks the psychologist, who barely holds her laughter, like a hyena about to be fed. Anna-Maria prepares to speak by sitting up straight and resting both palms on her lap with knees pressed against one another below her brightly colored dress. "I will, thank you. I sometimes yell at my teenage daughter, Cassandra. I once almost struck her with the toaster after missing her with a mug. She has a talent for rebelling against my good intentions and guidance. Maybe I'm a bad mother," she says with a slight sniff and a tear rolling lost from her eye. Cathy sends her a tissue, "Don't be so hard on yourself, sweety. Losing a parent's temper with a teen is quite normal. I did it all the time, yet every-thing worked out okay. I promise everything will be fine."

"Yeah, look at me. I turned out not too bad," confirmed Stephen while picking his teeth with his chewed-off thumbnail. Helga, who has no kids, withholds from giving false hope, "We are here for you, Anna-Maria. Even after your stay, we'll be here for you." I can't say I know how it must feel to be a single parent, nor should anyone ever try to imagine the hell single parents have to face. It's not only about the lack of money but also the fact that you don't have a map or book to guide you through the unknown with the hope of having your kid grow a spine.

I take my hat off to Jacob's mom, who had to deal with his rebelliousness after his father left. It now makes sense that Jacob went for a snip-snip at an early age— a lousy frame of reference he had growing up. "Thank you for sharing, Anna-Maria. Who would like to go next?" By now, you should be well acquainted with the fact that the psychiatrist tries to refer to them by name as much as possible because that is sometimes the only valuable thing people have left. Take this as a lesson and refrain from using Dude, Chief, Buddy, Bro, Sis, Ball sack, Dick head, Champ, Trooper, or whatever you think is appropriate to resemble your age or the midlife crises you face. Anny raises her hand proudly and with a smile. "I have masturbated on several national and international flights like Amerair, US Air, Difference Airlines, Middle East Air, Swiss, and many more."

"Swiss has good cabin service, though," adds Bob, who never lost a game against the AI when playing chess 35,000 feet up in the air. You may be tired of reading about the lust issues that Anny has, but it all's still secretive, as indicated by the clueless facial expressions of the group. "I can relate to that," bravely admits Jana, regardless of her past of sexual abuse.

Enlighten me, please: why do people believe that only those with a scarred past have above-normal sexual desires when evidence backs the claims neonatal nurses have regarding early development and self-pleasure, as shared by Jacob, who spent hundreds of hours adding to his knowledge when visiting NICU (Neonatal Intensive Care Unit) between 12 a.m. and 2 a.m. during his student years? Forensic psychologists will argue that Uncle Fred did what he did because of the trauma he experienced without taking into account the expected behavior and longing the body and mind had and still have as a predecessor of a life-changing event.

Bob also realizes this when people discuss the Big Bang with their assumption that nothing existed before the gigantic event. His beliefs toward returning to life aren't based on emotion but rather the curiosity associated with the possibilities of having a past before any given presence at any given time. Damn, that sounds deep, to be frank, but see it like this: there can't be a beginning if there is no end, there can't be a beginning if there was no end, and there can't be a beginning if there will be no end. Sounds gibberish, right?

That's why he is Bob, the man who can text while reading a book and following an intense scientific discussion at the same time while his mind focuses on calculating the amount of sleep he needs over a year to be productive. And you worry about not being able to sleep? There is no way under this moon Bob would be able to sleep throughout without relying on a sedative designed to safely transport the first cloned Patagonian mayorum, a titanosaur, towards Mars on the back of a raft propelled by snapping turtle tails. "How about you, James—would you like to share something?" asks the Psychologist. "Okay, I'll go. A friend and I almost burnt down a fuel storage facility. We were playing with matches in a nearby field by lighting a small patch of grass and extinguishing it. What we meant as fun turned into fear when my friend insisted we see how big the circle in the grass could go. I couldn't understand his pleasure in viewing the firetruck extinguishing the flames from a distance. I was never so scared in my life except for the time my father asked my mom to join him on a long walk, knowing he had a knife with him."

"That's confuckulated!" exclaims Bram, who commandeered pirate Steve's Miranda rights version where he typically swaps "That's" with "You're."

"I didn't mean what you did was confuckulated, but the knife part was."

"Thanks." Jacob also knew a few such kids when he grew up with whom he severed ties decades ago. He enters the room. "Ahoy, pirate! We were talking about you—have a seat!" barnstorming welcomes Dean. He takes a seat after helping himself to a small pack of his favorite candy, Nougat. "Hello, Jacob…' welcomes Anny while filing her concern among all her desires toward him."

"Oh yeah? What did I miss?"

"We were discussing our idiosyncratic talents," responds the man who relies on four hours of sleep daily. How does Hanna know about the erotic encounter they had, or is it perhaps a sixth sense women share when she mentions in an erotic voice, "Anny will fill you in later."

Remember I said maintaining a spring of water instead of just consuming it without replenishing it? That's a bit difficult with a woman who can turn a spring into a fountain; it's not impossible if you invest in a waterproof mattress protector. "Thank you all for sharing your private moments and thoughts regardless of whether you may have seen it as embarrassing. It takes courage to share things we hide from ourselves, hoping to forget about them eventually. I hope you can also share one good thing you've done for someone else without telling." Yet again, silence befalls the room for fear of the unknown, which requires a true leader by example, not because they need to be seen as such but mainly because order needs to be established in moments where people fear the outcome. The logic behind this approach has nothing to do with what people perceive as logic. Still, people who have been broken down find it challenging to share their good attributes since the world, those who determine normality without being educated, decide that which we all should be held accountable for… our weakness".

Helga's job is to ensure everyone has normalized thoughts, which doesn't mean they have to think the way you do, but rather that all should be able to see their way of thinking as normal, within reason. Don't for one moment believe I'm trying to okay anything that goes against the law since that kind of group therapy is reserved for people behind high fences and concrete recreation areas, hence my earlier argument of not having normal patients "locked up" in an institution which has such a resemblance.

"I'll go first. I once paid for someone else's groceries." Still, no one responds. "How about you, Stephen?" she asks while scanning the room. We all know our "bad" attributes will outweigh our good, which again is how normality shapes people. However, Stephen and the others need to focus on the good as he replies with discomfort, "I've done quite a lot of bad in this life, which will break my mom's heart, but there is one thing I believe was something good. A friend of mine's daughter contemplated shooting herself one evening in their backyard. After a fallout with the misses, I strolled throughout the neighborhood when I noticed her sitting on the backyard loveseat facing the forest. I didn't immediately notice the weapon when something persuaded me to join her, who was like a little sister to me. We chatted for a few when I noticed her about to direct what seemed to be a barrel toward her mouth. I talked her down and removed it, followed by a shot roaring through the clear winter sky—"

"—did she die?" interrupts Bob. "Nah, she already loaded the 30-06, and the safety was off. Those were the days before I knew anything about guns. The family rushed to the backyard, knowing the possibility of their daughter ending her own life due to several reasons private to them. I told them I was around the neighborhood and asked if I could use their gun to shoot a coyote I saw in their backyard. Until today, her parents see me as a loose cannon for what I did, if only they knew." You can hear a pin drop, Orangutan Joe, and the Urk breathing. "That's a heroic thing you did, Stephen— thanks for sharing."

"What happened to her?" asks Hanna with utmost respect and kindness. "She finished college and is doing her dream job—quite good at it, too. She has become a true inspiration for others," he concludes, knowing her parents will see him as a reckless man till kingdom come, but also knowing he saved the life of a girl who was a sister to him. "How about you, Dean? Would you like to go next?" Awkwardness covers the walls while uncertainty fills those who have done more "good" than "bad." "Yeah, I'll give it a shot. No paronomasia intended Steve," indicates Dean. "No what intended?" asks Bob, playing dumb to allow Uncle Dean to plow with someone else's Oxen. "A pun, son, a pun. It was a cold and stormy evening when I was driving home from my surprise birthday party hosted by my fellow KKK members. I noticed a one-legged disabled African American man on crutches trying to outrun the rain without much success. I pulled up and helped him into my old rusty pickup—he was soaked, cold, and out of breath. I handed him my shirt, pants, KKK robe, and a birthday gift towel set, hoping he could get body warmth. I then drove him to safety and gave him the only cash I had before credit cards. All this happened when it was frowned upon to help strangers from different colors—confuckulated middle-of-nowhere small-town mentality."

"Not to be inconsiderate, but I would find it truly interesting seeing my one-legged brother walking around like Casper the ghost in a town where racial inequalities are celebrated on both sides. Not sure you blessed him...," adds Alicia, laughing. "That is some funny shit when you think about it," adds Jacob having a tender stretched-out tongue and a stiff neck.

"You helped a brother in need, and that's all that matters," assures Cathy, followed by an "Amen!"

"Indeed! So, you were a member of the KKK?" agrees and asks Bram, who is learning so much more about the hidden gems of his dear friend Dean. "A Grand Magi…"

"We all screwed up somewhere in our lives…" reassures Cathy with empathy. "And sadly, it stays on our curriculum vitae…" Jana got lost with a few new words, "A curricula whatta?"

Bob saw this coming and responded just as fast as Dean did

when he saw the man in need, "A curriculum vitae is also known as a resumé, Jana." She flicks him the finger once again, confirming the emotional bond she has formed with him.

It's strange to think that one can come to such a conclusion when you take the history of a good Fuck-You finger into consideration. The French proposed way back in the 1400s to cut off the middle finger of every English soldier they caught. You can't shoot an arrow from a bow without a middle finger. This resulted in English soldiers mockingly displaying their middle fingers whenever they saw a French soldier.

Sometimes, because of the lack of emotional education, all we know is to say or do something hurtful, which may result in a damaged relationship regardless of intent. We should take ownership by studying our previous mistakes and learning from them as much as possible, knowing that we might repeat them if we don't effectively re-wire the thought patterns we created before we rose on our hind limbs and formed a sentence. Sure, it will hurt like a son of a gun when you start opening old wounds, but do so knowing you need to learn from it and, at the same time, refrain from including those you heard in your past from joining your learning venture since their ventures are different, and you have no right to open wounds on their behalf.

"Stays on our what?" asks Dean, who didn't get it the first time. "Resumé, Uncle Dean, resumé…"

"Wait—you drove naked?" asks Jacob. "Balls and all, neatly packed in my briefs."

"That's a noble thing you did, Dean. Thank you for sharing," adds Helga. Anna-Maria, who is no stranger to being labeled and bullied, agrees with the psychologist, "I think so too."

With a smile and confidence, Cathy adds, "I'm privileged to know you, Dean."

"May I go next?" asks Jana while tightening the elastics around her pigtails to hide her self-consciousness. "Absolutely, Jana," confirms Helga. "There was an old man with two teenagers living in a trailer park near the small apartment my mom rented. I visited her for Christmas, and she cooked us a lovely meal to celebrate the season and my visit, even though she didn't have much herself.

While having a morning blunt, I remembered seeing the snow-covered old man and kids walking the streets collecting empty cans and boxes for some extra money in what seemed to be an abandoned town since most were either with family or enjoying the warmth of the indoors. It broke my heart knowing we had so much more. With my mom's blessing, we decided to give them the blessing of Christmas. The joy in their eyes can't be bought—we ended up having spaghetti and sauce, which were truly delicious."

"What happened to them?" asks Bram with admiration and curiosity. Anna-Maria is just as moved, knowing the feeling of hunger too well, "Yeah, what happened to them?"

"I honestly don't know. Neither would I remember if my mom hadn't brought it up a few weeks ago."

"Seems you have a great mother, Jana," acknowledges Anny, who misses the idea of being a mom who's human after all and not just driven by lust. "If only we could be as genuine as we need to be. Thank you for sharing, Jana. Who wants to go next?" Bram, still moved, "I'll go." Even though it may come across at times that he wears his heart on his sleeve, he still has a particular locker where he keeps special moments such as the ones he learned as a young student. "I used to do odd jobs at several hospitals at night, ranging from washing linen to fixing wheelchairs, all to pay for my studies. I remembered seeing a man brave enough to endure the cold nights while standing next to an abandoned traffic light asking for some assistance—not money, but something else. One evening, I decided to pay him a visit with a suitcase full of clothing handed down to me as a teenager and student. He was truly grateful for helping him out, but what saddens me is my girlfriend being annoyed with my 11 p.m. gesture— guess she didn't understand."

"Perhaps she felt scared?" asks Anny, who for a moment placed herself in the seat of Bram's passenger. "The only way to truly comprehend a situation is to be acquainted with that situation yourself—and that's what makes a good pastor," shares Bob from his knowledge of wisdom. "Spot on Bob! Spot on! Our pastor used to do all kinds of stuff back in the day—the man reminds me of King David himself," compares Cathy thoughtfully.

Anny comes to terms with Bram's goodness while shedding a tear with a soft, warm voice, "A true man can walk barefoot alongside a stranger in a field of thorns. You are a good man, Bram!"

"Thank you for sharing, which is close to your heart, Bram."

"Thank you," he replies, slightly leaning forward with palms together and interlocked fingers on his lap with a humble head hanging as his thoughts are with the man who taught him right from wrong, his late father. "Bob, how about you?" asks Helga as he gets up fearlessly to retrieve a banana from the creature who barks at testicles and Joe's rain forest. "Anyone wants something?"

"I'll have a peach," indicates James. Bob, deep in thought, hands him a peach and banana just before making himself comfortable like a judge about to start with the proceedings. "You all know the no-name brand versions of Pringles, I assume…" Everyone gives some form of indication that they do, with Jana giving a thumbs up. "I was standing behind a man at a checkout counter when I saw him scanning the alternative version of the famous cylindrical container. I made a comment about that stuff being addictive, at which he mentioned it's for his Down syndrome son, who was waiting in the car—apparently not good in crowds. We started talking to realize his son was already in his early fifties, with the old man somewhere close to the age of a biblical character. He shared his concerns about his son's fate if he was to pass away. He also mentioned he doesn't understand the will of God anymore. I saw the concern in his eyes, pulled him aside, laid my hands on his shoulders, and started praying for him. I didn't give a damn who was watching or not. I told him

God has cared for his son for the last fifty years; he should continue putting his trust in the Almighty to look after him when he's gone."

An extended silence befalls the room when everyone realizes the impact an atheist may have had on a person who puts his trust in God. We are human; we will doubt, we will question, and we will repeat those characteristics. The moment you stop doubting, questioning, blaming, and arguing is the exact moment you will find peace in your heart. If you can do that, let either myself or Jacob know, for he will be able to make you a wealthy individual if and only if such a solution can be patented directly after the Elixir of Life. Tears are running from everyone's faces as they believe they are in the presence of a man who'll put aside his religious views, even just for a moment, to encourage those who may, for a minute or two, lose sight of the goodness they enjoyed in exchange for that which the body by natural design craves for. Perhaps it's also because Bob's rebellion against religion is driven by the absence of a father figure painted by an aged old book yet never presented tangibly in his and so many others' lives when all seems lost. Regardless, Bob isn't an emotionless, self-centered being but someone who will pause the battle and cross the enemy line to retrieve those needing assistance despite them being on the opposite side.

This, ladies and gentlemen, is where I kindly ask you to take a few moments to process and respect what just happened in a room filled with people seeking an understanding of why they are who they are. Go make a cup of coffee or perhaps Rooibos tea since that is what I'm about to do. Think about the uncertainty that the elderly man had for his Down syndrome son and what effect words instead of money or gestures can have on someone. "Wow! I'm truly moved right now," says Cathy, with the tissue box making its rounds. Alicia is without words but believes in asking what everyone else wants, "So you do believe in God?"

"I believe in paying attention to detail and showing empathy where we can," he responds, knowing quite well he can only be seen as a believer if he believes. Some brains work differently, but it doesn't mean he is superior. Be thankful for not being Bob, as his life is a living hell if you believe in hell. The angelical Helga fights against the tears as she responds, "Thank you, Bob, for sharing your personal moment."

"Sure, but please don't bring it up. I buried that memory…" he says with little to no emotion on his face, as mostly. "The supermarket experience reminds me of a similar one I had as a student," adds Hanna. "Please share," encourages Anny, who's still trying to clear the fluid the soul uses to wash your two windshields. "I'm not sure if this was the will of God or not, but I'll share anyway. I was shopping for items I needed for college when I walked past a woman in tattered clothes who seemed to be with her daughter in the stationary aisle. I assume they were shopping for back-to-school items. As I walked past, I stopped dead in my tracks, turned around, and engaged in conversation with the woman who was shy and reserved, and so was her daughter. It turned out they were shopping for back-to-school items but had very little money. I told her daughter to pick what she needed without looking at the prices of the items. She gave it to me, and I took care of it at the checkout. By the way, I told her also to take a yellow highlighter or two."

"Why a yellow highlighter?" inquisitively asks Alicia, who still dreams of attending college.

"Warm colors such as yellow, red, and orange have been found to have a greater memory effect on attention. Writing things down on a yellow pad or highlighting text in yellow makes it more likely to remember," answers Bob. Anny seems to be a changed woman, as evidenced by her response, "Hanna, you're a rock star for sharing your story. You just changed my life, thank you."

"I'm glad I could help. Thanks for the explanation, Bob."

"Anytime, Hanna."

"Amazing how our brains work, isn't it? James, would you like to go?"

"I honestly don't have anything to share. For me, it's only been about survival in a house run by the devil. I rescued a kitten once but was told by my dad to take it back to where I found it." Allow me to explain how James experienced the whole ordeal he summed up in a few sentences, shall I? James loves animals, regardless of their size or appearance, excluding spiders and anything he believes should be treated with respect in their environment. He found an abandoned kitten near the town's railway bridge on the coldest of nights while riding his bicycle back from a friend. He carefully picked it up and gave it warmth, excited to have a life he could help. Sadly, his father made him take the defenseless kitten back to the trench where he found it. That same evening, a storm swept through town and most likely swept the kitten away toward certain death. He cried himself to sleep behind the doors of a house in a town where no one ever came to his, his mom's, and his sibling's rescue. Seeing a living creature all alone and helpless is only one of the things that scared him. "Your dad told you to take it back?" asks a concerned Jacob.

"Yes." Jacob knows this isn't his BBQ and has the utmost respect for Helga, but he isn't the kind of person who will stand for the injustice caused by others on those who have no way of defending themselves. That, my dear friends, is why you never, ever try to fuck with Jacob, not then, when he was in the clinic, nor now that he is a successful man. Whatever he decides will include a middle-aged German with a yellow-stained toothbrush mustache, a Tyrolean hat, undersized chino shorts, flip-flops, and a t-shirt with a cartoon character who may just beat you to death with your amputated arm. "Now listen to me carefully. We can't control the actions of others, especially the ones older than us or appointed above us. What you can control is to ensure you don't follow in their footsteps. You did what was right, and you should never blame yourself, ever," says Jacob with both eyes locked onto James'.

"Amen to that!" agrees Cathy. "Okay, thanks," responds James, who didn't truly grasp Jacob's speech. Helga, so far pleased with the session, agrees, "Wise words…"

"May I go next?" asks Anny, who may just be cured of her sexual desires. "Please share, Anny."

"I was visiting a friend in what Bob will call a blighted area. We discussed his life, some religious topics, and how he faced financial challenges. He was a true and humble gentleman to whom life handed a shitty card. I took the liberty to share the scripture, hoping to ease his pain and confusion. That's when I randomly opened my Bible and discovered a $100 bill, which I gave him. I have no idea how it got there since I don't carry cash with me, nor would I ever take $100 for granted and let it lay around. It's almost as if the money was 'planted' by God or some angelical being."

"God works in mysterious ways, my friend. Can I get an AMEN to that?"

"AMEN, sister!" supports Alicia. "I honestly thought you'd be sharing how you bought a stranger a vibrator," remarks Bob without blinking an eye. "I'm not all about a high libido, Bob."

"I second that."

"His statement or hers, Jacob?" asks Hanna trying to keep up with the back and forth as described by one of her song requests she had at Fangs and Fags. "Anny's," assures Jacob.

"You don't perhaps have your Bible with you?" jokingly asks Bram. Jana also jumps in, "I can do with 100 dollars".

"I think that's a kind gesture, Anny," says Dean.

"Having her Bible here and scanning for some money or her story?"

"Her story, fellow moose knuckle spotter."

"Gotcha…" responds Bram. "You definitely added to his life, Anny. Thank you for sharing," acknowledges Helga. Stephen asks with curiosity, "So where is the guy now?"

"No idea…"

"May I go next, please?" asks Alicia with excitement, knowing she will get the chance to be seen through your eyes as someone good. "Absolutely, Alicia, and feel free to take your time," says Helga, realizing the excitement can result in a distorted version of what she wants to share. "Maybe you've also experienced what I have. It was dusk and raining like crazy when I noticed two lost dogs through my bedroom window. You know those dogs with the long ears and sad-looking eyes…"

"Basset hounds with dipsticks almost touching the floor…" confirms Stephen. "I loaded them into my mom's 1980s VW Golf and took them home. I went from door to door searching for their owners for days and eventually had to take them to the ASPCA—I couldn't have them and Charlie in the small apartment. It broke my heart to part from two beautiful animals. Days later, I received a call from the ASPCA confirming they had found the owners. It made me cry from joy," shares Alicia, with joyful tears forming behind her obicularis oculi muscles as directed from her lacrimal sac via the canals toward her tear ducts. "Awe, that was a kind thing you did!" says Anna-Maria, who shares a love for animals with droopy eyes, like the basset hound who struggles from time to time with dry eyes, just like some humans who get diagnosed with ICD-10 code H04.129.

"I also would have cried," remarks Hanna. "How did they find them?" asks Bram with honest curiosity. "No idea…"

"Most likely RFIDs," answers Bob.

Confusion overtakes Dean, "Come again."

"Radio frequency identification tags."

"How do you know all this stuff?" asks Hanna in amazement. "You know it as well—you just don't know it…" informs Bob to enlighten those who still live in the maze of confusion.

"Aliens use that shit," jokingly remarks Jacob with a straight index finger as he tries to mimic what everyone associates with "Alien Anal Probing."

"Like real aliens?" asks Alicia, who is losing the plot. "Not the racial profiling aliens?" asks Dean, adding more to the confusion. Stephen, with his chest pushed outwards, says. "I had to shoot one once." Jana, a sucker for conspiracies, asks, "How did it look like?"

"Green and slim with big eyes?" asks Anny, who most likely will end up wondering what their sexual endurance is. "I'm referring to a drug bust…" Heads are moving left and right as everyone tries to get some confirmation of the confusion Jacob intentionally introduced, with Alicia almost indicating her will to stop asking, "I'm lost."

"I don't know if I dreamt it or not, but I shot the motherfucker."

"I'm confused—do aliens sell drugs?" asks James, with no intent ever to follow that path of addiction. Helga, entertained, decides to bring some form of understanding without interfering too much in the session. "He's referring to a person from a different country who was dealing drugs." A light goes on somewhere in Alicia's head as she responds, "Aha, like a pharmacist without a qualification or a pharmacy?"

"More like an illegal pharmacist who pointed a gun at me." The group settles down as the cockroaches floating inside their brains find their way back onto their corks, with Bob and Jacob enjoying something they managed to create as a team. "Anna-Maria, would you like to go next, or can I?"

"Please, go ahead, Cathy."

"Thanks. Our church was packed during our service, and our choir and band filled the house with spirit, with colorful and bright lights blinking to the beat of the drums. Our pastor laid down hands-on people who needed healing and blessings when I decided to join in. I bravely walked to the front, placed my hands on both shoulders of a woman, and started blessing her—she fell to the floor, and a demon left her body—she shook uncontrollably and foaming from the mouth. I believe I performed an exorcism."

The group is mystified by what she claims and waits anxiously for more of the story. "Was it night?" asks Bob. "Indeed, it was," she answers, annoyed with Bob, who seems to have an answer for everything. "And did she shake all night long once she fell?"

"She did, yes, but only for a few."

"That's intense," adds Jana, who is now on the edge of her seat, just like most.

"Happened to my mom once," adds Alicia as if it's some form of achievement. Bob, o, Bob, he will toy with you for as long as possible but with good intentions. "Don't go to an 'Alternating Current Direct Current' concert when they use flashing lights and you're menstruating. You'll be having convulsions all night long." "What do you mean?" asks Cathy, who is as lost as a silkworm on the top of an elephant's back. "Yes, what do you mean, Mr. Encyclopedia?" asks Dean with concern for Cathy. "There's a term and a code for when the spirit of the lord fills you, as determined by the Pentecostal Church of Goddesses headquarters in Bangladesh," adds Bob with derision. "And what's that?" asks Hanna on behalf of everyone intrigued by his wisdom. "Idiopathic and the code is ICD 10 R56.9."

"How do you know all these things?" asks an amazed and naive Alicia. In all fairness, at this stage, everyone is stunned, yet again, except Helga, who only observes. "Let me guess, we all know it—we just don't know it…" answer Jacob on Bob's behalf with a hint of sarcasm.

"Couldn't say that better…"

"Anna-Maria, the floor is yours. Let's be respectful of her turn, okay?" asks Helga, who notices the possible deflection of these sessions even though it has repeatedly proven their success. The group settles down, and those on the edge of their designer chairs sit back, almost like passengers who curiously await an answer to the news of the pilot possibly spotting a mountain goat at cruising altitude. "I'm in the same boat as James—don't have anything important to share."

"Come now, you seem like a kind person—you surely have something," encourages Stephen, who has multiple times had to rescue women with little self-esteem due to previous and current domestic violence. I'm unsure how you perceive Stephen, but allow me to enlighten you. He may come across as a self-centered police officer, but he will go out of his way to defend those who can't do it themselves—I guess his upbringing taught him that.

"Wait, I remember this one thing… I was doing the night shift at a private emergency clinic, checking in patients, and processing the payments after their visit. An elderly lady entered with a bill for which she needed clarity. The doctor billed her for performing an ECG using a special device, which is more expensive than a normal ECG machine. I knew the practice quite well and the equipment the clinic owner had, who turned out to be the same doctor who charged her. The bad part was that she didn't have private medical insurance and couldn't settle the bill for the charge of an ECG using a special device. I suggested she start looking at finding another medical practice since I discovered previous suspicious billings from that same doctor, and largely because I knew we didn't have such a device among our assortments. I took her bill and settled the outstanding amount using my money."

"Wait a moment, they can do that—charging for things they don't even have?" asks Stephen, supporting her turn. "The world of medicine isn't exactly what you think it is, Stephen," responds Anna-Maria. Almost simultaneously, everyone looks toward Helga. Are they thinking she's one of those bastards, or are they waiting for an answer to disprove whatever they believe?

"What's the difference between God and a doctor?" asks Hanna, clearly pissed off knowing firsthand the narcissistic behaviors associated with those who think it normal to speak down on those who have enough manners not to retaliate with a bitch slap attributed to the power of eleven wise women and men. "Tell us," encourages Jacob like a little pussycat about to drink milk from a saucer beside a giant Irish Wolfhound. After all, he knows a pissed-off woman when he sees one. "God doesn't think he's a doctor…" answers Cathy in response to Hanna's question.

Helga is aware that some perceive her as a medical doctor, which she isn't, but allows them to form their own opinions. She has several PhD behind her name but never shares that information. Some people enjoy throwing around the PhD title as a form of manipulation. My answer and stance on that is simple, and I will say it as always: all you need to do is to add a BfD behind your PhD. I'll let you figure it out. "Co-payments and payments in general suck!" exclaim Dean, who has never made a copayment since he stopped going to the doctor. It seems like a legitimate way of saving money, I guess. But then again, I'm not your provider, nor am I you or your body. "It felt awesome sharing my thoughts," says Bram, who noticed the session ending after Anna-Maria shared. "It did, didn't it?" adds a cooled-off Hanna. "In a way, it did," confirms Bob with a faint smile, which some may perceive as sarcasm. Cathy is just as excited as a kid about to go home after putting away the playdough, "God is—"

"—is what?" asks Jana with a cynical tone and mocking look. "Good, all the time," completes Alicia, knowing she has several things to be grateful for, including her deaf dog, his snores, and farts. Helga notices the stretching of legs and arms as the session comes to an end, and, with her trademark voice, says, "I want to thank each and every one for sharing things that are close and dear to your hearts, even if you felt it might put you in a bad light. The idea behind these exercises was to allow you to speak about something that may make you feel uncomfortable, making you realize all of us are human, and so is everyone out there. So many people worldwide share the same challenges, secrets, and success stories, and you are the few I have the pleasure of meeting. You may think you're bad or a failure, knowing that you may have deeper and darker secrets, yet you can do good for people in need without taking credit for it. Your intentions for helping someone in need outweigh whatever you may see as failures. I am very proud of you and want to encourage you to do more acts of kindness."

For successfully conquering a nation has less to do with enslaved men and more with controlling their women and language. By design and nature, women are emotional and seek stability, safety, and the possibility of bringing life into this world. It may take several years to establish such a level of trust when conquered, but it will eventually materialize. When razing a language, you remove the emotions and understanding of something unique to that specific way of life or culture and replace it with a variant way of thinking unique to Victor or Victoria. One can attempt to conquer a kingdom with a physical approach, which may extend over several years as you systematically try to demolish high-rise stone walls bit by bit without any guarantee of triumph. Or one can infiltrate a kingdom such as a cicada nymph, subsequently using a slower yet more effective way of conquering. As previously said, the latter is more probable, considering who determines normality.

ORANGUTAN JOE ON BEHALF OF BOB

11

MOSQUITO, THE LOVE DRUG, AND A BALLERINA'S HERZ

July 2023

My dear friend has had the pleasure and privilege of traveling the world, which gave him critical insight into what we know very well: the Mosquito. Whenever he travels, irrespective of where he goes, he snaps a few close-up photos of this well-acquainted pest as a replacement for memorabilia. Let me be clear: he doesn't find them fascinating since he still threatens to tear their wings off and make them walk back home if he ever were to catch one.

That said, he knows the impossible task of capturing and torturing every single flying nuisance in a well-furnished hotel room with a size designed for just that, which in itself made him realize to seek a permanent solution to ensure adequate rest and being free from itching and worst case, Malaria.

After some informal research, he came to various conclusions and a game plan he still sticks with. Whenever he books a hotel room, it has to be, if possible, as high up as it can, preferably closer to the water heating systems. Secondly, the first thing he'll do when preparing to head to bed is to turn the air-conditioning system to its coldest setting, at which point he will return perhaps thirty minutes later. He will leave the air conditioning running throughout the night to ensure the effectiveness of his approach.

What is the logic behind this? Mosquitos, or at least those that prey on humans, tend not to fly higher than 7.6 meters, 25 feet from a surface, reducing the possibility of having more than an acceptable number of bloodthirsty parasites in an elevated room. The likelihood still exists based on the pseudo-intelligence of those who followed the upward staircase.

That is where the cold room comes into play, backed by studies indicating this blood-sucking nightmare becomes lethargic in colder temperatures due to the inability to self-regulate body temperature. I wish I kept the picture he shared with me, which he took somewhere in a rural part, showing around fifty to eighty mosquitoes against the inner of the window when he opened the curtains the following day with their hope of reaching the outside warmth.

The picture resembled his perfect approach and many possible Malaria-carrying mosquitos powerful enough to have you intubated to a ventilator stored next to the room with the cardiac ice machine and where the plastic surgeon makes out with his assistant. On the other hand, I don't have this issue as a deep sleeper who seldomly notices the annoying sound associated with this nuisance, which achieves this by rapid wing movement generating a sound that falls within our auditorial range of 20 Hz to 20 kHz, referred to as high frequency.

Hz denotes Hertz, the scientific symbology derived after Heinrich Rudolf Hertz, a brilliant German physicist born in Hamburg on February 22, 1857. Hamburg is known for its beautiful waterways, opera house Staatsoper Hamburg, and the legendary Ukrainian heavyweight boxing brothers.

He is a man who enjoys hours of pleasure watching heavyweight boxing, ballet, and attending symphonies. He does so not because he has a love for pain, skinny men wearing fake bulges, mooseknuckle women, and elegantly dressed females blowing on something, also resulting in a sound being produced. Still, he does so merely because he understands and respects the hundreds to thousands of hours these people had to commit before being allowed to partake in the form of perfection few people appreciate.

You may disagree with heavyweight boxing being part of a list describing elegance. Still, you would do so based on the opinion that two fully grown adults take pleasure in the form of savageness, resulting in lacerations and blood painting the ring's canvased floor.

On the contrary, if you are a heavyweight walking into the ring with the intent to destroy art that took years to perfect, you'll lose the 1st round and be dismissed just as quickly as a man or woman who didn't spend thousands of hours perfecting the study of biomechanics and human predictability.

Boxing has never been about pain since that is only a result. Yet, it has everything to do with prediction, self-control, finesse, and endurance till the last sound of the bell, which can be associated with the bell found in graveyards that saves not only those buried alive but also the boxer about to lose a round, hence again, saved by the bell.

Ballet has an extraordinary place in his heart not only because he enjoys being in the company of other cultured and sophisticated people but predominantly because it gives him a soothing sensation his soul craves. If you've been to a ballet production and loved it, you'll surely be on your way to enjoying that which smooths the soul. Make it a habit even if it means you must go alone. Several production houses offer season tickets at discount prices.

Sadly, he no longer has the emotional strength to attend productions in a particular State he frequently visits due to several consecutive events overpowered by the sounds of candy wraps, beer cans being opened, and crowds cheering with high fives, fist bumps, and loud whistles when the principal dancer makes their appearance.

No, I'm not contradicting myself by encouraging you to go, followed by sharing the reason for Jacob's absence. He can sometimes be quite difficult, to be frank, and doesn't torture himself when exposed to the lack of refinement at such events, especially if he needs his mind to rest.

Not so long ago, he attended a "The Legend of Sleepy Hollow" production. The entire week, he kept on sharing his excitement about revisiting Irving's short story in the form of a ballet. The town of Sleepy Hollow is a place he frequently visits, especially the large cemetery where he reads history from the fading headstones and spends time with The Bronze Lady.

However, he decided to leave the production when a degraded version of a headless horseman and his pierced chick wearing Steampunk and an LED belt joined the cheering by raising their beers. Sophistication can't be bought, as evidenced by those wearing jeans, goth makeup, and sneakers at such an event.

If this makes Jacob a snob, then it makes those the reason why civilization will eventually be governed by individuals who feel entitled without any form of endurance in their past, be it practicing or commitment.

I'm not suggesting in any form that some are better than others, but I suggest that you start teaching your children about the finer things in life. No, you surely don't need to pay hundreds to achieve that, but instead, use YouTube or watch "My Fair Lady". Start small if you want.

The example you set for your children, as a spineless parent, will be your downfall, just like the sound produced by a candy wrap being the downfall of a venue supposed to cater to the needs of the sophisticated and the humble mosquito being the downfall to five-star hotels, for both are under the top ten antagonizing spectrum of which your offspring will top the ten.

No, it's not okay to attend events like these in your sneakers or flip-flops. Men, invest in something more appropriate to wear, even if it is the shitty suit from prom night. Take the lead and communicate the dress code.

If Jacob could have his way, he would strap those who confuckulated his ballet and symphony sessions to a chair, facing a large white wall with a single dot in the middle of a room filled with one bloodthirsty mosquito who doesn't have a proboscis. He will use that sound to make you realize the pain you caused when you tell your children that mosquitos bite and elephants can fly, directly reflecting your intellect or absence.

Alas, the blame shouldn't be on you but rather on the organizer of a prestigious event for allowing punks, kitty cats, and those who regrettably were the fastest swimmers into a venue, such as an egg produced in the ovaries or painstakingly well-rehearsed ballet production…

Helga's attention shifts to a knock on her consultation room door. She is slightly confused and caught off guard for possibly overlooking an appointment at the hour after glancing at her Breguet Reine de Naples. She pulls her business suit skirt straight and gathers her posture, heading to the door when a person with a familiar smell slowly enters. She couldn't place the scent regardless of it soothing her soul and with a pleasant pinkish shine over her skin with the torment of being aroused as a result.

Jacob, who has visited this room multiple times as a teen and into his mid-twenties, dressed in a black suit, close to Vantablack, complimented with an intimidating red tie even though seldom, enters Helga's dimmed and warm private consultation room furnished to give the traveler's aura with keepsakes and relics from every she visited, which makes you feel at ease. He has a Corsage in his right hand showcasing her favorite flower, the Saint Joseph Lilly. A Calogero bronze arc floor lamp overhangs an Ox-blood Winchester

Chesterfield leather sofa while the Greek god Atlas balances a globe on his neck.

On her desk is a collection of Montblanc accessories and several patient files. A bookshelf displays medical and philosophical works, family photos, and achievements as a principal dancer from her ballet days, with a scented wax warmer filling the room with the calm aroma shared by the three wise men shortly after the king's birth.

A space like this doesn't come cheap and results from dreams being lived. Hers has always been to help those who struggle to make sense of this world regardless of the wealthy doctor's family expecting her to pursue what they are legendary and respected for.

I guess you can call her the black sheep of the family. He hands her the flowers accompanied by La Bise. They pause momentarily, studying the changes in age since the last time they had face-to-face contact. Helga abruptly invites him to sit on the Ox-blood sofa after she extends her soft, cold hand before making herself comfortable on the leather accent chair.

Both of them understand the craft behind a perfectly cut suit, with hers balancing professionalism with a night out studying the latest fashion from a Via Monte Napoleone catwalk or the more intimate Via Della Spiga, next to Milan's Duomo, also frequently visited by him with his favorite being Fontana del Piermarini, referred to by locals as the four-one fountain…

"Thank you for my beautiful flowers," she says with a subtle blush. "You are most welcome." I hope it means something to her, he thought. "It has been quite some time since we saw each other, Mr. Van der Linde. You look healthy and elegant. How have you been?" she asks as she studies his facial expressions hidden among the change of age with a five-o clock shadow, using his last name to establish distance. "Feels like yesterday to me, Ms. Psychologist. It has been a while indeed, but you still look like you did when we first met, beautiful and professional," he replies, intending to play along to whatever book knowledge she thinks might overpower his natural ability to blend in just like a chameleon about to snatch its prey.

Some may dismiss his longing to challenge her emotionally as something associated with an obsession. Still, both are attracted emotionally for some weird reason, something that doesn't fade away like headlines on the front pages of the Manhattan street vendor. They share something unique that time can't erase regardless of moving on and possibly starting a family, which either avoided with a hidden hope to reunite emotionally.

"I've been doing the same as always, Helga," he responds, using her name, hoping to turn the table to suit the foundation on which he built something that only contains furniture and nothing else. She still struggles to accept that he just walked through her door after all these years. Her smile, which has become mischievous, reveals an emotional desire to have him challenge her introspective psychological upper hand, not considering his ability to twist the fabric of nature toward a surreal experience, resulting in her begging for more.

For him, this is a significant step toward overcoming his fear of being rejected when he walked through the door. His search for the meaning of life may end here regardless of whether someone tries to convince him that the meaning is 42, which they obtained from a famous screenplay.

Unfortunately, he tends to challenge those supposed to keep the key to his emotional prison, resulting in bidirectional resentment. It is as if something in his soul sometimes wants to intentionally sabotage any form of an emotional relationship or test if you have enough intelligence to engage in some form of an intelligent conversation, ending with a crap load of regret while he tries to come to terms with why he got rejected.

Some may call it mind games, and others may call him batshit crazy. There is another possibility as to why he may challenge those who long for his mind and success like with her: the probability of both actually realizing that they can be themselves. That makes more sense than the mind games or batshit crazy opinions.

Yes, I'm now 100% sure that is why. And that, my dear reader, is why you decided way back, in the beginning, to trust me as your personal oracle who doesn't have a pointy hat with holes for eyes.

Allow me to elaborate on my assessment of the latter probability; it's not that you have a choice, do you? At work, we all tend to come across as professional, or at least most of us, and shy away as far as possible from exposing our emotions, which may result in someone taking advantage of our weaknesses and also because it is a professional setting. He does the "challenging thing" with the hope that the other party, her, shows some form of vulnerability in order for him to let his own guard down in certain aspects.

It's simple; he wants to communicate like a normal human being and not sit opposite some well-dressed person who will have his vulnerability in their hands. This is why he is more attracted to her emotionally than sexually. Still, for both to be themselves, there should be a healthy level of challenge; call it playfulness if you want.

However, his uncontrollable urge to have her submit to his sexual authority burns like a large piece of malted lava on top of a barrel containing a mixture of gasoline and oxytocin. He needs to be emotionally challenged not because of a drive to win, for lack of a better word, but because that turns him on when the lava burns through the barrel, which both seek.

If that connection isn't there, the connection of emotional exploration resulting in her barrel exploding, he will walk away after respectfully shaking her hand and making his co-payment. However, suppose he were to walk away, away from your session. In that case, you can see yourself as someone who may be perceived by angelical beings as being a fucking idiot with a psychology qualification and nothing more since you most likely had no idea what to study.

Don't get me wrong, I'm not judging, but I'm saying that some are born to change the world, and you might not be it unless you are a natural dark horse like them. This is a wicked game only suited to those who see an orgasm as a union of neurological chemicals transferred telepathically and not a wham-bam-thank-you-ma'am. "Have you enjoyed bringing a new idea or invention to birth?

I remember vaguely reading an article some time ago discussing your possible solution to human-torpor," she adds to the question using "vaguely" with the intent not to come across as someone truthfully impressed by his out-of-the-box thinking, even though she does regular internet searches. She concluded after studying his facade years ago that he has the power to turn any respectable woman into someone who begs to be late for work accompanied with the hope to have inner thigh love bites as close as possible to her flower. "Disappointingly not."

"And how does that make you feel?"

"I'm not sure how I'm supposed to feel, Helga. One gets to a point where you give up on trying. Why I fail every time is a mystery in itself. It's almost as if I'm supposed to experience the bad this world and life has to offer." Some, like him, will bring forth something they know they are very good at, painted with failure, to receive a compliment, just like how a man will fish for a bra size, hoping to experience the softness of Bell-shaped, Asymmetrical, Athletic, East-West, and Side Set breasts has to offer those longing comfort and safety to the soothing sounds of an enigma, for which he has no preference for. You may dismiss the fishing part, but know this: he is a well-respected inventor who solves things we only get to read about, and his intentional show of some form of vulnerability puts him in the position a kitty cat wants to be in when a soft-hearted woman may offer him milk.

"What challenges do you still face since we first met?"

"When again was that?" he asks while tearing time apart and intentionally determining her interest since she has no file or notepad with his name written close by.

"10 years ago, when you were 25," she responds with a perfectly memorized memory, only toward him, just like "Navy Frogmen" would memorize a map before heading on a secret mission with the intent to capture. "Time flies! It's still a struggle processing rejection and submitting to authority."

"You still sometimes fail to distinguish between reality and dreams?"

"Rarely, but a new thing presented itself—I have dreams that playoff within the first four hours after starting my day. It's not that I can confirm what will happen in the first four hours after the dreams, but rather something in the line of cryptomnesia. I also started sleeping with my bedroom doors locked."

"Why is that?"

"I would wake up at night and see someone stand at the bedside looking down on me. I would get so frightened that I'd jump up and start kicking and swinging." Imagine him using force instead of having Dieter shoot whatever moves, including a cross-eyed mosquito or bow-legged squirrel. He doesn't have a violent streak in him in the least as a result of seeing life leaving a kid hit on the side of the head during a bar brawl. "When about did that start?" she asks, knowing that fright herself. After the passing of my dog— weird, right? You may just be into killing shit for fun, but he is on the opposite spectrum, with Dieter doing whatever you may see as necessary.

Once you've seen emotion through the windshields to the soul or experienced the call a cow gives toward her calf who wandered off, you'll think more than a hundred times before accepting a BBQ hosted by a friend about dying from elevated cholesterol and coronary artery disease while sucking on the thirty-first cigarette of the day, unless you want to use the oblivious card. "I don't think it's weird at all, Jacob. Trauma has a different effect on people's minds. I'm truly sorry for your loss. I know both meant the world to you, and I can't even start to imagine the setback that was caused."

"Thank you. Yes, that was a massive setback which not only

broke me emotionally but also changed how I look at religion." You may think that it was just a dog, and if you do, I have a word or two of encouragement on my dear friend's behalf; Go fucking fall on your neck and die, as simple as that, after you gathered the balls to watch 1986's film version of Sir Percy Fitzgerald's *Jock of the Bushveld*.

"Have you found a girlfriend since we last met?" she asks with no hidden intent but merely out of concern for his social interactions, even though her subconscious feels different.

"Nothing has changed since then—I'm unable to keep relationships and would intentionally sabotage them, almost like thinning out the herd. But how about you, Helga? Are you not married since?" She sees the reason for his question as a way to change from being "interviewed" to being the "interviewer," which will make him walk away once achieved or perhaps stay if he intends to turn the conversation towards making it all about her with the desire to treat her like a queen, which he learned way too late in life. But, for some strange yet assumptive reason, he will challenge every qualified person to determine their level of commitment to learning more about how difficult it is to maintain being occupied in a study that may or may not require a superior level of intellect. Confusing, right, but allow me to explain; he will never consider your line of work if you come across as someone not seeing a commitment to their occupation as vital. Remember, he still has no idea what he wants to do in life, with retirement not an option. You can build a swimming pool filled with his dollars and naked women, yet he will never understand or appreciate what he has achieved in life.

"Why do you think that is?" she asks while intentionally refraining from answering him.

"I guess it's because I want to ensure they are truly prepared and committed to staying in the relationship with a broken man. It always ends with a crap load of regret and the cockroach falling off the cork. I don't know how to accept love. And to make it worse, I struggle to maintain a normal and healthy libido," he says, knowing his last burst of oxytocin was more or less one year before Anny decided to milk him to the extent of guaranteed failure.

"Aha, the cockroach we all have floating in our brains—rowing around on a piece of cork," she remarks with memory from the past and with a smile and little wrinkles to the side of her eyes, portraying her, after all, as human. "We all have that little bugger exploring our serotonin levels and ripping our Axon Terminals from our Dendritic spines—destroying our Synaptic clefts," he adds.

"Do you think you still have issues with perfectionism?"

"Absolutely! I have to create something to feel worthy of the exact specifications needed to be nothing but perfect. It frustrates me to the point of insanity, knowing some people don't get what it is to take pride in their work. Perhaps it's not that I'm perfect. Still, maybe I'm seen as such simply because the majority have stopped developing, either by choice or by circumstances such as solving murder mysteries from the comfort of their living room while neglecting their partner's emotional needs?"

"Perhaps, and I can imagine how it must frustrate you. And what about the math problems you like solving—Calculus, right?"

"Can't live without it…Basic math is too difficult for me—seven times eight is still unsolved and will remain a mystery until I die."

"That is indeed interesting, Jacob. Ever thought of associating numbers with colors, like yellow or red?" she asks, aware that he is inside her head, seeking the ideal moment to expose her vulnerability. How do I block emotions toward a man I genuinely care about, she thought, with the underlying need to be satisfied as a queen after the lava reached her volatile mixture.

"Warm colors do work from time to time," he responds with the thought of exploring the colors her emotions will radiate once she realizes who he is: a wolf in sheep's clothes. Red or perhaps purple comes to mind. "I remember you mentioned being unable to tell black from navy blue?"

"I can tell the colors apart, but not when those specific two are next to one another. I can see the difference but cannot verbally confirm which is which. I must separate my suits with lighter suits such as grey—the only high-value items in my house." This is your queue, dear reader, to test your knowledge obtained from watching hundreds of episodes covering psychology, which you tend to use when hanging with your buddies to come across as a psychology guru; where in this conversation did he manage to get into a mind which tried to establish distance? Bloody hell, I don't think I know either, but if you know, keep it to yourself unless you deem it necessary to risk your reputation as a saggy-breasts or balls crime solver. "And most likely your colognes too?"

"Eau de Parfum or Elixir," he adds, knowing who she is behind the smell that masks her angelic soul. "What's the difference again?"

"Eau de Parfum has between 10 and 20% aromatic compounds, and Elixir has between 15 and 40%." She realizes she is heading in a direction so many professionals warn against, even though it has been some time since they spoke eye to eye. "So what percentage should women wear?"

"It has nothing to do with gender but rather with what doesn't annoy your nose—like someone else's fart," he says jokingly, taking them back to Bob's explanations during group therapy. She starts laughing as she recalls the same moments. "Strange, isn't it…I shared an elevator once with a man who thought it was okay to pass gas—horrible experience!"

"It's almost like someone behind you in an elevator picking their nose and not realizing the doors have reflection," he adds, referring to what Steve also mentioned years ago.

"But what you are wearing perfectly suits you," he says confidently, knowing he analyzed her fragrance when he walked through the door. "That being?"

"The top notes of your perfume contain Orange Blossom, Peach, Plum, Neroli, Brazilian Rosewood, Mandarin Orange, and Violet. I'm not 100% certain what the middle notes consist of, but I believe the base notes include Sandalwood, Amber, Vanilla, Musk, and others."

She slightly blushes, not because he can point to what she prefers to wear but because she realizes he could notice the slightest change in her body aroma during this conversation, being aware that he already saw her enlarged pupils and skin tone change around her lips. We all, or the majority, enjoy it when someone asks us more about ourselves, especially on a date, which this isn't. You may see this as strange, perhaps weird, but what if you can date a man who knows what you want or crave even before you whisper it, whether obtained visually or by smell? Think about it, but not for too long, as you may be perceived as someone willing to be enslaved by Vlad the Impaler or a man who would spontaneously pleasure you either in a dressing room or in the middle of nowhere during on-the spur-moment road trips. "And do you still talk to yourself?" she asks, hoping to redirect the conversation. Jokingly, with some sarcasm, he responds, "About what?"

"Touché," she reacts to what may be seen as a rhetorical answer. "I love it when you smile," he remarks like a Cheshire cat, bringing his dimples forth and admired teeth. She's blushing yet able to focus on steering this conversation in a direction that excludes possible regret. "How about friends—made any?"

"Only a few I'd like to see on the 30th of February," he replies, using the exact date you can claim ownership of a bar of gold you managed to lift from a display at the world-renowned Gold Reef City in Johannesburg, using only one hand's fingertips. "You like keeping your distance, or is it because you want them to keep theirs?"

"The less people know about me, the better." You may think you'll understand Jacob after completing this book, but sadly, we will never truly grasp the complexity behind what makes him who he is. Yes, he may come across as self-centered, arrogant, or condescend-ing, but that would result from my inability to describe him to a sociably acceptable extent. He does cry, he does care, and he also doesn't give a flying fuck if there is none to give. His emotions toward other people, regardless of your opinion, are sincere to the extent of checking up on you occasionally to avoid damaging your door's threshold. "Why is that, if I may?"

"You know my past, Helga—it's not precisely something people will understand. The value of damaged goods is low for a reason. You're the only one I trust, even if we haven't seen each other in a decade." Allow me to highlight your goal again, mentioned at the beginning of the book: "Someone will murder him, and it's your job to figure out who and why," which by now should be at the brink of solving. If not, join the club, get the T-shirt, and burn it. How can he possibly trust me after seeing me ten years ago, she thought. What made him say that is a result of adding several observations in a short period since he walked through her door.

"But what if I'm no longer here?" she asks, concerned and flattered at the same time.

"In that case, I guess I'll keep my emotions locked away until some cult persuades me to write a book or script using a pseudonym."

"And do you still study the Bible?"

"I did but gave up trying to understand how BS could be written in the form of a library and compiled in a singular book. I don't get how people can follow mindlessly without verifying the content. It may just be the norm, but then again, normality is determined by the majority of people, and the majority of people are lazy as hell, uneducated, and naïve. Let's rather leave well enough alone…However, I believe there's something after this, perhaps a Hindu cow or a gander looking for a partner. But how about you, Helga, found someone to share your life with?" he probes again after failing to recognize the presence or absence of a wedding ring impression on her ring finger due to the dim light. By the way, Europeans typically wear wedding rings on the opposite ring finger than you are used to, so keep that in mind when clubbing in the EU.

"You know I'm not supposed to share my private life with you…" she answers with the burning desire to shout her status from the top of the highest mountain with the hope of him flying like a Superman to rescue her while being swept from her feet. "We have known each other for ten years, Helga, and you know every secret and detail in my life. I think it's only fair to learn a little about you."

This is the confusing part where you rightfully ask how they could have known each other for ten years without contact. Souls like these never accept life as it is and commit to frequently checking up via searches, anonymous flowers, or news articles. Then why don't they know the status of each other's love lives? Stalkers do shit like that, checking who has a ring that compresses the build-up of lust and who doesn't. It is indeed an infrequent occurrence to meet someone who you undoubtedly know is the one made for you and vice versa.

"Okay, I'll share some. I'm still waiting for that special one. I haven't dated for three years or so."

"And why's that?" he asks, focused on making it all about her, for her need to be treated like a queen has to be realized along with her longing for touch. She responds while quickly shrugging her shoulders and touching her nose, "My work pretty much keeps me occupied."

With a faint smile and eyes staring at her soul, he adds, after observing her body response following the question, "All work and no play make Helga an interesting woman to explore. You may have had an epiphany of what we both feel." She shows discomfort governed by professionalism and looks at the wall clock, knowing this may ruin her reputation. Still, at the same time, her urge to play with madness is filling a bottomless pit meant for two willing to play with a mixture of lava and oxytocin while they become one and exchange neurological chemistry, which, in their case, will take several hours.

"Something like that—look at the time, I most likely have patients waiting. Shall we meet again in 6 months from now?" she asks with her Herz increasing its Hertz, which he is aware of when she changes her crossed leg position from left-over-right to right-over-left at the same time her arms gently cross and gives visual protection over her suit's jacket and in front of her breast with the hope of hiding her erect nipples. "I hope so. I'll schedule with your assistant once I'm back in the office," he answers, understanding that six months is nothing but the typical interval suggested by many.

Perhaps I have it wrong, or maybe she is not as intelligent as I believed, he thought, driven by the knowledge that he has been wrong too many times. When you thought you had him figured out, he doesn't have a physical preference for an ideal partner but rather an intellectual one. Bimbos, not his kind of thing…

"Perfect," she responds with what seems to be a faint glitter in her eyes. He gets up from the sofa, ties the "button-one" of his jacket, and slowly turns toward the door, ready to conclude their consultation with the understanding and acceptance that they'll never cross paths again. She may see me as the boogie man under her bed or the voice that comes from her pillow, he thought, dismissing the possibility of her heart burning. She realizes the window to soul exploration is about to close as she gathers enough courage to speak, even if it is toward his face, conveniently facing the door. "Wait—can we perhaps schedule visits every three weeks? I'm concerned about your health, Jacob."

He slowly turns around with hope and realizes he wasn't wrong. "Admit it, Helga—you feel something for me. When you look at me, your pupils are the size of Jupiter, and your work doesn't keep you that busy."

"How would you know, Jacob?"

"You quickly shrugged your shoulders, touched your nose, used distancing language, rearranged your legs, and covered your breasts while darker red lips laid claim to an elevated heart rate."

"You're right—I have feelings for you—not the Florence Nightingale effect but something different…" she responds with the weight of the world lifting from her shoulders and a dream about to realize. He finds her vulnerability as a successful professional attractive and her analogy quite cute. "Florence Nightingale never fell in love with a patient," he jokingly teases, realizing that more than just her beautiful lips are changing to a different kind of pinkness. "She didn't?" she asks, surprised and lost in the battle to prevent her brain chemistry from wanting more in a room with the perfect setup for mastering the Kama Sutra. Perhaps this is why she chose the furniture the way she did years ago, he wishfully thought. "Nah, Nightingale didn't, but I'm glad you could finally admit how you feel—I do share that same feeling, Helga," he responds while slowly approaching her at the same time she is taking small steps in the direction of a Judas Goat, who knows the path to sexual pleasure without having him experienced the fruits of climax since he has never found the partner he wants to commit to emotionally. She is most vulnerable when she replies, "But we can't…it would be wrong of me—you're my patient…"

She pauses momentarily and stares through his eyes and into his soul. A moment turns into an extended one as both stare deeply in the absence of sound, hoping to hold each other's soul. They are trapped in a space where the only certainty is loss. They are face to face with foreheads against each other and palms of each pressing against the other with fingers interlocking to the sides of her hips. Their breathing increases as it fills the room, the only sound preceding possible whispers while his right-hand moves toward her face, followed by a gentle pull of neck hair, complimented with the warmth of his breath covering the skin below her ear.

Her body trembles to the simultaneous enjoyment of chemicals experienced within their brains and down their spines, with his reassuring lust pressing against her pelvis as a result of a deep emotional connection. He gently bites her bottom lip, simultaneously, his hand supports her head with fingers intertwining with her hair.

"Three weeks it is," he whispers, which we all know will eventually turn into him serving her breakfast wearing nothing but an apron and with a raspy morning voice shortly before quenching their lust in a steamy shower with breast and palm prints against the glass, resulting in her having to move appointments, or so you were raised to believe. For the first in a very long time, she feels safe in the presence of a man longing for a soul heaven can wait for.

By the way, shower fun or in a pool sounds quite the adventure, right? If you can pull that off without discomfort, you'll be part of a small group who can, just like these two.

Sadly, Jacob will leave knowing he made a mistake; deep inside him the inability to accept love but with the burning will to give.

12

REDEFINING CONFUSION AND THE ART
OF CUMMING AND GOING

The following is rated R—not sure by whose definition, but let's assume it's determined by someone in the Amazon who is easily offended by our vocabulary. I believe this entire book should be rated R for the language used, sex talk, and the lack of ripping someone's heart out just after someone yelled, "FINISH HIM," like in the game Mortal Kombat, but let's continue with the mental stuff, shall we?

Are you happy. If not, fake it. Are you longing for a Margarita with some friends, if not, fake it. Are you looking forward to the Hawaii vacation your Uncle Fred decided to join at the last moment, if not, fake it. Did you enjoy your mother-in-law's food, if not, fake it. Did you appreciate having your sister's kids over, if not, fake it.

All these questions lack a question mark, therefore removing the possibility of questioning yourself as being wrong, and all solutions end with fake it, of which this solution, fake it, has been imprinted in your brain when you learned from the best: your parents. Remember those days when your parents tried spoon-feeding your collard greens while at the same time pretending it has an appealing taste even though the Chinese God Zao Shen would swop nationality with Japan, just so he could visit the Aokigahara, the Sea of Trees, to avoid having that stuff as a meal?

Our parents laid the foundation to accept that which isn't true with the hope of not offending others, resulting in pretending. Let me refer to what I previously said about sharing your recollection of events backward. Your brain IS NOT equipped to process things that didn't happen unless you are part of some covert organization specializing in neurological manipulation or someone who can manipulate their own subconscious with no guarantee of being successful.

Also, you may have heard the famous saying "fake it till you make it," with fake it presenting itself yet again. The danger around this word is not taken seriously enough, considering that most aren't even aware of what psychological effect this will have in the long run, regardless of how this word is being used.

Those living by the ethos, *fake it till you make it*, rely on this word more often than the usual citizen so they can be accepted into a system carefully grafted by the majority, for which we already established the level of intellect the majority has or lacks. Some even see the "fake it till you make it" as the most extraordinary way to rebuild themselves and shed their "skin of failure" in exchange for a "skin of opportunism" made from something thinner than the 0.01 mm Okamoto Zero One condom…it will eventually tare and expose you.

Ultimately, their worlds may collapse at random times, leading to an overload of self-doubt, disappointment, and, in some cases, self-destruction, not because of choice but simply because of a rude awakening caused by your brain's inability to organize a life which doesn't have any tangible history, resulting in the person's subconscious distancing itself from the all-powerful computing capabilities of a supercomputer.

When adopting the ethos of faking everything to make it eventually, you run the risk of your pseudo-life spiraling out of control due to the fantasy world you created. I will go as far as to say your downfall will be inevitable.

The world you created doesn't exist, nor will it ever, unless you have two brains, one of which can manage the real and the other your fantasy world. Your fake world will become so convincing that you will start believing what you want others to believe. You will also introduce entitlement without even realizing, therefore believing without a doubt that you have the right to certain things that should come with the world you created.

You may also end up hating yourself for not being able to achieve what you tried faking the entire time and perhaps also the people not submitting to your persona of entitlement. The only way you will get where you need to be in life is through hard work and not through illusions.

You may fool the world, but not those who have committed a serious amount of effort to understand what is needed to live their dreams instead of living in a dream. You may even cross paths with someone who also lives in their own version of fake it till you make it. Both of you will have a fantastic time together since you will know exactly what to say and how to say it, what to do, and how to do it.

Perhaps you are lost right now with the above, but this will be understandable to a reader who lives by this ethos. Eventually, you will get called out by someone who has lived that kind of life or perhaps a seasoned "fake it till you make it" veteran who has more "wolf suits" than the devil himself, hence the saying: "You can't bullshit a bullshitter."

This might also be a big issue or gamble when learning how to steal with your eyes and your ears, as the 25-year-old Jacob suggested to 16-year-old James, who will eventually misplace his personality, not that he had one to start with, resulting in him being lost in a world with perhaps one or two friends and none at the time of his death.

All this is because he will have no idea who he was supposed to be from the time he was growing up and because he got addicted to solving the chaos he created in his mind as a rehearsal for having an answer when his intentions are being questioned. Some get addicted to creating chaos just to be able to restore order, almost like someone who enjoys presenting a perfectly ironed shirt moments after removing it from a basket containing wrinkled clothing, for which the ironed shirt represents a perfectly tailored answer coming from the mouth of someone, like James, who rehearsed over and over.

Psychologists, or perhaps yourself, will argue that it's an attribute of someone who wants to be in control, but to the contrary, it's someone who got addicted to whatever brain chemical gets released while establishing order. It can be compared again to not getting addicted to masturbation but rather to oxytocin.

Also, another issue with being fake can be compared to someone putting several thorns into their heels and telling the world it's a new kind of track-and-field shoe. They'll either experience severe infections or chew off their legs, knowing it doesn't belong, and simultaneously prevent them from running instead of crawling.

Your brain, in return, built up more hatred toward the track you intend to run, not because the layout changed, but because you prevent yourself by pretending you have new athletic spike shoes instead of inverted thorns. This example supports the notion of preventing you from living your identity while putting someone else's honesty below yours when trying to avoid hurting feelings. Your mother-in-law made a lot of effort to prepare the meal honestly, with yours masked by being fake, putting your emotions at a higher priority by avoiding a possible family debacle. You hate her but mask that feeling, going against how your brain processes honesty or the lack of it.

The thorns in your brain will stay there for as long as possible, thereby increasing the negative thoughts toward her: not because her persona changed for the worst, but merely because your brain is inflamed by being fake, just like your foot about to fall off due to the thorns having no place in your tissue.

And this, my reader, is why Jacob is despised by many, not because he fakes, which he can, but because he can be deadly direct, therefore getting to the point and respecting you as a person who deserves the truth from a friend or a has been friend after he gave his honest opinion. He values honesty and will give that in return, not to hurt but to show his concern toward what you may perceive as fine, be that you are excessively overweight, increasing the possibility of making your wife a widow and children fatherless. He will also decline a night out guaranteed by breaking several shot records when not in the mood since faking does more damage to yourself than your friends.

If that doesn't make sense, you should approach it as giving a flying fuck if any was to be given. The solution to this problem arose from exploring sexuality the way it's meant to with turning from "Cumming to Going," which can also be applied to your life.

Ladies, you might be under the impression that only a woman can fake an orgasm. Still, I hate to break it to you, but men can, too, as my dear friend mastered over the years. But this excludes what some women or men prefer when having their load's warmth felt on their skin or visually enjoyed as a goal some work toward either using the pull-out method or the well-acquainted titty fuck.

Some women can't be fooled nor allow it due to their visual enjoyment of having an eruption, also known as the money shot, with or without applying gentle pressure to the prostate, accompanied by him being at his most vulnerable during the sensation of a momentary death.

At the same time, the smell of bleach or the Pyrus Calleryana tree stimulates some partner's senses, as shared by the mysterious

Hanna, who claimed her goldfish Jimmy going missing, which turned out to be remnants of a zucchini called Jimmy as indicated by ICD-10 Code T19.2.

How can a man fake an orgasm, and more importantly, why? Wearing a condom is an absolute must when attempting whatever position you both enjoy while avoiding getting pregnant or growing an extra eye.

Suppose you know your body and ejaculation response as a man. In that case, you can pretend "dying" followed by quickly dismissing yourself to the restroom, or you can fake the momentary death followed by going down on her. Weird as hell, right? But like our inventor friend says: "Suppose I have a problem needing a solution. In that case, someone else most likely needs it, too, considering the number of people on this planet. Hence, I will pursue the solution and have it patented." But why would a man fake a volcanic eruption? That is the question.

Some may pull it off to avoid feelings of regret, guilt, or emptiness and perhaps to get it over with. Still, some fake it to extend the session over several hours even though the feeling of emptiness is inevitable but to see her climax over and over. The latter, however, doesn't dismiss the fact that you haven't been honest.

Also, a man's thought pattern and emotions change immediately after the climax, which may result in complete confusion once he declines your request to go down on you or do the horizontal monkey dance. It's not a question of whether he still likes you or not but rather why he did not spend more time pleasing you to have you experience several consecutive orgasms while being honest. Maybe these result from failed communication or his limited knowledge of the subject.

Regardless, men should spend more time studying the fleshly desires of women and the art of pleasure because it should not be about you but rather her. A friend once said, "A quicky can be fun, but a four-hour session is addictive when intentionally holding back as long as possible," for which James will one day compile a four-hour intimacy playlist.

Going down on a woman should never be done feeling compelled but should be experienced as something that gives pleasure to your primary senses, such as taste, smell, sound, touch response, and so much more, which you deprive both you and your partner of when faking. After all, fake is associated with pretending, the same action needed to screw with your own or someone else's brains, preventing a genuine emotional bond since there is no tangible history of being vulnerable with someone you trust.

You may fool your partner, but it will not change the fact that you lied about how good the meal tasted or that you are trying to run on a track that you will end up hating every time your thorn erects. Men, do yourself a favor and learn the following: make it all about her, make her feel wanted and cherished, flatter her with sincerity, buy her flowers, give her hugs and unexpected touches, listen to what she says without advising unless asked, attend to her spiritual needs, don't fight over her but on behalf of her, protect her, give her safety and respect. Never expect her to ever undergo plastic surgery for whatever reason unless it's her wish, for your concern regarding seeing her in pain should be your number one priority.

Finally, study the female body as best as possible to discover the hidden gems that will leave both satisfied with mastering your endurance to have her guide you to her pinnacle of climax. Most importantly, enjoy every moment and extend it for as long as possible, and then you can lay your claim of mastering the art of "Cumming and Going," going to explore her most precious gift, love.

Change the way you see intercourse with the understanding that her flower is the only place you should never want to leave, for which you can also register your new address . When you have mastered the proposed list and long to see your unborn children in her eyes, that is the moment you know what love is.

So why did I decide to use foul language, assuming it will send you to hell, excluding the Amazonians due to their lack of under-standing of a language we believe they should know? I used these words without including pussy, cock, titties, tits, fucking, fuck me or you, and so forth for the following reason with a frank answer; some men and women, including myself, like to use these words during intercourse and refrain from using words like I'm climaxing, I'm orgasming, I'm arriving or would you like to kiss me down there.

Case closed, I'm not a sex-ed teacher but only someone trying to avoid giving hugs and, at the same time, someone who can recom-mend the Amazon position that my ex-boyfriend introduced me to. By the way, now that I think of it, have you ever seen the genitalia of any dinosaur represented in movies? Neither have I. Perhaps science got it wrong, and they all have it on their foreheads, flapping around like a 220lb flaccid pool noodle or a massive flower, which looks more toward a five-story satellite dish than the mystical eye itself…

It's a clear sunny day with the twelve patients relaxing beneath the shade of lush trees while engaged in chit-chat and sharing stories. At the same time, some verbally contribute to the actions needed by white dungaree-wearing men to complete the painting of the large and modern building's frontal face. Jacob, as always, sucks on a rocket while admiring the small red coal fueling the burning of bakka as the smoke leaves his nostrils, associated by many as a dragon running out of fire. James, now well-practiced in speaking while having a fag hanging from his lips, sits next to him with the rest enjoying the soft lawn in a half-moon facing the bench. Several patients are strolling the grounds while others check out after their three-week session or their outpatient program. "So, I told her to go further, and she asked where to…" adds Bram to a discussion covering the lack of sexual phrase understanding among those who think it's a microphone used for nothing but missionary or perhaps calling home. They burst out with laughter, with Hanna remembering her first "fool around" session, which led to a disappointing outcome after seeing the helmet-wearing villain for the first time. It could've been worse if I blew instead of sucked, she thought, even though she never went as far.

Her thoughts do make you realize we have everything backward. But then again, which of the two sounds more attractive? "Makes me think about the time when I told my ex-husband, 'I'm cumming!' He had no fucking idea what I was talking about and asked: 'Where to?'" shares Anny, who refers to her squirting as cumming, something some men love, especially those with the hidden fetish they didn't get to choose, something that makes every person unique, yet again.

Feel free to brush it off as being weird, but also take into consideration that whatever turns you on may just be associated by some as being abusive. Some women, like me, do like it when a man pulls my hair, slap my ass, or restrain me in some form or the other while teasing whatever works for them. Cathy, wearing a paper Pope hat made by James, can't keep her composure, realizing she's been in that same boat twice.

"That's hilarious!" she laughingly adds, knowing her fetish may turn this whole conversation on its head if ever disclosed. "I don't get it," says James, almost dropping his cigarette from his mouth, proving he still has a long way ahead of him in perfecting the look associated with telegraphers from the late 1900s to mid-2000s who wore green dealer visors to protect their eyes. He is slowly but surely forming a habit that he will eventually regret once he realizes the only addiction we struggle to start is that of going to the gym, where cigarettes aren't allowed.

"Want me to explain?" asks the all-knowing Bob while trying to count the licks it takes to get to the chocolate-flavored core of a renowned lollipop. "Yes, please," he answers just as he kills his cigarette against the concrete leg of the bench. "During coitus, there'll come a time when you will experience a sensation called the little death as described by the French. I believe they call it 'Le Petit Mort.' That is also known as cumming or climaxing, and people use that term to indicate to their partner that they are very near to enjoying the best feeling ever while being vulnerable at their most." Alicia, even though she had a boyfriend, has never been in such a situation, leading her to ask, "Wait—you actually die?"

"And resurrected at the same time," adds Cathy.

"All the fucking advantages Christians have!" remarks Jana, who has never experienced one nor bared witness to one, or so she claims, even though she can perfectly mimic giving fellatio. "That's quite a description, Bob—the first time I understood what you said," adds the long-bearded Dean, who most likely got introduced to the word coitus just before the French Revolution. "Remind me again, who uses the word coitus?" asks Stephen jokingly.

"Those who pray before and after the deed," answers Jacob. Anny asks with confusion, "Wait, there are motherfuckers who pray before and after eating out?"

"Absofuckinglutely," assures Stephen, who once almost joined a cult with the promise of endless fooling around but tapped out, knowing he won't be able to afford a flower farm. In a way, he still is old school and believes in buying his wife fresh flowers twice a month. "Hey James, remind me later to tell you the definition of a motherfucker, like that fucknut I punched in the throat." An African American woman in her late twenties sneaks up behind Alicia with a bicycle and dog trailer. It's her sister with Charlie, the English bull-dog. "Turn around slowly, Alicia," suggests Jacob. You know that feeling when everyone stares at you when they notice one giant ass spider on your left shoulder? This is her reaction when her body freezes out of fear toward something scary or perhaps dangerous, sneaking up on her as she asks, "Why?"

"Just do it," he instructs with a smile and a wink.

She slowly turns around and leaps to her feet, her face showing all possible signs of excitement, revealing the child all of them may have hidden somewhere. "CHARLIE!" exclaims Alicia as Dopamine communicates between her brain's nerve cells and her body. Her sister opens the trailer's canopy with Charlie moving his pig-tailed bum in all directions a Wind Rose can point toward. She embraces her best friend, who snorts from excitement while she paints his face with kisses and gently holds his big, old body. She gently assists him out of the trailer and onto the lawn for everyone to meet and enjoy. Dean quickly points out what he observes as different, "Ahoy! Where's his pistol's ammo?"

"His what?" asks Anny, who has heard it all, yet not this one. "His testicles," explains Bob, holding an imaginary set of balls in his right. "Gotcha."

"He's adorable!" says Cathy with awe. "And slobbery…" remarks Hanna as Charlie sniffs her pants. Are you thinking of getting an English bulldog? Invest in wipes and satin wall paint. "Come here, boy!" calls Bram to rescue Hanna. It takes a bit for Charlie to respond due to his hearing issues, which Alicia reminds them of, "He's a bit deaf, Bram. You may have to add some hand signals, too." The whole group is in awe of this beautiful, funny-looking dog greeting everybody as if they were toys or treats. Helga can be seen taking notes through a window. "Best surprise ever!" energetically adds Alicia, who is scratching Charlie's ears, bum, and back, all things English Bulldogs love, like most dogs do. "Helga made this meeting possible, Alicia," shares Jacob, just as excited while lighting a fresh cigarette and offering James another one. Hell, I still can't believe I'm smoking with those possibly holding The Old Dog or The Meerkat license cards, he thought while watching Anny pulling on a lady-like cigarette, which some seniors at his school call a mouse tampon. My thoughts are that I don't think he can believe that he's hanging with the cool kids. "Who?" she asked with a bit of confusion and uncertainty. "Our psychologist," he answers. "Wait, she has a name?" asks Stephen, just as lost. "Didn't know that either," says

Jana, about to light her third. The quick-thinking Bob responds, "Not only does she have a name, but she also poops."

"He's indeed a big boy!" says Dean while admiring the beauty and the beast combo, resulting in memories wandering toward his granddaughter, whom he still has to meet. Perhaps I should buy her one, he thought, but dismissed it just as quickly as the doubt of seeing her settled in. Jana is just as excited as Alicia when she says, "I've never seen you so happy, Alicia! You are glowing with joy!"

"Coitus is impossible for English bulldogs."

"Eeeww, Charlie doesn't do that stuff. He is a gentle giant!" responds Alicia to Bob's remark. "So how do they pull it off?" asks Anny, likely trying to fish for a new position.

"They don't pull at all—someone else does it for them. It's called digital simulation in the presence of an estrous bitch." If you were ever to get yourself a male English bulldog, you should respect the fact that humping someone's leg or something else may result in cardiac failure. How do I know? A German told me. "Do you think they'll allow me to keep him here?" she asks enthusiastically. "Unfortunately, not—already asked," answers Jacob, lips indicating regret. "This is still the best day of my life ever!"

13

JACOB'S COCOON AND A WORD FROM OUR SPONSOR, PART III

December 2023

I have two words for you, son: "Fischereischein" and "Sportfisherprüfung." I know you'll find both understandable once you've mastered the art of reading something the majority of 83.31 million people in 138,100 square miles can. Not only will it take you time to master the language, but you will never be accepted as one of them, or so I was told by Dieter's hairy cousin Uta, who happens to end most of her sentences with "Nein-Nein-Nein" if you were to finish too fast.

These two words come down to one essential thing: you are not allowed to fish in Germany without a license, which requires around 40 hours of supervised fishing lessons, fish biology, the treatment of the catch, and the equipment. Sure, this seems easy if you can speak German, but that is if you can speak German and find a spot in the bi-annual exams with you registered at a fishing club. Bloody hell, you'll say, especially when you ask yourself who managed to fuckup so big that caused these requirements as a result. Perhaps it was Uta who beaved a beaver, or maybe it came because Dieter's great-grandfather decided to go fishing using "Handgranate."

Regardless, it doesn't change the fact that "Hast" can either mean hate or have, and "Geil" can mean either horny or relaxed. Most of us, including you, understand the basic equipment requirements when heading to your favorite mart shopping for beer, tampons, and an inflatable dinghy. All you'll need is several hooks, a pole, sinkers, and perhaps a knife to put the poor fella out of its misery before you fuckup your first fillet attempt using that same bread knife.

Opening up a fish can be pretty traumatic if you've never seen the insides of a recently deceased being or if you have spent some time down under with Uta. It can be a life-changing event, not Uta's, but the insides of your first cold-blooded catch that can't regulate its body temperature. Maybe you have also had the experience of gutting a warm-blooded animal, resulting in you noticing the emotional differences when comparing fish gutting to Bambi's. Some may even show emotions of regret or sadness once they realize they killed a warm-blooded animal. Strange yet true.

Many years ago, Jacob showed some of his colleagues in Osaka a photo of his latest hunt just to be ousted by the majority who don't have any issue with deep frying a live fish. These examples show the different emotions of gutting cold-blooded versus warm-blooded animals. But whatever you do when fishing in Japan, don't fish where you see Koi, and always remember your protection against the universal nuisance that stings and does not bite.

There are a few things in life that almost everyone finds annoying, such as the previously discussed mosquito, regardless of where you may find yourself in the world. Another annoying thing is the famous paper cut, which we all can agree can confuckulate your day not only because it stings or burns like hell but also because it results in a small amount of blood, possibly tainting whatever piece of paper lays on your desk.

If you share the same feeling, you should try to imagine how it must feel when you accidentally cut your testicles or chin while shaving. It isn't that painful but rather quite messy when your blood decides to greet the world just before you head off to work or prep for your date night. Frankly, I won't be able to confirm or dismiss such claims as waxing is my preferred method, and I don't have a scrotum, penis, or a beard.

Two things you should never try: don't offer to help someone manually empty an inground pool, and don't ever try to shave that prestige bush or beard using a straight razor. As to why not assist in emptying a pool, I can't answer, but you need to take my word, just like I took the word of a skinny Piears many years ago. About the straight razor, you will end up cutting yourself, which may lead to infections and, worst case, death. Some may find it sexy when offering to shave their man's beard using a straight razor, knowing he will be at their mercy.

In contrast, others, just like one of Jacob's exes, found it sexy when she offered to shave his beard using a state-of-the-art electric shaver, which, in my opinion, is like bragging about milking the bull statue in Frankfurt am Main.

So, just what makes it sexy when a woman holds a highly sharp blade close to your throat? The idea of trusting her not to sever your external jugular vein makes it sexy, according to those who most likely also take pleasure in wearing a candy-floss thong backward. If you were to ever ask Jacob as to who his favorite inventor of all time is, his answer would be 1904

By the way, I intentionally refrain from using a full-stop, or period as known by Americans, behind 1904 since my understanding of mathematics strangely prevents me from doing so. In 1904, King Camp Gillette realized the need to invent something that could replace the straight razor for several reasons, such as the mentioned infections and excessive bleeding, for which both had a high possibility of arranging a meeting with Joseph-Ignace Guillotin and

Musashi Miyamoto. Also, Gillette was a shitty door-to-door salesman whose boss encouraged the idea of developing a product that needed replacement after several uses.

The safety razor invented by Gillette changed the shaving world. It inspired Morgan Parker from Bard-Parker company to patent a two-piece scalpel with a handle and removable blade in 1915, forever changing the medical world.

The word "scalpel" derives from the Latin "scallpellus," a term introduced during the pinnacle of Roman surgical skill. The development of such a fine product, the scalpel, makes me realize how fortunate I truly am for being in the medical field since 1998, not because it pays well, but because I got to attend some of the more sophisticated medical procedures some can only dream of which doesn't entail using the breadknife you chose for your first fish fillet.

I do get it from time to time that folks ask me if it would be possible to join me for surgery, for which my answer is simple: no. Why do I decline such a request, and would my answer ever change? I deny it for a particular reason related to the interested party finding it fascinating. Medicine requires years of studying and commitment to be your best while adding "practicing" to your title, where applicable.

Not only have I been asked permission to join a surgery, but I have many a time been asked about the possibility of attending an autopsy, which again is seen as attractive by some. There is a huge difference between seeing a fish or buck being gutted and viewing something that goes completely against what you learned within your first seven years. Parents pass down the importance of your health and well-being, which automatically puts you and many others on top of a hierarchy built on religious principles from a book that Bob knows quite well.

This importance is printed deep into your belief system regardless of whether you were raised by adopted parents or the dysfunctional parents of Bob. I will use the following to back my dismissal of your attendance request.

Let's pretend you have to go for abdomen surgery or, better, cardiac bypass surgery. Your obstructed field of view from your body during such an event is for several good reasons, such as protecting the surgical field from contamination.

Let's pretend I am about to remove this temporary partition called an "ether screen" followed by waking you up. What will your response be? What would your response be even if you were on a high dosage of analgesics while being awake during the surgery when I was to remove this temporary partition?

The answer is simple: you will freak the fuck out once you get to see something that goes against the value of human life. You will be traumatized for quite some time due to trauma caused by seeing the workshop tools used and your intestines winking at you. This trauma should have been managed by dissociative amnesia, as previously mentioned, but it wasn't.

The same goes for postmortems, except the fact that a postmortem will completely fuck with your head till the day Helga gives up on your psychology sessions. Remember me mentioning the reason for Steve's emotional setback as a result of walking into the postmortem dissection hall when his sister's kid was taken apart the way you would gut a fish?

Postmortems, alias autopsies, are performed on all unnatural deaths with a small amount by request. All unnatural deaths, which include anything that may deform, stretch, hamburger, explode, roast, boil, suffocate, and the list goes on, will undergo a gutting session using equipment you would think less of once you see it on your shopping list. Nothing is natural about a postmortem that you will realize once you walk up to the slab while seeing the opening of a Bambi-Fish hybrid. It would be a glorified butcher table if you were to ask Steve who has had his messed-up experience.

I also believe that humans should never be used as exhibits by individuals with questionable intentions, just like that famous international traveling body exhibition. Medicine is a profession so many pursue just to drop out the moment they attend the dissection of a decapitated mother whose body was found two weeks later in the middle of nowhere, accompanied by a smell you can't possibly imagine.

As said, there is nothing normal or interesting about post-mortems, but only that which some actor or emotionless forensic pathologist may describe in an episode during your saggy sessions. Don't get me wrong, it's not the most traumatic experience, but only one, depending on your stomach. Some fall apart once they see blood, others when they accompany their hubby to the ER after being stabbed by his bar buddy, and some when entering an ICU to be greeted by an irresponsive body connected to engineered equipment with lights, sounds, and smell.

Your interest in serial killers falls in the same category until you visit a crime scene or see the photos or, better, the bodies, resulting in you coming to terms with the fact that you are intrigued by a sick monster—birds of a feather flock together. The only reason these monsters come across as masterminds is due to the sensation created by the media and some overrated documentaries. Suppose you still find it interesting and want to attend medical procedure sessions. In that case, I can give you a quick suggestion: stop fucking about and get yourself into medicine since nobody likes a graphic designer who didn't study graphic design.

Medicine is a profession built on commitment, facts, and pioneering. Stop telling doctors that it has always been your dream to one day study medicine. No, you didn't end up doing something else because of circumstances. However, you chose a life that never included medicine, driven by the fact that you still struggle to consult the dictionary for the few foreign words used throughout this journey.

That said, perhaps life did give you a card that is not part of a regular poker pack, and all you need is some inspiration. If that's you, make your dream your priority, which will also depend on how much you want it. Never say: I am where I am because of my circumstances, but rather, I am where I am despite my circumstances…

Gnomes and ornaments populate small bedside tables specially placed next to each bed by a thoughtful facilities manager and her elves, besides Jacob's, whose table only has a bobblehead Jesus who still bounces by the touch of a mysterious visitor and almost to the synchronized sounds from life subvention units. The faint sound of a QRS complex stabs a stake through Helga's heart as she gathers enough strength to enter his room, welcomed by several tubes extruding from his body and a recliner that doubles up as a bed. She sits down with eyes locked onto his face, tears filling her as she holds onto a hand that once had movements toward gentle touches.

Sorrow paves the way for a river that no amount of base can hide while leaving a differential in color. I know this hand, thought Jacob while her thumb stroked his. His chest slowly lifts and descends to the guidance of HIS ventilator, carefully adjusted by black sheep Cassandra. "Please don't let this be it, God," whispers Helga, whose emotions have become undefinable to any writer worth their salt unless you've been next to possible death, which won't help you because everyone experiences trauma differently.

Have you ever visited someone connected to life subvention units in a cardiac ICU? Life subvention, by the way, is a fancy word for life support, as previously mentioned. Again, whatever you do, don't take children with a deficient immune system, which is all of them, to visit Nana or Opa—it's a place full of diseases and all kinds of other stuff. Instead, let them stay in the car or give each of them a knife and tell them to go play. I guess the idea of him dying terrifies her. I'm sure Anny would've offered a quick hand-job with Bob describing the ancient art of self-pleasure without using a vacuum machine and KY. Do you think that's weird? Trust me, I've seen it all.

Would you give one last hand job? Think about it, but longer than usual, especially if you have given the first yet last chocolate treat to your dying dog moments before the veterinarian performs euthanasia.

By now, you are highly likely convinced that the author of this book has something seriously messed up in their head. Rest assured, I'm only telling you what has been shared with me, and I also address those things many think about, including perhaps your better half who can't possibly hide their thoughts or wishes from you. Yep, Anny would've offered a quick hand job regardless of the Foley Catheter.

Keep Me Hopeful but Empty Me from Morbidity

ANNY

14

SOUP KITCHEN AND AN INTERNATIONAL TRAVELER

July 2010

Nightclubs are where you can choose when you fall over and who'll join your VIP corner if you have the fabric or card to flash like Jacob has and does. This is also where he met Sara Brady, who bartended for a few months until she called it quits after accepting a transfer back as an officer in Langley.

Word on the streets of underground London is that the foreign bartender from the States had to defend herself one late evening against a self-proclaimed scuttler who had ties with the underworld kingpin, Jimmy the stingy fucking Rose, known for arms smuggling and occasional hits.

Now let me also mention something very peculiar about stingy fucking Rose. He goes by the name Jimmy Rose, which he prefers, but little does he know that everyone in his gangster mansion knows by now that he wears his "Knickers" more than once to save on detergent. Nevertheless, the punk approached her as she was about to "Mind the Gap," brandishing what seemed to be a perfect weapon for "Glassing."

Fortunately, she escalated first with a balisong she buried into his spleen, not because she knew where his spleen was located but by pure luck. She has always been seen as a "Top Totty" by those who believed "She'll get it" after a few "Pints." After the "Coppers" did their investigation, they came to the conclusion, as backed by cameras around the club and streets, that he specifically waited for her and stalked her like a rogue one-eyed lion who got kicked from the pack.

This whole ordeal didn't sit too well with Rose, who has eyes like a Celestial eye goldfish, not because he feared the "Bobbies," also known by many as the "Fuzz" and "Pigs," to name a few. Oh no, madam and sir, his concern was toward the Butcher of North Rhine-Westphalia, Dieter, known for leveling the playing field by donating pieces of your family's organs to some flesh-eating Papua Islanders, or so the legend goes, also complimenting his name.

You see, the thing about Dieter isn't that you have to fear him since he is just the effect to a cause, but your fear should be toward fucking with anyone Jacob takes under his wing, who also relies on the advice of the 5'2 Sicilian with a mustache between a Dali and a Hungarian butcher with slightly waxed tails.

It's a unique setup, just like trying to understand the complex coagulation cascade, which will torment you. Luckily, the whole situation was de-escalated in weeks by the pancake size areola Alegria, which resulted in the momentary decline of stabbings around London. The UK, unfortunately, is well known for stabbings for which you can do your research due to statistics not being my thing.

Stabbings are not limited to knives and broken glass bottles but include any sharp object that doesn't bend during the quick movement of an arm and wrist, almost like you would when casting your magic spell using your "special" wand. Cases of sharpened toothbrush handles, miniature stakes, and the well-known ballpoint pen have been reported, which changed the world just like the condom and salt.

I still recall the first writing utensil that formed part of my armory, getting that association from our first-grade teacher who always compared your forgetfulness to pack your pencil to a soldier forgetting his weapon: "A soldier can't go to war without his gun." I'm convinced she was into some form of pegging portrait by her "dominatrix" personality. Every day, you had to have your well-sharpened pencil displayed next to your sharpener, eraser, and 30-centimeter ruler, for which all had to point in a specific direction.

I hated my teacher, who gave me all the reasons under the sun to book myself into the special-ed class, also known as the spit-and-paste class, mainly because scissors were too complex of a tool, and glue was associated with getting high. Not only did I intentionally book myself into that class to escape the authority of Mrs. Rotten-meier, but mainly because this class had a soup kitchen serving soup and white bread for financially challenged children during recess.

You can say what you want about me being an opportunist as a kid, but you'll do so, driven by your ignorance toward the feeling of being hungry as a six-year-old child. The cool thing about being in the spit-and-paste class was that you got to speak funny and pretend that you couldn't read, which unfortunately materialized just as quickly.

That didn't stop the teacher from conquering that which many may see as a lost case since she abolished the finger-painting sessions by writing a letter to an imaginary friend session. I'm still unsure if the kids around me had imaginary friends, but mine never intro-duced himself.

The fun part of writing these letters in my mother tongue was that it could be as fictional as you can make it, like asking the presi-dent to take you away to a family with white bread and new shoes. I quickly got the hang of it and dismissed myself back to the "normal" classes where children had no fucking idea how to cut on the outside of a line. Perhaps we weren't allowed scissors in the special class out of fear that we may start a revolution in cutting shit just for fun.

I developed a love for writing letters not only to my mom or dad but also to my cousins scattered throughout and the occasional one to my granny, whom she wrote more letters to her kids, grandchildren, and great-grandchildren of which she had thirteen, forty-two and twelve, respectively somewhere in my late teens. Her letters always smelled like mothballs and "old people," which I didn't care for as my main focus was to try and decipher her handwriting.

In all fairness, enough of the BS; I only cared about her letters around Christmas and my birthday, as any kid would, knowing the possibility of getting a $1 note, which I used to buy six granny smith apples for my family. Those days were when people took time to put their thoughts on paper regardless of how much erasing or correction fluid they used.

We have come a long way since then, as evidenced by your children wearing pajamas to school with no fucking idea how to communicate without made-up abbreviations and emojis. I'm genuinely blessed knowing that my children only see a cell phone as nothing more than a device that will allow the evolution of bent thumbs and 60° bent necks…

Today is a special day for group therapy, while Orangutan Joe and the Urk left for a well-deserved vacation somewhere where oxytocin is served as skin patches. Everyone is excited and energetic with the three-week treatment coming to an end. This is the height most patients look forward to, even though it's accompanied by uncertainty.

Entering the "normal" world after such an extended stay will make you realize how broken those who judge you genuinely are while they hang on to the hope of being promoted while stepping on others. Helga, dressed in a well-tailored suit, enters the room with the same sincere smile since she entered this world as a presumed angelic being. She carries a large brown envelope, placing it on her lap after taking her seat on the square where everyone, including herself, is equal and free to voice that which is more appropriately associated with saying: on the square. Dean finishes voicing his concerns regarding today's youth while Bob serves the group Lakritz from the snack bar. "Yeah, who the hell goes to school in pajamas anyway?"

"Failed parents' offspring," responds Bob. Alicia has built quite the confidence during her stay, responding, "I used to go to school in Pajamas, and my parents were not too bad." Stephen quickly adds, "How do you tell someone what chaos is when raised in chaos anyway?"

"Now that I think of it, you are right," she responds, who never viewed it like that.

"You all are only jealous that we are the future of this world, and you are not—

old dinosaurs," adds Jana, wearing what seems to be a combination of goth impregnated by steampunk. Bob sees this as the ideal moment to show his feelings toward Jana strangely, "And that is just the thing; we aren't jealous but somewhat concerned about your safety in a world where wolves will always be in charge." She responds with a sarcastic smile and a big middle finger with a black painted nail. "Oh, dear lord, here we go again", thought Cathy, who plans to introduce Dean to her family later. "And what's up with the banana, peach, and tongue combo emojis?" asks the just as interested Hanna. "The banana and tongue combo means I want to lick and suck your meat-gun, and if you add a fountain emoji, it means till you explode.

The tongue and peach combo mean you want to eat her out like a Sir," answers Steve, who has mastered the art of sexting with his wife during his late-night stakeout sessions. I wonder if I should ask if candy-floss G-strings truly exist, thought Bram. Helga realizes the hype and takes control of the session using her subtle yet excited approach.

"Good afternoon, my favorite group of people! Had a good morning?" she asks, knowing they all are about to get something extraordinary. The entire group responds with a good afternoon, as one, driven by their excitement to try their new life coping skills.

"The best ever! Charlie came to visit us! Thank you so much for arranging it!"

"It's a great pleasure, Alicia. The group made it happen—I only did the paperwork."

"Thanks, guys…and girls," says Alicia with genuine gratitude toward people she now sees as no different than herself. "He lost his ammo on his way here."

"His what?" responds Helga to Dean.

"Testicles," answers Bob with little emotion on his face out of fear of being seen as jolly.

"Aha, interesting observation. I have a surprise for all of you this afternoon."

"What's in the envelope?" asks Stephen, who is quite the observer when it comes to foreign items and choosing flowers for his misses. "It contains letters addressed to each of you, sent from different places worldwide."

"A pen pal!" cheerfully remarks Alicia.

"I knew I had a kid somewhere in Nam…"

"I think it's the KKK asking for your robe back," responds Cathy toward her darling.

"Or a dick pic," remarks Anny, who has no issue sharing dick pic selfies with her ladies.

Attention, men, we already justified your need to share your antlers or beautiful feathers, but remember to keep it classy. It does help to hold back at times. There is no need to display your crooked stick as if it has no worth. Please treat it with a little more respect and yourself.

Bob responds with hope, "Perhaps it's my acceptance to study in Germany?"

"I never arrested or shot anyone who lives abroad," remarks Steve with concern.

Evangelical Cathy gets a bit impatient even though her excitement hides it well. "Let's see it then!"

"I'll hand it out, but on one condition. You have to share your letter with the group. We don't keep secrets from each other."

"Fuck that! What if it's a check with a million bucks?" asks Jana, who has considered breast implants for quite some time. By the way, every breast and penile implant comes with a serial number, of which penile implants are quite the surprise during a postmortem, so no worries if someone were to ever plan on stealing your implant. "Then we cross that bridge when we get there. Ready?" Stephen has his finger in his nose as he responds, "Ten-four."

She gets up and hands each an envelope with their names written on it. They open their letters and scan through the sentences, followed by Anna-Maria going first at reading out loud.

"This one's from Japan. Dear Anna, I want to assure you that Cassandra will turn out just fine and that you'll become a successful business owner of a cozy diner in NY. Please go easy on Cassandra and take comfort that you also had her challenges, yet you overcame them, and so will she. By the way, I tried cooking like you but sucked at it. Thanks for your kindness and the coffee."

"I'll go next," says Jana while everyone is following with attention. "This one is from England. Dear Jana, I had cocktails with friends the other evening when I thought of you. Nothing I say can take away the pain you have or change the fact that you got abused as a child. I will carry your pain as long as I can. I assure you that you'll become a successful businesswoman with a beautiful family. I'll never forget the fun we had—being reckless at times."

Tears run down her cheeks, knowing that someone recognizes the pain she has to live with on a personal level. "This one's from

Germany. Dear Dean, you are a legend among us and will never be forgotten! Your family dearly loves you but is just as confused as you. Don't give up on them! Know that you are about to get a beautiful and kind woman. Treat her like a diamond. Thank you for accepting her the same way she accepts you. I look up to you and cherish every moment we had."

For the first time, the group sees a giant weeping like a child while Cathy sends the tissue box. "This one is from Italy. Dear James, my friend, I believe you will like it here in Italy when your time comes. They smoke like cannons! Life is full of uncertainties, not only for you but for all of us. I'll try to guide you on the road even though there may come times when you forget about me. Remember, you will become an inspiration for many around the world once you have accepted not to fear success. As an aside, your first stay in New York, a big and beautiful city in America will be at the Ritz Carton across from Central Park. Explore the park and remember to save a few dollars from your granny since hotdogs are for sale at the baseball fields and Granny Smith apples are not.

"May I go next," asks Cathy.

"Please do," answers Bram on everyone's behalf. "This one's from the motherland—South Africa. Cathy, my dear Cathy, you made me laugh all the time. Forget about the things you did in your past and accept that you can't change it. The office baptizing was fun even though we freaked out a shit load of atheists. Love your new boyfriend even though he confuses Vietnam with Namibia. Either way, he is a great man, just like you, and an inspiration. Thank you for accepting him just the way he is."

Cathy wipes a tear, knowing that whoever wrote this letter has a connection with God.

The group is moved by every letter while excitement turns into a more profound meaning they all searched for. "Who wants to go next," asks Helga, who also has a tear of emotion. "This one is from Milan in Italy. Dear Alicia, your innocence is pure, and your love is unbreakable. You're worried about Charlie and the day he leaves you. That day will come, and your heart will be torn to pieces. Please take my hand as we take that journey together. I want you to know that I love you dearly and that everything will be fine regardless of how you may feel now."

Bram gets up and reads his while fighting tears. "This one is also from Germany. Hi Bram, getting to know you through my life's journey has been a pleasure. Your dad was a great man, just like you. You are stronger than you think, a good husband, and a caring father. They will need you more than ever to overcome the uncertainty of stability. I'll make sure I have your back, buddy. Love you!" Bram bursts out with tears, and Dean joins him in an emotional hug brothers give, the only true love some will ever know. They return to their seats, followed by Hanna reading out loud. "This one is from Japan. Hey Hanna! We had a great day in Osaka, and I could see how much you enjoyed yourself. Perhaps you should investigate opening a Green Tea ice cream shop, considering the amount we enjoyed in Kobe. Please don't harm yourself again, and know that you do mean a lot to me. Life is a journey without a true and reliable map. Carve your own with the tip of your heart."

Steve takes his turn after meditating on what Hanna just read. "This one's from Germany, too. Stephen, my man! It seems we had some good times in Frankfurt! Go easy on the bourbon, brother. You can't get your disability with no liver. By the way, don't put your heart on getting disability benefits, but rather find the family of the man you shot and ask for their forgiveness. They won't kick your ass —I have your back. Remember to wash your hands after picking your nose."

The group burst into laughter while snorting the tears this anonymous person brought to their souls. "No dick pic, but this one is also from England. My dearest Anny, I truly enjoyed having kinky conversations with you and sharing whatever you wanted. Please remember always to be safe and enjoy your body as much as possible. You will meet a nice guy who will treat you respectfully and give you the love you need. Please don't choose the word **RED** as a safe word—choose **MOIST** regardless of how weird it may sound."

Anny is just as moved when she realizes someone has addressed her genuine need: love. "I guess I'm always last. Greetings Bob! You are always last and as sharp as a knife. I thought of you during a business meeting in Osaka. Nothing around you will ever truly make sense—the sooner you accept it, the better. Forget about fighting religion and be respectful of those who believe in something you don't. I'm proud of your level of intellect, considering you had to teach yourself what you know. You freed your mind! By the way, it's a good reincarnation choice!"

The room is ruled by emotion, something people with scars or without should have regardless of whether you're a prisoner in solitary confinement or a father buying a no-name brand of Pringles for his Dawn syndrome child. Nothing in life should ever allow for status to determine your right to emotion. If you can't extend your hand to the janitor just like you do with the CEO, you'll die with the uncertainty of where you'll be going and remorse toward who you became. Jana realizes that Jacob didn't get a letter when she asks, "But what about Jacob? You didn't get one?" Jacob responds with a faint smile, "Correct, yes. Life isn't fair, and we should accept that. Your kindness, love, and support are more than I could ever ask for. You made me realize how fortunate I am to be associated with you. My letter will arrive someday, and I'm sure of that."

We don't always get what we want or what we expect. I personally have been there many times, coming from a broken home where the only certainty was uncertainty.

15

JACOB'S COCOON AND A WORD FROM OUR SPONSOR, PART IV

December 2023

Misdirection ensures a beautiful wedding gift just before you exit the ramp

UNKNOWN

Is the glass half full, half empty, or full to the brim with a perfect faded line on the inside, separating the upper half from the lower of the glass? Do you see things through the eyes of a pessimist or the eyes of an optimist at the same time as avoiding a Parallax error, the error that occurs when your eyes aren't correctly aligned with the perfectly faded line?

Mindfuck, is a slang term describing the intentional destabilization or manipulation of another person's mind. Subliminal messaging describes hidden visual or auditory messages, which are small or hidden, resulting in the brain discerning without processing.

Eyewitness misidentification describes the brain's inability to accurately record sensory events, leading to some innocent person taking the fall for someone else with a possible death sentence hanging from a rope or a droplet extending the tip of a high gauge needle. Did you hear Laurel or Yanny when you listened to it on YouTube? Did you see the dress as black and blue or white and gold? Did you turn left or right when your GPS clearly said the opposite?

What do all of these things have in common? To truly grasp what these things have in common will require you to view yourself naked in a mirror, followed by asking thousands of people to view your nude body while live streaming. Please don't do this literally unless you're already an OnlyFans content creator, which I personally don't approve of. Their opinions will differ, with some describing you as perfect, beautiful, saggy, firm, and perhaps godlike.

Their perception will differ from yours based on several factors, such as experience, time of the day, honesty, intent, history, and qualifications, to name a few. Brain structure, brain chemistry, genetics, and environmental factors can also be added from a medical viewpoint. Lust and the craving for a burst of oxytocin may even play a role, especially when thousands of people are attracted to your gender. Their opinions may even change the next day or so, depending on norms, values, and perhaps guilt.

Our brains may be seen as supercomputers, but sadly, we can't always calculate something like a calibrated machine would. Therefore, we will never be able to outsmart the next generation of computer intelligence since we have too many factors influencing individual brain performance.

Do the following if you want: Lay on your right side and try to fantasize about something, then turn on your left side and do the same. Stand and text, then lay down and text. You should be able to recognize a different thought pattern, even if it is almost imperceptible. This is also one of the reasons most employers worth their reputation will only employ a qualified engineer, a qualified mathematician, a qualified physicist, and so forth, not because they are better human beings but because they can speak the same language driven by facts and not emotion.

Jacob, for instance, relies heavily on solving problems using certified individuals for that particular reason but just as much on others to assist in conceptual designs or brainstorming possible new products.

If you go back several sentences, you will notice I included the word "saggy" as the third, describing how people may see you with the intent to make you believe that it's a probability only after I used perfect, beautiful, and before using firm, and perhaps godlike. We do this all the time, and the term for it is called a shit sandwich. Or is it? Perhaps I do so to promote a new mirror Jacob invented, or perhaps I used the word specifically in that position governed by my culture, the Western culture where "fake it" comes into play.

Don't get me wrong, I'm not saying we should destroy relationships by being dead honest, but rather that the positioning of words doesn't fall short of the definition of "Mindfuck." Our "Western civilization" is arguably the reason why we are naive to the extent that we will trust the agreements made with terrorists, convicted or not, since we are raised to believe bad intentions driven by terror are temporary.

The world is indeed a playground ruled by those who recognize the vulnerability associated with being naïve. Adding all the terms and descriptions above will make you realize that some of us have the ability to harvest the power of mindfucking when manipulating subliminal stimuli and the sciences describing why people perceive sounds differently and perceive the same color differently. Does this make the "mindfucker" a bad person? You may come to that conclusion if you know their intentions are dark, or perhaps it makes them a true friend looking out for your best.

The sad reality is that most will agree with the former, that being a bad person, without having any evidence of malice. This is indeed a topic for debate, which will cause more frustration since nothing in the debate will be backed by mathematical, scientific, or engineering principles but rather that which the person taking the podium perceives.

Not being able to scientifically prove the intent of mindfucking backed by calibrated "facts" makes it the deadliest weapon known to humanity. There are exceptions, though; serial killers and pedophiles have never had good intentions, nor will they ever have. Their malice is that of a broken mind.

I forgot to mention a comment Steve may have made sometime under the tree about pedophiles being exceptionally good at remembering your kids' names wasn't meant as a joke, nor should it ever be told as a joke, but rather to give insight into what many Law Enforcement Officers have to deal with, knowing it could sometimes be too late.

Once you've finished this book, you'll come to a conclusion regarding the content and the author, but nothing about your conclusion will ever be driven by calibrated and tested facts. Therefore, I can suggest keeping your opinion to yourself, as no one wants to be seen as a self-proclaimed whatever. And by the way, ladies, if you ever were to ask a man on a dating app what he likes or loves to do, you should pay attention to where, among all his interests, he places anything to do with intimacy, even if it seems remote.

That, my dear reader, is how someone perfectly hides a word or interest to test the waters. And if someone includes "good hygiene" as something they prefer, it points toward being waxed with no hidden cheese and a fresh breath after you drowned your body with soap on a rope.

To intentionally change the subject to something different, what do Serra Norte, Samarco Alegria, Sishen, Prince Albert piercings, a goat, and Stephen have in common? The answer is relatively straightforward, especially since you most likely did an internet search, for which you could eliminate the goat and Stephen, except for his Prince Albert and Jacob's Ladder piercings.

Iron ore is what they have in common: a rock from which metallic iron can be extracted and processed to manufacture various steel products such as pipes, angle iron, square tubing, and beams, to name a few. In 1932, a photo of eleven men having lunch 850 feet above the ground on the sixty-night floor of the RCA building in Manhattan depicts one such product.

It remains a mystery as to who the photographer was, but some claim Giovanni De Luca, who occasionally turns into a bat, as backed by "calibrated" claims of children who dismiss him as the Chupacabra. And where does a goat come into the equation? If you recall, I mentioned at the beginning of the book, in the first chapter: *"Shoulder to shoulder and with little emotion, they rush through a straightened Serpentine Ramp with one day closer to retirement or perhaps affording that one-bedroom apartment Manhattan boasts about."*

The two relevant words in the sentence are Serpentine and Ramp, a chute designed by Temple Grandin in 1974 to ensure the humane treatment of cattle, thereby eliminating the use of prods and noise. Eliminating these two methods ensures no panic and self-injury, considering that these beings, cattle, are aware of their fate, which can be seen in their eyes' knowing death is only minutes away.

It happens from time to time that the animals, including sheep, need some guidance, not only toward pens and trucks but also the slaughter floor. This is where the goat comes into play, which isn't just an ordinary goat but a trained one that will lead the animals down the chute.

At a specific point, the goat will exit into a side passage, sparing its own life. Think about it; it almost resembles a politician. This goat is referred to as the Judas goat with reference to Judas Iscariot, the apostle who betrayed Jesus Christ with a kiss on the cheek, according to the New Testament.

For some or other, people have a way of turning a goat into a legend, just like the scapegoats mentioned three times in the book of Leviticus, of which one of two male goats had to bear the sins of the Israelites while being sent into the desert for Azazel. Azazel was and perhaps still is seen as a fallen angel responsible for introducing humans to forbidden knowledge, as described in the Book of Enoch, conveniently left from the Bible if you were to ask Bob or Dieter.

Anton Szandor LaVey even took it one step further when he founded the Church of Satan back in San Francisco on April 30, 1966. He chose the logo of his creation to be the Sigil of Baphomet, depicted not only on famous materials found throughout but also on the book jacket of the bible he finalized around 1969. His works are still followed today, all thanks to a goat.

Take this as you see fit, considering that neither I nor my dear friend support any form of religion that has a thick book with hundreds of pages; when I refer back to previously said: "God save the Queen and California, the place known for solutions." Regardless of whether you want to follow a goat or toss one to Azazel for consumption during your desert adventures, you'll still find yourself in a place where Jimmy Cooper's perfectly mowed lawn with beautiful blooming plants guiding the occasional visitor to the front door is non-existent.

The desert can be quite unforgiving with its harsh conditions, emptiness, and boundaries set by nomads searching for greener pastures. It is not a place where you want to start a cattle farm.. What do you think they will eat? You could visit the wilderness of Sinai, Sin, and Paran to formulate a plan for feeding thousands of big-bodied cattle. These kinds of environments have always been feared by most, as depicted in books, screenplays, and stories carried down from generation to generation just to be shared around a midsummer night campfire.

Little do people realize that one book in particular shares such an event where hundreds of thousands had to walk this barren land for forty years, with a substantial amount of people succumbing to age and illnesses while clinging to the possibility of entering a promised land.

The book should not come as a surprise, taking that it has been around for thousands of years, or at least that which we know of and should be celebrated as one of the oldest works of literature we have, depending on which Victor or Victoria you ask.

In the book of Exodus, Moses is tasked with leading thousands from captivity to a promised land, Canaan's large and prosperous ancient country. Exodus pledges hours of entertainment should you ever wish to indulge, but do so after you finish the first book, Genesis, from the library called the Bible.

Modern-day Christians, including most of our parents, refrain as much as possible from learning that which the first half of the library offers and focus more on the second half due to several reasons, which I'm not going to discuss but can mention the biggest reason being shocking.

Regardless, the first five books from the Bible should be studied, not just read, to understand why the world is what it is and why we are destined to repeat our own mistakes. Asking you to imagine walking the desert for forty years would not be just unpractical but also without any value, taking into consideration that neither you nor your great grandparents were treated as enslaved people for several hundred years before embarking on the 40-year journey, which in all practicality should have been less than 12 days.

Why did this journey take this long, and was it truly because they lacked faith? Around 600,000 people left the safety and security of their homes in a direction where none of these were available, nor would it be. Their lack of faith in the almighty was just one of the factors preventing them from making a quick journey, which I will discuss. Remember, these people were treated like slaves, lived like slaves, and believed what enslaved people believe.

When you add this together, what do you get? People who are unorganized and defenseless without self-value, not by choice but because of oppression. Even if they took the 11-day journey, they would just as quickly perish, not only because they would not stand a chance against any armies, but they would eat every single animal in the promised land without thinking about the long run, therefore preventing them from flourishing and defaulting back to what they know best, being enslaved.

It took them forty years to shed their "slave skin" to become one of the strongest nations in biblical times. But not all were good in the forty years because they rebelled against their God and their leader Moses, who broke the Ten Commandments tablets the first time around. Moses had his challenges, just like most of us, ultimately preventing him from accessing the promised land determined by God even though he spent more than forty years of his hundred and twenty dedicated to the instructions of God.

King David, father of King Solomon, for instance, was not allowed to erect the final house of the Lord due to his past faults and failures. He was, however, allowed to provide ample material to construct the temple. We don't always get to enjoy the fruits of our labor and, at times, will be seen as the Judas goat or perhaps even a scapegoat, for which I'm sure some will agree when referring to Moses, who lived about 1336 years before the birth of Jesus or Iscariot.

Jacob, also known as Israel, is a shiny example of someone who didn't get to enjoy the fruits of his labor, even though it was only a blessing he bestowed, which back then carried more weight than doing something physical. No, I'm not referring to Jacob Van Der Linde but rather to a man of true wisdom and courage. Israel blessed his son, Judah, resulting in the birth of Jesus of Nazareth, yet Israel never got to meet the Messiah. I want to encourage you to read Genesis 49: 8 – 12, emphasizing verse 10, which Bob will obviously dispute.

People tend to be captivated by a charismatic leader and end up selling all their possessions to ensure their stay in a cult with one outcome: none. Why is it that we willingly follow mindlessly? Is it perhaps that we seek to be led just like cattle behind a goat or have our faults projected onto a scapegoat? Conceivably it may also be as a result of brainwashing or mind fucking if you were to ask one of Jacob's exes.

Planting an idea into someone's head and capitalizing on the results isn't just reckless but also one of the more selfish acts you can imagine. That said, some need to be led to achieve a certain goal, just like you are being led to solve the murder of Jacob, which I'm sure will leave you speechless once you finish this book.

Things aren't always as they seem, such as looking at a piece of rock mined from an iron ore mine. The rock can be used to stone someone or to manufacture forceps and hemostats used in life-saving surgeries, and your romantic wife can also use the processed product to sever your outer jugular, or it can be used for hours of indulging in Thanksgiving cuisine using the best utensils your grandmother stores in a Mahogany box.

See it the way you want but remember the Double Slit Theorem, The Copenhagen Interpretation, the Observer Effect, and Color Constancy, for which you'll need to do some research. You may observe or experience the same thing differently than others now that I got you in the chute…

Dieter, the middle-aged German with a yellow stained toothbrush mustache, a Tyrolean hat, undersized chino shorts, flip-flops, and a t-shirt with a cartoon character, stands beside Jacob's bed with tears rolling into his mustache. Pancake size areola Alegria holds his hand while both monitor the QRS complex on the vital signs screen. Jacob's heart stops, which triggers alarms and codes at the central monitoring station, resulting in several staff members rushing to his bed.

Their unsuccessful resuscitation attempts result in them calling the time of death, followed by leaving the room. Cassandra enters and engages in conversation with Dieter and Alegria. "He used to visit us quite often as a student. Ultimately, his way of life destroyed everything he stood for during his 20 hours of staying awake as a student, attending lectures, doing extra jobs to pay his way through college, and observing the staff during patient treatment. He wanted to become the best and nothing less," says Cassandra, trying to hold her composure.

Dieter internally fights to come to terms with what just happened as he responds with how he saw Jacob and with the hidden knowledge of Jacob having Somniphobia since he was a kid, "The man with nothing to live for besides his inventions and dogs. He added to Alegria's and my life—the man who created me."

Alegria cries profusely as confusion sets in while Bob and Anny enter with an English bulldog named Bella Milano. Hanna, Bram, Alicia with her bulldog print pajamas, and Charlie Figs enter shortly after trying to pull him from aiming at a pot plant next to the central monitoring station. Yeah, right, no Charge will ever let dogs into the unit, but be reminded that money talks, and I'm telling the story. Cathy, James, Dean, and Jana, with her Superman cape, join, followed by Anna-Maria. Dean and Bram pick the dogs up and put them on Jacob's bed. Everyone is emotionally moved, seeing how the dogs gently lay beside him after softly licking his ears. Sad but true, they were the only family he had or wanted to be associated with. "Did you guys know him too?" asks the German, who has proved to be more human than human.

Alicia, overwhelmed with confusion, asks, "Where's Jacob? Will he be joining us?"

"You are looking at him, sweetie. He wrote the letters," says Bram while comforting her with an extended hug and trying to hold back his tears. "Thought we lost him in Nam."

"Yeah, the motherfucker pulled a disappearing act on us."

"That can't be him. He looks so old, and what the fuck is that tube in his mouth?" asks Jana while holding Dean's hand as her brain struggles to process that which lays perfectly still with taped eyes and a slightly raised head, better known as an empty vessel.

Hanna realizes the confusion set in and responds with care, "Honey, it's a tube connected to a machine to help him breathe."

"But it doesn't seem like he is fucking breathing!" responds Jana, who doesn't seem to get used to this sight.

"I wish we spent more time together," softly adds Anny, battling to direct her fluids to her eyes.

"For the first time in my life, I can't think of something intelligent to say except that we had so much fun getting the smoking licenses laced by you, Anny, and approved by Piears, even though I quit way back."

Anny hands Bob her pacifier, "Enjoy it, Bob, time isn't on your side, and make sure you use mouthwash afterward."

"I'll always be grateful for his kind words," adds Hanna, whose face represents that of someone who just smelled a foul odor. "God is good—"

"—all the time. All the fucking time!" adds Jana with both middle fingers pointed toward Cathy. Anna-Maria, lost in emotions yet trying to set an example for her daughter, "I'll miss him dearly—what do we do now, Cassandra?"

"We bury him, Mom," she replies, with no one noticing the return of a faint QRS complex, not frequent enough to be perceived as a living being about to pull the string attached to a graveyard bell. Don't ask me how the hell that works: being "clinically dead" and returning back to life like a 1600s warlock. "But where's Helga?" asks Anna-Maria, knowing their love relationship. "She is stuck in the Manfuckinghattan traffic," responds Steve, who is trying to arrange a police escort through peak traffic. "See you soon, brother," remarks James while sucking on an unlit rocket. Hanna dismisses herself from the room, trying to escape the smell she associates with death, all thanks to Hyperosmia. Anny walks up to Jacob's bed and looks at Bob with questioning eyes. "No, Anny, not when he's dead—you'll have to wait a few more days before you can give him a hand. I'm sure he'll have your legs over his shoulders again," whispers Bob while showing some form of respect.

Yep, I told you Anny would want to lend a hand…

16

DEOXYRIBONUCLEIC ACID AT A FUNERAL

December 2024

Regardless of whether you decide to quit on life or smoke yourself to death after you have already destroyed your heart due to pharmaceutics to stay awake, we'll all face the uncertainty of what comes next. We tend to fear the only place no one has ever entered and reported back, regardless of the claims of individuals visiting death, which led them to believe that they have an answer.

We get carried away when philosophizing on what the possibilities are, to return to reality with no progress on creating a viable solution to cheat death. Embrace it and sing your death song, that is, if you aren't unlucky to have a breathing tube down your throat like Van Der Linde did. It's almost Christmas as I finish this book, knowing many worldwide are fond of the white Christmas idea even though most have never experienced snow, nor will they ever have the possibility, like most living in Africa, excluding South Africa and Egypt.

Believe it or not, on the 13th of December 2013, Egypt and some surrounding countries were covered in a white blanket, which local media claimed to be the first in 112 years. We are mesmerized by the gentle fall of snow as we prepare for Christmas, the only day in the year we choose to be generous, excluding Thanksgiving, where families no longer share what they are thankful for, as shared by Jacob, who has attended quite a few by invitation.

Perhaps people feel sorry for him, only having a family of dogs, or maybe it's for some mysterious reason, such as getting to meet the mythical orangutan or Urk. Regardless, he always appreciated the gesture shortly before Christmas, the same time so many people commit suicide. We decorate our trees, homes, and office spaces with small memorabilia representing the humble snowflake, even though it can create destruction, as seen by the after-effects of snowstorms and avalanches.

Very few people know that DNA (Deoxyribonucleic acid) has something very particular in common with snowflakes, which I will discuss shortly. The sad reality is that "snowflakes" have become a term for describing a person with a unique personality, just like all of us are unique.

Yes, you don't have to agree with what you don't want to, nor do you need to support that which you don't agree to, but assigning a beautiful word as a derogative term is nothing different than me calling you a Christian, which you very well know the destructive history and carnage of, just like an avalanche.

For some fucked up reason, we always want to put someone in a box, just like when people classify someone as a narcissist or sociopath. I once had an in-depth discussion with a criminal psychologist assigned to evaluate a "gun-for-hire" who killed a political leader of an opposition party in his country.

Her assessment is what you would expect from a professional specializing in "the mind"; professional and factual. What makes her different, just like some, is that she has empathy. She made it clear the court believed he should rot away in prison but that it was her clinical opinion that he is a reformed old man who should enjoy the last of his days among those of his family who are still alive.

We want justice, we want a "quick drop with a sudden stop," and we are just as fast to label someone as confuckulated in the head, even though we haven't studied psychology. And even if we did, there should never be a motivation to put someone in a box except from serial killers and pedophiles, which I will argue for with the following. What makes snowflakes unique is that none of them are the same shape or size, which is widely accepted by researchers and scientists, regardless of what you may have read in between your internet porn sessions.

Their uniqueness is what gives it beauty, therefore keeping you more intrigued than the bland Christmas representation, which some even use to cover their nipples at semi-nude pool parties at Jacob's mansion in Spain. When interlocked or stacked, their unique shapes give us one of the most visual satisfactions you can possibly describe: snow. Just so is DNA, which makes all of us unique, with no two people having the same.

When put together, we resemble creation, destruction, and evolution, to name a few. How you look at it is your choice, and I have no right to dismiss how you see it, just like none of us have the right to assign a term to a group of people we don't agree with. Sure, Bob doesn't like children, nor does Stephen believe they should attend school in pajamas.

Regardless of how they may view you, they'll never assign a term to someone or a group different from them. The reason is simple: for their entire lives, they have been called names and treated as if they have the most contagious disease that could wipe out humanity. Some of these words include Psychos, Depros, Crazies, Insane, Luny, and so forth. Your DNA makes you unique, and you do not get to choose your upbringing.

You are shaped by various factors of which our parents and their parents have the right to raise their children, which should exclude harm, destruction, and physical abuse even when the snot noses screw up, and even though I blame grandparents for the lack in backbones for their grandchildren. You are allowed to disagree, and I assure you I won't cancel you or call you something as long as you understand your place in this world.

By the way, I absolutely and with exclamation despise my neighborhood at Christmas—uniformity is out the door with their decorations, of which proportionality is an absolute must in certain people's lives. If you are one of those who illuminate the tree to the left of your house, you should plant one to the right and wait for it to be fully grown before you continue displaying your shitty lantern lights, please. Your only asymmetrical love should be toward a woman's breasts despite being saggy, small, big, perky, puffy, or whatever description you can add…

It's a cold winter morning somewhere in a small eastern European town. Surprisingly, it has a large graveyard with fading Lunettes on headstones dating back to the early 1600s and a few fresh flowers marking random graves. Friends, slightly covered by gently falling snow, are gathered next to an open grave, ready to say their last goodbyes. The pallbearers, Bob, Dieter, Bram, James, Stephen, and Dean, remove a cheap casket from an old Hearse and position it over the lowering device. Tears of grief are on their faces as the funeral director, Piears, with a hanging lit cigarette in his mouth and a green visor hat, starts the lowering. Bob, Dieter, Cassandra, Alegria, Anny with Bella Milano, Hanna and Bram, Alicia with Charlie, Cathy, James, Dean, Jana, Anna-Maria, and the 39-year-old psychologist are gathered next to the open grave.

Helga steps up and perfectly places fresh flowers on the casket, which Hanna handed her. "DJ, what should I play?" asks Bram, holding a guitar. "Miss Cathy, will you do the vocals, please?" asks

James, pushing his St. Michel glasses closer to his eyes. "I will, sweety," she responds while balancing the thought of her missing goldfish, Jimmy, the rose of her life. "Cobain's Lake of Fire," instructs James, remembering Jacob's 150 GPA chiseled jaw, followed by counting down, "One—two—three—four." I honestly hoped he would've chosen "If I Were the Devil." After the song concludes, Hanna, through the tears and in remembrance of excellent and satisfying times, wisecracks after turning toward Anny with a whisper, "Do you think it'll be okay if I have your role next time?"

"Why is that, Hanna?"

"I also want to enjoy a bit of an erotic adventure."

Alegria quickly adds, whispering, "And I seriously need a boob job. I understand that I represent fruitfulness with my helicopter landing pad areolas, but being perky would be nice."

"But I like them, my Horsy—the best for target practicing," says Dieter while shivering in the cold, realizing he conforms to the definition of "Lion cold," even though with hands in his pockets trying to keep the helmet-wearing villain warm.

Jana, with fieldmouse ears, adds, "Perky-puffy is the way to go. We can swap, but only with the blessing of the sponsor."

"Your memories don't last that long, do they? He ate you out pretty good in the entertainment room with a tongue like a giraffe's, didn't he?" asks Cathy, whose tears turned into joy.

"Keep it down," reprimands Bob.

"Yeah, keep it down motherfuckers!"

"For fucks and broomsticks, Bob, I don't have a crooked broomstick to keep down! You're disturbing the force! Let's make snow angels, shall we?" softly suggests Jana to Alicia after giving Bob the finger. Stephen realizes this is the time to submit your wishes, "Hey Bob, how about borrowing your encyclopedia for the next version?"

"Jeeeaaaasus fucking Christ, behave yourselves and keep it down! This isn't a book written in the back of a party panty van! Have some respect for the dead!" responds Bob while trying to comfort

Helga, who seems frozen by overwhelming emotions. "Bob, what's up with the bell and string Piears is trying to mount on that rebar?" asks Bram, hiding his tears behind his St. Michel glasses. "Saved by the bell as far as I can remember," responds Bob, with Helga clinging onto his designer suit jacket with hand-picked stitching.

"This funeral sucks! Who the hell forgot to bring the devilled eggs?" softly asks Piears to James.

17

FORMULA $(X^2+(Y-((X^2)^{(1/3)}))^2=1)$ AND JOHN 20: 1-2

December 2024

Even though seemingly trivial, one of life's mysteries is the question of whether women like fresh flowers. This is also a good topic for debate among those who just met their "bird" and those who no longer open the doors for their "queens." Some women apparently don't, whereas most absolutely love them, as evidenced by polls and statistics, of which I don't have the faintest idea for determining the latter.

From my experience, I haven't met a woman who doesn't like fresh flowers. I personally experimented with this over and over and over again till the cows came home. Men, if it's her birthday, make sure you go out of your way to get her a fresh bunch and for any other special occasion, which pretty much should be twice a month. And if you can't afford a bunch, you can pick a flower from Anny Du Preez's bush in Vintage City or pay a quick visit to a graveyard where there'll always be some flowers, just like a friend I had back in Varsity did.

Whatever you decide, stay away from plastic ones, and

remember which of your girlfriends prefer roses and which prefer St. Joseph Lilies, with roses always available after a burial. Once you have made peace with robbing a grave and embracing the fact that it is a Class H felony, which may or may not give you the opportunity to spend some time alone with your thoughts or with the jailhouse "love doll and in-house disk jockey" Alberta, the sooner you'll be able to graph the formula above in this chapter's title, which shouldn't take a rocket scientist to draw. However, you may just return to an empty house once released from captivity.....

It's a cold winter afternoon as Helga, dressed in bulldog print pajamas and accompanied by a nurse, steps up to the bench where Jacob used to sit. At the same time, Piears, with a hanging lit cigarette in his mouth and a green visor hat initiates the lowering of an imaginary coffin. The nurse hands her fresh flowers, which she carefully places on the bench.

Helga's smile is soft and warm as always while memories play through her head. She stands at the bench for several minutes, ensuring she placed the flowers perfectly on top of the casket, just like confirming a letter made its way into the USPS box's bag, the belly of the beast. The nurse gently touches her shoulder, which is covered by gently falling snow, indicating it's time to return to the building, which needs a fresh coat of paint.

"I forgot to mention not to use the word moist except in the bedroom," reminds Jacob.

18

WHEN IN ROME...

December 2024

Whenever moving to a new country, Jacob makes finding a house the number one priority, not only because of his two dogs, who'll need a fenced-in backyard, but also because he'll need a place to recover with his own duvet and pillows when sick. So many employers forget the importance of having the new employee check that off their list as soon as possible, therefore allowing them to appreciate their own smelly pillow and tissue box.

We all need a place we can call home, a place with warmth, perhaps having a loved one, and children taking turns to ride on the back of a big fluffy dog. Our homes don't need to be perfect, but one thing is an absolute must for a perfect home: love.

Love allows us to express our emotions without demanding, share ideas while listening, care without conditions, guide without dictating, and replenish each other's fountains without consuming.

We are not meant to be alone. We are meant to enjoy one of the most precious gifts life has to offer, that being in love, even if it is conceptual toward a cockroach. None of these he'll ever be able to do since he has a house containing furniture and nothing more. Unfortunately, both his dogs, Charlie Figs and Bella Milano, left and joined Lassie, Hercules from The Sandlot, and Cujo up in a place that could just as well be down since the earth seems round.

The only thing he has left from his two family members, Charlie and Bella, are their ashes and some toys, which won't sit right with him to toss in the garbage. He cherishes each moment he had with them as a small family traveling the globe. Their snores, farts, slobber, and potato-like bodies are what made his house a home. He could've had the shittiest day ever, but once he entered his home and saw them, all the concerns of life left his mind, almost like that happy feeling caused by a smell you can't place. Their love was unconditional, the kind of love Kings, Queens, and poets ponder on.

Sometimes, we only have a pet through whom we experience unconditional love. I intentionally used "whom" in the previous sentence, not because Jacob is one of those pushing dogs on strollers but because he is someone who can recognize the possibility of reincarnation. I agree; it doesn't mention that anywhere in the book containing 1200 pages, also referred to as the Bible, nor does it mention Giraffes entering Noah's Ark. However, dismissing the possibility is limiting the capabilities of our Almighty God.

I have had endless discussions on this topic with several scholars, including Bob, who all embrace the various possibilities and the evidence supporting the notion. I also highly recommend a book I once read, "Return to Life," as support. For us to place limitations on our creator is to dismiss the universe and all other possible creations out there.

The devil argues like a man, or so some claim, but God doesn't need to argue regardless of what is written in the book of Job, who was left with ashes. If you were to say that I'm wrong, you disregard the fact that only a few would read the book if it had 1200 trillion pages. Those who compiled the biblical library did so to highlight what they saw as important and what should be conveniently left out.

In essence, we all hold onto something that makes sense to us, such as our own pillow, a scripture that gives meaning, and perhaps something else like a cape associated with memories. But whatever you choose, share that with someone without implementing a sophisticated formula that contains your credit card PIN, as there'll come a day when you'll forget it yourself since you aren't "I am who I am"…

A luxurious room with patient art against the walls, a Bernhardt queen-sized bed, and flesh flowers on a nightstand next to an orangutan clay sculpture by Johannes Morris alias the Sculptor. Psychologist Helga, dressed in bulldog print pajamas and a Superman cape in her hand, stares through the window at the bench with the fresh flowers. She turns toward a small desk with a bobblehead Jesus. What appears seems to be several manuscripts, each with dates separating them by three weeks. One such manuscript, the one currently open on her desk, displays Chapter 22.

19

∞ ≡ ∞ → ∞ ANTEROGRADE & DISSOCIATIVE AMNESIA

December 2024

To be honest, I'm running out of ideas since I already know the ending, and I'll be making stuff up with the hope of still capturing the imagination, your imagination. The closer we, or most, get to the end of our lives, the less we focus on perfection, not because we gave up caring but because we realize life is too short to fill with unnecessary nonsense. Or perhaps I'm entirely wrong, and people just don't give a flying fuck, or maybe the majority of elders still manage life to perfection, and I just made everything up.

The possibility of having an epiphany while taking a leak at 2 a.m., 3 a.m., and again at 4 a.m. is also likely, thereby giving you the true meaning of life. This may or may not be 21 when dividing a number by two at the same time you fall to the floor caused by an aneurysm stealing your perfection.

Looking at Jacob's mom as she gets closer to the other side isn't necessarily the most satisfying thing to do, considering she is heading toward being a child again. In contrast, her small children developed into adults who now seem to have the answers just like she once did.

Then, we also have parents who get trapped in the same loop, over and over, due to changes in brain functions and so forth. But what about patients who seem to see things or hear voices? Did their brains crash, for lack of a better word, or did a past traumatic event lead them down that path of distortion?

I personally have met several people who seem to live in a completely different world, one we can't see or hear. I even met the second coming of Christ, or shall I say, "Jesus Version 2.0," whom I dismissed just as fast by pointing toward another patient as "Jesus Version 2.0", who staked his claim two days earlier. This brings forth the possibility that their worlds may just be the "correct" ones which we dismiss even though we tend to do the same shit every day, over and over. No, I'm not referring to the Messiahs' worlds, but others who seem to be lost somewhere in space and time, just like that small stone annoying your foot after fitting your shoes.

Imagine, if you can, that you saw or experienced something so traumatic – an event which gave you insight into a world ruled by demons, angels, or a mythical orangutan. Will you still see life the same way, or will you distance yourself from normality, knowing you are surrounded by something we can't possibly imagine? After all, some things can't be unseen, and some can only be seen once. Then we have people claiming to hear voices, like someone claiming the reason for the murder was due to voices telling them to. What do you make of that?

In my opinion, I believe they don't hear physical human voices but rather those of characters they created to overcome loneliness, trauma, or anything that needs some form of management, just like when writing a book with multiple characters.

Everyone speaks to themselves in some way, such as out loud or internally. What can happen, which I support, is the creation of several characters as a coping mechanism, with each having a unique persona and voice. This opens the possibility of engaging in conversation not just with your characters but also among themselves while narrated by you.

As a result, each character develops based on the amount of "empowerment" you assign without knowing. Eventually, they become real, not because they are, nor because you think they are, but because you developed a world in which they are the masters, with you becoming the slave, feeling compelled to support their needs.

Sooner or later, this coping mechanism will claim a part of your thought patterns, almost as if each character claims a part of your brain, for which each has its own way of thinking. It's almost like the small stone returning to your shoe every morning with you not knowing how it got there in the first place. Sounds bonkers, right?

Just to be clear, I AM NOT describing Multiple Personality Disorder. If you think I do, you should instead choose a different career path since your diagnosis will be based on nothing but that which supported torture as a form of treatment.

Several scholars will disagree since what they know is governed by "facts" obtained through years of failed psychology. What do I mean by this? Someone will assign an ICD-10 code based on studies and information gathered, but no one ever asks the patient to have a look at the codes, explain it to them, and choose one with you they see fit if they are willing and able. "Fuck that! I didn't study that shit, and I pay the bonkers doc enough to do their job—no fucking way that shit will work for me. I shoot confuckulated motherfuckers for a living and not diagnose. I'm not a pavement wanker patient who thinks I know shit I don't," adds Jana.

But then again, some practitioners have a God Complex, and sadly, we put our trust in that same person. The only one who knows what goes on in your head is you, and only you. Some may just be trapped forever while others seek a way out through some form of "re-living" as a result of trauma.

Please don't get me wrong. I'm not a clinical psychologist or psychiatrist, nor will I ever pursue that direction since my life is based on mathematical facts and facts alone, as shared by the legendary Urk, who doesn't support any form of occupation relying on statistics. What if you could trace back your trauma and find a way for your characters to safeguard you while one in particular is tasked to find a way out regardless of the costs…

Psychiatrist Jimmy Cooper and the hospital superintendent, Dr. Vullis, both professionally dressed, observe Helga through the window of her bedroom door while she stares toward the outside bench with flowers. This isn't a room with a door window like in prisons, but rather a door with a window where the patient can open the small blinds from the inside if wanted.

"How did she end up here, Jimmy?"

"Severe trauma."

"Caused by?"

"Apparently, she was bathing in a completely relaxed environment, the rose petal and candle thing, when something in her house exploded…I believe it was some kind of water-heating device. Her state of mind changed from being relaxed and calm to a sudden overload of Norepinephrine and Cortisol. Her amygdala, hippocampus, and prefrontal cortex were severely affected during the event—it's almost as if she is stuck between Dissociative and Anterograde amnesia. She is also experiencing delusional disorder, which makes her believe she's treating 11 patients, representing the life of one she treated and fell in love with. He tried committing suicide 11 times—Jacob Van Der Linde. Her whole world is imaginary and restarts around every three weeks."

"Prognosis?"

"Not looking good—all we can do is to let her relive her imaginary sessions over and over with the hope she'll 'snap' out of it. After all, she was one of our best and would've agreed with us," answers Jimmy with no confidence in what he just said as he crosses his arms and takes a step half a foot backward, just like Richard Nixon did.

"And what happened to Van Der Linde?" asks Dr. James Vullis, taking a few notes as the new hospital superintendent who has mastered micro-expressions and deception detection throughout his career. Needless to say, he sees straight through Cooper, who has built up quite a reputation for invading patients' privacy by going through their drawers.

"He basically murdered himself over several years—taking all kinds of stuff as a student to stay awake and smoked thirty-one and a half a day. His heart eventually gave in. I believe he's locked up somewhere deep inside her head, and we can't truly know for sure what else she's experiencing besides the 11 suicide attempts."

"The brain is indeed mysterious at times," remarks Dr. Vullis while pondering on the mysteries we know so little about. "Anything else you believe I should know?" he asks with full attention on Cooper's posture and facial expressions.

"Apparently, she has been writing a book."

"About?"

"The same thing over and over, which she also repeats every three weeks or so. I'm not sure what it's about, though," says Cooper with raised shoulders, which he maintains for several seconds, and a quick scratch to the left of his nostrils. "Don't you think it's your job to know Dr. Cooper?" asks Dr. Vullis, annoyed. "Come on, James, she's just a patient."

"I thought you said the best we had?"

"Had, yes, but obviously not anymore."

Dr. Vullis isn't interested in the lack of psychiatrists' motivation nor that of someone who has a reputation for sowing his seed around town when he is supposed to be committed to his wife, who happens to be Dr. Vullis' sister. Just as a reminder, the woman with three kids and a big fluffy dog is currently getting into a shuttle toward an airport, ready to start a new life, which Cooper will realize once he texts on his way home, the same home turned house.

"May I make a suggestion, Jimmy?" asks Dr. Vullis, not really wanting an answer.

"Sure," he responds with confusion. "Someone brought to my attention that you made a comment of a sexual nature toward our patient, Helga." A sudden rush of blood heads to Jimmy Cooper's cranial, accompanied by a shiver down his spine, knowing very well he fucked up and didn't see this coming. "I'm sure it was a misunderstanding, James."

"That may just be, but this is a top privately owned facility which can't afford to be dragged down by accusations—"

"—What are you getting at?" interrupts Jimmy, hoping to get out of this one.

"Let me be clear, Dr. Cooper; this is a place which one bad apple won't ruin regardless of what that apple may think. I need you to pack your things and leave the premises."

Jimmy, shocked as can be and just as confused, "When shall I return?"

"Don't!"

"Is this because I fucking don't know what she is writing and the comment I made?" asks Jimmy as he loses control and with a raised voice. "Watch your tongue and temper! The fact that someone saw you going through a patient's drawer is what led you here and the inappropriate comments you've made before I joined. Also, never use the word apparently when it's your responsibility to know the facts. But let's not make this bigger than what you can handle, Cooper. We both know you'll be pulling on a short end. I won't suggest leaving again!" assertively reminds Dr. Vullis while glancing at his Hora Mundi 5717 by Breguet.

"Understood," responds Jimmy, who for a moment stares toward the floor in shame, followed by dismissing himself from the premises and heading toward his house.

Helga turns away from the window and walks to the seat behind her small Natura walnut desk with the manuscripts. She momentarily stares at a blank page in Chapter 22 and writes a heading: A Day at the Beach, using the Montblanc pen she got from JJ Van Der Linde as a gift.

She sits for a while, her brain computing how to turn into a superior version of herself, which triggers a moment with life returning to her eyes as she returns to the window with a subtle smile and tears clouding her vision. Dr. Vullis notices her actions, removes his cell phone from his pocket, and dials a fascinating contact.

20

CATCH HER ON THE FLIP SIDE

December 2024

Shapeshifting and the Chupacabra go hand in hand whenever you intend to portray something science doesn't support. You may remember reading a book or watching a movie where a character changed either into a cat just before being threatened with being turned into a pocket watch or before entering the armory in an attempt to steal as many possible devices while being perceived as a General with a direct line to the commander and chief. These are all for entertainment purposes, which will most likely lure you to obtain all the "baseball cards" associated with the various character possibilities a specific character offers.

Just imagine having a complete set representing the mythical orangutan or Urk. Perhaps the Urk has a scuba diver card, a bank robber card, a horizontal monkey dance card, and much more with imagination limiting the entrepreneur to pursue this idea, which I will claim 51% royalties if successfully trademarked. But what about one person representing several, all of which can define the others, almost like when you decide to multiply seven with eight when eight can also result from multiplying four by two?

Please raise your hand if you believe your pocketknife can be used to gut an animal and carve your name into a tree on your first date somewhere in a forest. Achieving both these, gutting and carving using your knife, makes you realize two things: a statement and a question a jury needs to answer.

The first emphasizes gutting and carving as attributes of your knife, which can also be used as a throwing weapon while still knowing it's yours and not a second or third knife introduced. The second, which isn't a statement but something the jury has to answer, is: "Who the hell takes a knife on a first date in the middle of the forest anyway?" Welcome to the sinusoidal world of mistaken identities, ladies and gentlemen…

Rays of sunlight promise a beautiful day through high-rise buildings onto lower Manhattan's busy, jagged sidewalks. People dressed in suits and the occasional tourist rush to the end of a maze, which leads to a return journey in the late afternoon. Taxis, Suburbans, and limos are bumper to bumper with horns honking as if communicating in Morse code; A few short honks for getting your ass moving and several extended ones for emphasizing how to get the fuck out of the city.

Food vendors are selling the best heartburn has to offer while some patrons sip on disposable coffee cups, not realizing the lack of hygiene from the pot. Shoulder to shoulder and with little emotion, they rush through a straightened Serpentine Ramp with one day closer to retirement or perhaps affording that one-bedroom apartment Manhattan boasts about. Bob, wearing a recently cut grey suit, joins the rush, picking up the pace toward a USPS postal box where he needs to insert the letter as promised. She approaches it, stops, and removes an envelope from her inner pocket. He carefully inserts the envelope and explores the opening for an extended time, ensuring the letter has made its way into the belly of the beast. Helga waits a few more seconds and carefully crosses the street, jaywalking between the slow-moving traffic towards Anna Maria's Diner.

21

ENGLISH AND THE DEVIL

Acrophobia is the fear of heights, aerophobia is the fear of flying, and several others such as but not limited to are aquaphobia, astraphobia, claustrophobia, mysophobia, and nosocomephobia, all of which someone somewhere in our "perfect world" fears also known as a phobia.

What terrifies you most, and do you recall when that fear started? Before you answer, it is vital to understand that I'm not referring to being scared of earthworms or giant ass spiders but rather something along the lines of heights, inability to breathe, or perhaps the dark, of which the last is better known as Nyctophobia among the scientific and medical community.

Let's assume, without it being the mother of all fuckups, that you fear darkness for some or another reason. Why is it that you fear the dark? Is it because you've seen a genuinely horrific horror while babysitting, or is it perhaps your inability to come to terms with the fact that your environment is still the same, even in the absence of light?

Some folk's reasons are far more complex than most due to theirs being of a destructive nature, including sexual abuse as a child, a paranormal event, and even the fear of being lonely as a result of their parents neglecting their calls to be picked up from their cot at 3 a.m. This makes me think of movies where paranormal activities pester families once they move into a big old house, for which such a possibility is the wet dream of certain movie producers striving toward a number one production for October.

The catch, however, is that people tend to believe such a production when accompanied by credentials associated with millions of dollars at the box office, even though the storyline goes against reason. Does it go against reason? Yes, who in their right mind will return home, specifically at night, if they believe they aren't alone? Let's call it how it is, absolute bullshit! Sure, some legendary families will claim years of torment from entities, but human psychology goes against that, at least how Bob and I see it. Allow me to explain. Earlier in this journey, I referred to Chinese water torture described by Hippolytus De Marsiliis in the 15th or 16th century.

Our normal response when confronted by something that goes against us feeling safe and in control is fight or flight; consequently, it simply doesn't make sense that you won't leave a haunted house when not restrained, as in the water torture process. Come rain or shine, there are circumstances that will prevent you from leaving such a dwelling, such as a 3rd reaction, that being succumbing, when confronted with a fight or flight scenario, of which the family who submitted to the paranormal torture should each receive a medal of honor from the "scary-as shit-community," regardless, I'll still call it BS. This view demonstrates why the book's introduction and the amount of time required to be successful in mathematics mention 87.2% and 12.8 %.

Thus, it would be best to dismiss a movie as 87.2% factual when "based on true events" refers to a production that is either good for dry-humping or questioning religion. If I managed to confuse you, I did achieve what I set out to. The only time we know something to be real is when we can relate to such an event or events and not to the possibility of something Hollywood wants us to believe.

No, a human can't change into a frog or the mythical Orangutan Joe, regardless of what your priest said. Shall I call them liars if they claim it to be the truth? I guess I could, but the alternative I also support is to embrace the fact that being naive (normal) will make you believe anything with a half-truth for a foundation.

The more interesting human response is submitting to an environment, a person, a group, or even a philosophy when you fear for your life, knowing no possible solutions, or when you seek meaning among the madness that can result in having sympathy for the Devil, referred to as Stockholm Syndrome.

In this case you end up supporting the cause after spending ample of time among that which goes against your fundamental values served on a platter called kindness. Please don't confuse this with the possible reality some psychiatric patients perceive since I am not referring to an imaginary world created by potential exposure to an alternative realm but rather to an environment where everyone is on the same page and experiences the exact same events.

James' fear of the dark comes as a result of an abusive father and events that made him realize the possibility of having their entire family murdered by a "thing" that is supposed to love and not hate. You can compare this "thing" to an Iron Maiden, a mythical medieval torture device that very well depicts Pit and the Pendulum, the "thing" being his father and not a metal coffin with spikes.

You would walk past their house and not see it differently than others, just like James viewed others: Perhaps that's how dads are, and we're just naughty, or perhaps we are being abused, and their dads don't want to help? We see this all the time with domestic violence, where the only place of safety seems to be the only place we know: hell. Regardless, such an environment may convince you that the pit is how it should be and that the pendulum is your reward since you have never experienced something different.

Describing James' house growing up to an audience would not be the easiest or a fair thing to do, not only because we can't possibly imagine the fear he, his mom, and his siblings had growing up, but also because your brain won't be able to process and congest that which small-town libraries refrain from having in their collection. Physical abuse was the order of the day, accompanied by the worst thing ever: psychological abuse.

Since no alternative was available back then, James's solution was to sleep with a dagger below his pillow while trying to fall asleep to a song describing his question of why God still protects him even when he doesn't deserve it. Again, if what I said from the beginning of this chapter to the start of this sentence comes across as confusing, then I managed to give you an insight into the life of a 14-year-old Jacob who didn't have a proper solution, a place to go or help he could've asked. All these are a result of a family trapped under the oppression of a Tyrant who made them believe the world wasn't big enough to hide.

What added to Jacob's worthlessness in those days was the pleasure town folk took in degrading a family which they knew very little about, which happened to be the same small-town people with a shit load of churches where you can choose to ask forgiveness for not stopping promptly at the stop sign on your way into town followed by either turning left or right toward the church's bell tower. No, Jacob's family wasn't part of the town's prayers.

The sad reality is that even extended family members on his mom's side had a quick fix for Jacob's inability to be obedient: snap out of it and stop blaming the past despite him still being part of it. Can you blame them?

The answer to this question is: They all support having a book describing their purpose at ages very close to the end. As said, *"If you can't recognize the scars of a broken person, what use is your purpose anyway?"*

What they gave their children is love, joy, and so forth, whereas what James, Jacob, Bob, Jana, and Anny got was the absence of love substituted with fear, worthlessness, and rejection, over and over, as Somniphobia slowly but surely got tamed by the sign of the cross…

It's a late evening when a 14-year-old Jacob, dressed in plain pajamas, sits behind a small study desk against a simple single bedroom wall. Against the upper of the walls are posters torn from magazines, which some publishers included in the middle. On the single bed's head hangs a Superman cape, representing his early life wish to have him rescued from an abusive household in the absence of white bread and new shoes. He tries studying multiplication tables even though he has no interest, which leaves his pencil, ruler, sharpener, and eraser untouched and pointing in the same direction. His boredom overtakes him, resulting in opening an engineering magazine from below his desk. He carefully examines the pictures but doesn't attempt to read the descriptions.

There's a knock on his door, it's his mother, and he quickly hides the magazine. With excitement she enters and hands him an envelope with his name and their address on the front. "This came for you in the post today—from New York." He is excited yet confused since nobody ever writes to him except his grandmother, whose letters smell like mothballs and older people. "For me? Who will write to me?"

"Do you need help reading it?" she asks, just as excited as him. Getting a local letter from Grandma is a blessing, but getting one from another country specifically addressed to her son is far beyond her expertise. "Where's New York?" he asks, hoping it will be where Clark Kent gets to live his full potential as the caped hero. "I think it's in America—a place overseas."

He carefully takes the envelope and scans the front, which has a stamp he doesn't recognize from his collection. "That's so cool! How did it get here, Mom?"

"A postal worker dropped it off."

"But where did he get it from?" he asks, just like a three-year-old will keep asking, "Why?"

"I'm sure it was delivered to his office by a truck or something."

"It scares me to think you must throw a letter into a box, not knowing what happens to it. What if it doesn't fall into the bag, or what if you think you put it in, but it falls back out when you walk away? What if their machines swallow the letter without anyone knowing?"

"I'm sure they have a process which takes care of all those things," she responds with a smile, knowing her son's questions are those of innocence. "But who takes care of the process, Mom?" he asks without opening the letter. "Some clever people, my son."

"Hopefully, it's a perfect process, like that dad tries to follow," he says, not realizing his frame of reference does contain something vital to his future success, but just so will that same attribute be the reason for so many of his failures. She looks at the small clock on his bedside table, "Look at the time—it's already late, Jacob. We will have to wait till tomorrow for the letter. I suggest you quickly get ready for bed before lights out. I wish I could give my children a better life where fearing their father isn't part of it, she thought, sharing that same fear of the Devil. "But mom, it's only ten…" he protests, hoping to have her read the letter. She realizes his excitement and responds teasingly, "Don't argue with me, Mr. Young Van Der Linde!"

"I'll try to read it tomorrow after school."

"You sure you don't want me to read it for you tomorrow night?" she asks, knowing he struggles to read and understand the most basic English has to offer, with her skills being slightly better. After all, a small town like theirs doesn't cater to anyone except those fluent in their native tongue. Old folk refer to English as the language of the

Devil since their forefathers had to fight British colonialism, resulting in thousands of Afrikaner deaths not only on the battlefield but also in concentration camps, invented by those with crooked teeth and necklines burned red. Yes, those are the same ones who refer to an African vacation as a Safari. If you refer to Safari, you can have an L tattooed on your forehead. Instead, say: "We will visit a country in Africa for sightseeing and game drives."

"I'll manage," responds Jacob, trying to come across as his talented sister. He doesn't even have the faintest idea of how to spell English. She places the letter on his table and leaves the room, "Good night, my son. Finish up and get to bed before your father walks in here."

Just as she walks out, his father yells with a bouldering voice, which can be associated with fear for your life, "GET TO BED BEFORE I COME IN THERE, BOY! YOU'RE COSTING ME ELECTRICITY!"

22

____

A DAY AT THE BEACH

February 1999

Every city, town, or desert has a hangout spot for teenagers different from those with promising futures, or so Bullhorn Margret, the 69-year-old spinster and aunt of Piears, would say while perfecting the art of gossiping and secretly trying different size Zucchinis when not at work.

The local hangout spot for rebel teenagers in their small town is below a railway bridge with graffiti against the walls, empty beer bottles and cigarette buds paving the floor, and a ruddy cat with scars, occasionally making an appearance. Cars can be heard overhead while a Diesel engine slowly pulls into town.

The 14-year-old Jacob makes him comfortable on a knee-high

brick wall to the side of the track, running parallel to the opposite where the cat bakes in the sun. The bottom of the bridge, stained black from diesel smoke, offers no sign of life, just as the graffiti against the bridge's pillars rejects whatever is taught during the weekly one-hour religious studies.

This is the spot where you'll complete the Bare-Frog and Bare-Pears, also known as the BF and BP Card, if you are a freshman, which is the license for entry-level smokers without hair down there yet. He retrieves the letter from his hand-me-down backpack, opens it, and tries to read the first line. My Lady Helga sneaks up from behind and startles him when she softly whispers in an erotic voice, "Let's see your Happy hair, shall we?"

"For the sakes of fucks and broomsticks, Helga, don't do that!" he responds with fright which turns to calm once he realizes the softness of his best friend's voice. Helga notices the letter and asks, "Who is that from, Jay? Your Gran?"

"You give me a rocket, and I'll let you have a look," he negotiates, knowing very well she may ask him for a smoke if she were to read it. "I can do better than that Jay—got you a soft pack of Luckies from Piears," she says while tossing it toward him. "Wow, My Lady, why did you do that?" he asked, never owning such a consumable's quantity. "God, I wish you would stop calling me that, Jay!" she responds teasingly. "Perhaps I do that out of respect, My Lady," he says while trying to figure out how to open the soft pack.

She can't help but start laughing when he adds his respect toward her with his inability to open something he tries to treat like a bride on the wedding night. "What's so funny?" he asks without looking up, with eyes focusing and his brain calculating how to go about should a superior way of opening a soft pack ever be needed by humanity. "Nothing, my dear Jay," she says, keeping on giggling and realizing something special about a boy she slightly seniors.

"I see our friend is taking a nap in the Sun. Our neighbor had a similar cat years ago who sneaked out while pregnant to have her litter somewhere in town on a stormy night," she mentions as she retrieves a honey-filled pacifier from her backpack. I wish I could call her by her name, thought Jacob, who subconsciously senses the presence of an emotional connection toward a girl who accepts him for who he is.

Her natural scent has trust as the base notes, sincerity as the middle, and compassion as the top, all three cords creating a longing for his soul to be comforted by her gentle touch with the knowledge that nothing compares to her.

Some people just have a connection we can't define, only envy, while we tend to dismiss it just as quickly. But what if we can access an elixir that can awaken and manipulate the emotional senses to something superior? Or you may be already familiar with this feeling, which is more than just being in love; something more profound, the same something thousands, if not millions, of artists sing about as a wish.

I still recall the day I met the love of my life more than 30 years ago, whom I haven't seen since that day. We both, even for a moment, shared the feeling of knowing each other for decades, even though it was only ten minutes.

Just so is this relationship with two young souls not truly realizing their souls fading into each other. She delicately puts an imported zippo with his family crest into his pocket without him truly noticing as something emotionally awakens in his subconscious. Helga sits beside him, observing his meticulous handling of the packet as he finally and precisely removes the first cigarette about to be put in his mouth. She gently reaches toward his hand and guides him to refit it upside down into the soft pack without any resistance from his right. "It's called The Lucky—smoke that last," she says softly while his hand holds hers for a moment.

She realizes the possibility of a kiss to be shared and interrupts by being her silly self, "But first, stand up before I read—want to admire your six-pack and happy hair," she says, referring to the hair running from his naval to the top of his pants. He gets up, stands in front of her, and lifts his shirt, with her pretending to scout the presence of happy hair and dismissing the thought of an emotional moment. "Yay, it seems we have a winner, Jay—you'll soon be having a paved way toward your disco stick! Are you ready for your BP Card license next week?"

"Why wouldn't I be?" he asks while pulling his shirt down to prevent her from teasing his Stoneys with her nails.

"Don't worry, Jacob, I won't bite, I promise," she jokingly adds, aware both are trying to mask what they believe the other feels. "I'm not worried, My Lady. It's quite tender and annoying to have this shit behind my nipples," he responds with a fake sad face, adding to their silliness on a Tuesday afternoon below the bridge. "Who's it from?" she asks just before she starts to read the letter from a mysterious individual. "No freaking idea!" She looks up for a moment and gently touches the laceration on his bottom lip without him making eye contact,

"The Devil did that?"

"You should see him, but fuck him—let's read," he responds with a smile, knowing she has no confidence in what he just said. She turns her attention back to the letter even though her concern for his safety is growing exponentially in a town where neither the police nor the welfare has a solution for a situation like his, not to mention the church folk who would rather rush their house with pitchforks and gasoline. "Dear Jacob. I am writing this letter hoping you find value in what I will share. I need you to listen carefully to ensure you don't end up lonely and unloved. Support her in what she does, lift her, and encourage her to achieve her goals. She isn't perfect, nor are you; love her for who she is and not for who you think she should be. Always remember your roots and keep that close to your heart. Be kind and respectful toward others, even if you don't share the same beliefs. Every person walking this planet has some form of coping device, and you have no right to try and persuade them differently.

Don't search for God as you'll have no success, and accept that you'll never find him, and don't try to understand who created who, since our brains can't argue that riddle. Nothing in this world is worth taking your own life for, and get a tattoo to remind you of that. Rejection will cut to the bone, but seek to understand the challenges those who reject you face. The world isn't just about you or your goals, but it's about everyone else's, too, which you should always consider. There is hope, there are opportunities, and there is love."

Helga stops for a moment when tears cloud her eyes. She closes the letter momentarily while her imagination sees something she never knew existed—the silhouettes of two people and two dogs. She continues reading, "Whatever you do, stay away from shit that'll destroy your heart since that will lead to heart failure at an early age and kill you! You will be chasing success to prove to yourself your true value. You are good enough; you are valuable, but ultimately, you are just human. Don't ever say I am where I am because of your circumstances, but rather, I am where I am despite my circum-stances. Learn how to steal with your eyes and your ears, take owner-ship of the wrongs, and strive not to repeat them. Helga, thanks for reading this letter. He will eventually develop a love for reading and writing. My best wishes, your pal in New York, JJVDL. And before I forget, your buddy baking in the sun is the same one you tried rescuing as a child," concludes the pregnant Helga, walking hand in hand on a Spanish beach accompanied by two English Bulldogs, Bella Milano, and Charlie Figs, months after accepting the last name of the 38-year-old self-made millionaire, James Jacob Van Der Linde.

December 2024

...Dr. Vullis stares through her door's window, lifts his right wrist, quickly scans the time, removes his cell phone from his pocket, and dials an intriguing contact. Will he pick up, or is he already doing "pick-ups and deliveries," he questionably thought. The phone rings a few times with a mysterious voice answering, "Some are so unique that neither God nor the devil knows what to do with them."

"This is Vullis. She's ready," he responds to a man who saves and trains people but for an arm and a leg. This mysterious man is no stranger to being called the one responsible for balancing good and evil. Interpol has made peace with the fact that they won't be able to bring him to justice. Is he a myth, a legend, or perhaps the one some call the replacement equivalent of Vasily Zaitsev? Regardless, when he gets turned loose, he will bring sorrow to the families of hard-core criminals on the run and murderers, but he will bring justice to families who the system failed.

"We'll pick her up at 20:00 sharp, Grüß Gott," says the mysterious man in a raspy voice just as fast as hanging up.

———

THE END

My name is HJ Harrison-Vullis, a friend to a victim and survivor of 11 suicide attempts who can't tell what seven times eight is and who doesn't believe in Christmas either. This is his life, his coping mechanisms, and how he manages to survive by creating characters from tragic events and people he has met in various clinics, like Anny, to whom he gave his word to share some of her adventures someday. Call it his wand carved by a 200-year-old blind wise man, if you want. Nothing said or used in this book is to dismiss any form of medical treatment, scientific facts, mathematical models, or religion, even if it may come across as such. Instead, it is intended to ponder on what we know as "making sense" and perceive as accurate and that which normality determines, and nothing more. The biggest question, however, is: did I intentionally use 87.2% real and 12.8% somewhat accurate to lure you?

Be kind, stay humble, and strive to be a better version of yourself. Nothing in this world should give you a reason to harm yourself when hope is always there.

Challenges will come, and your heart will be ripped from your chest, but that will make you stronger, and time will bring healing. Your mind can be an enemy; learn how to master it. Turn that which you struggle with into creativity.

Lastly, a polished pair of shoes can complement a $150 suit while wearing a $13 French cuff. If you can maintain this, you're on your way to success…

References

Bob's Brain.
Bullhorn Margret.
The life of a victim and survivor of 11 suicide attempts.

Credits

Jacob's mother.
All Jacob's Exes.
The on/off switch from a vacuum.
Jacob's father alias Devil.
Orangutan Joe.
Urk, the navel dweller.
Anny's pacifier laced with moisture.
Jesus V2.0
Jacob's favorite band.
Shitty peanut butter products.
All failed exorcisms.

THE SCULPTOR AND SCHWEIZER'S DEVILS

December 2024

It is 18:00 on Christmas Eve when a yellow cab slightly covered with snow pulls up outside an orphanage to escort a young boy to what will become her training ground.

It is 20:00 on Christmas Eve when a yellow cab slightly covered with snow pulls up at the entry of the psychiatric clinic, ready to transport Helga and the girl trapped in a boy's body toward their new home, Dieter and Alegria's training facility.

Dieter turns to Alegria, „Oder Sie könnten als Zikadennymphe in ein solches Königreich eindringen und dann eine langsamere, aber effektivere Eroberungsmethode anwenden."

If you managed to find this last chapter, which you obviously did, it's either because you were intrigued or bored to hell with the hope that you'll eventually make sense of the gibberish, not that I believe in such a place. If your reason is the former, I invite you to explore with me the other coping characters created in two unique adventures exploring your morbid fascinations.

"I am the King of Failures and Faults, who points out what I recognize in others," says Jimmie Morries, the historian of Schweizer's secrets. "And justice shall be ours," adds Morris, the Sculptor.

———

*"…The grace of the Lord Jesus be with all.
Amen"*

———